Pride and Proposals

A Pride and Prejudice Variation

By Victoria Kincaid

This is a work of fiction. Names, characters, places, and incidents are products of the author's imagination or are used fictitiously. Any resemblance to actual events or persons, living or dead, is entirely coincidental.

ISBN: 978-0-9916681-2-0

Chapter 1

Miss Bennet, I must tell you that almost since our first ...
No. Too formal.
You must be aware of my attentions ...
Would that assume too much?
You must allow me to tell you how much I admire you ...
This came closest to expressing his sentiments, but would she view it as excessive?

Darcy guided his stallion along the path to Hunsford Parsonage, anxiety increasing by the minute. Somehow the perfect words for a proposal must come to mind. He was close by the parsonage.

Almost out of time.

He took a deep breath. The master of Pemberley was unaccustomed to such agitation of the mind. But Elizabeth Bennet had a habit of unsettling his nerves as no one else could. Not for the first time, he wondered *why* that should indicate she would be the ideal companion of his future life. However, he had wrestled with his sentiments all day and finally concluded that it must be so, despite his objections to her family.

He had not slept the night previous and only fitfully the night before that. Practically his every thought was occupied by Elizabeth Bennet. Every minute of the day, he would recall a pert response she had made to his aunt or a piece of music she had played on the pianoforte. Or the sparkle of life in her fine eyes.

Yes, at first she had seemed an unlikely candidate for the mistress of Pemberley, but his passion could not be denied.

He no longer made the attempt.

Strange. He had been angered with himself for months that he could not rid himself of this ... obsession with Miss Bennet. But once he had determined to surrender to the sentiment and propose to her, he felt almost ... happy. Despite the fleeting sensations of guilt and doubt, he could not help but imagine how joyful it would be to have her as his wife.

He pictured the expression on Elizabeth's face when he declared himself. Undoubtedly, she was aware of his admiration, and she had returned his flirtatious banter on more than one occasion, but she could have no serious hopes for an alliance. Her delight would make any of his misgivings worth it.

The woods on either side of the path thinned, and Darcy slowed his horse to a walk as he reached the clearing surrounding the parsonage. Initially, he had been bitterly disappointed when Elizabeth's headache had prevented her from accompanying the Collinses to Rosings for tea, but then he recognized a perfect opportunity to speak with her alone.

Excusing himself from the gathering had not presented any difficulties. His cousin, Colonel Fitzwilliam, had received a letter that day with word of an unexpected inheritance of property following the death of his mother's sister. Darcy was well pleased for his cousin, who had chafed at the limitations of a second son's life. Richard had excused himself to plan for an immediate departure from Rosings the next day so he could soon visit his new estate. Darcy had seized on the excuse as well – since, naturally, he would be taking Richard in his coach and would necessarily need to prepare.

Darcy turned his thoughts to the task at hand.

You must allow me to tell you how violently I admire ...
No.

You must allow me to tell you how ardently *I admire and love you ...*

Perhaps ...

Darcy swung his leg over the pommel and slid off his saddle, tying his horse up at a post outside the Collinses' front door. Pausing for a moment, he breathed deeply, willing his body to calmness. Then he seized the door knocker and rapped.

The maid who answered the door appeared unnecessarily flustered. As he followed her down the short hallway to the Collinses' modest drawing room, Darcy had a dawning sense of wrongness.

Voices already emanated from the drawing room. Darcy immediately recognized Elizabeth's lovely soprano. But the other voice was male, too muffled for him to hear. Had Collins returned home unexpectedly?

Darcy quickened his stride, almost crowding against the maid as she opened the drawing room door. "Mr. Darcy, ma'am," the maid announced before swiftly scurrying away.

Darcy blinked several times. His mind had difficulty understanding what his eyes saw. His cousin Fitzwilliam was in the drawing room. With Elizabeth. With *Darcy's* Elizabeth. In actuality, Richard sat beside her on the settee, almost indecently close.

Why is Richard here? Darcy wondered with some irritation. *Should he not be packing for his departure rather than preventing me from proposing?*

Richard and Elizabeth had been smiling at each other, but now both regarded Darcy in surprise.

For a moment, all was silence. Darcy could hear the crackling of logs in the fireplace. He had the nagging sensation of having missed something of importance but could not identify it.

"I ... uh ... came to inquire after your health, Miss Bennet." Given the circumstances, Darcy was proud that the words emerged at all coherently.

"I am feeling much recovered, thank you." Her voice was somewhat breathless.

A look passed between Richard and Elizabeth, and she gave a tiny nod. Darcy's sense of mystification increased. Finally, Richard sprang to his feet with a huge grin on his face. "Darcy, you arrived at just the right moment. You can be the first to congratulate me." At that moment, Darcy started to get a sinking, gnawing feeling in the pit of his stomach. "Elizabeth has consented to be my wife!"

Chapter 2

Elizabeth opened her eyes, staring at the canopy of her bed, unwilling to face the business of donning clothing and descending for breakfast just yet. She wished to review and savor her memories of the previous day's events before facing others' reactions.

A chance encounter with Colonel Fitzwilliam the previous day had revealed the distressing news that Mr. Darcy had conspired with Mr. Bingley's sisters to separate Jane from their brother. The anguish that followed had brought about a headache, preventing her attendance at Rosings for tea.

Elizabeth had been grateful for a reprieve from Mr. Darcy's company, being uncertain if she could treat him civilly. Instead, she had occupied her time reviewing Jane's recent letters, noting how out-of-spirits her sister's words sounded. Although Jane wrote nothing in particular to elicit concern, her entire manner lacked the enthusiasm her sister usually displayed. As Elizabeth peered out of the window, worrying that her sister might never recover her spirits, the maid had announced Colonel Fitzwilliam's arrival.

Initially, the colonel entered and settled on a chair near the fireplace, only to vacate it and wander about the room. They spoke of inconsequential matters: her health and that of her family. Elizabeth found herself concerned about the colonel's health. He displayed a kind of nervous energy that she had never before encountered in him.

Finally, he settled once more in a chair, leaning forward so that his eyes caught and held hers in an intense gaze. When Elizabeth had first met the colonel, she had thought him pleasant, but not handsome. Now she was forced to reevaluate this opinion. The energy that lit his face transformed it; she could not tear her gaze away.

"I received a letter today." He paused, and Elizabeth nodded. "My mother's sister, Rebecca Tilbury, died unexpectedly last week."

"I am sorry to hear it." Elizabeth was mystified about the import of this conversation; he did not appear to be mourning his aunt's passing.

The colonel waved away her concern. "I barely knew her. My family was not on good terms with her, and I had not seen her since my boyhood. The letter I received was from her solicitor. The terms of her will stipulate that I am to inherit her estate of Hargrave Manor. It is only an hour's ride from my parents' home in Matlock." His eyes were unfocused as he contemplated the vagaries of fate and capricious relations. "I did not expect it."

After a moment, the colonel returned his attention to Elizabeth. "The estate is quite good. Several hundred acres, producing a steady income of some four thousand a year." Elizabeth nodded and smiled. "And a house in Town as well. I will sell my commission immediately so that I may take possession and manage the estate."

"I am very happy for you. This is good fortune!" she said warmly. Now Elizabeth better understood why the colonel appeared so abstracted. He was coming to terms with his unexpected good fortune. However, why was he sharing the news with her now? Surely it could have waited until she visited Rosings on the morrow?

Colonel Fitzwilliam's eyes fixed on Elizabeth's face, provoking a blush from her. "Today, when we walked in the Park, I told you that younger sons did not have the luxury of marrying where they would like."

Elizabeth's breath caught.

"This thought has often tormented me this week. More than once I considered ignoring the needs of an income to follow the dictates of my heart. But today, I need not make such a choice. I can marry where I would. And I would marry you, Miss Bennet, if you would have me."

Elizabeth's whole body flushed. Thankfully, she was already seated, or she might have fallen. She opened her mouth, but no words emerged. This was the most unexpected event. Well, no, the *most* unexpected would be a proposal from Mr. Darcy. She almost laughed at the thought.

The colonel scrutinized her face anxiously, his hands absently kneading the gloves in his lap. "I can perceive that I have surprised you. Do not feel compelled to give me a response immediately."

Elizabeth swallowed and found her voice. "Yes. That is, yes, this is a surprise." Why was her throat suddenly so dry? Every word was hoarse to her ears. "Such an honor is quite unexpected." Her mind was in turmoil as she attempted to sort through her feelings about the man before her.

"Miss Bennet, let me assure you of my sincerest affection." He reached out across the space separating them and boldly took her hand in his. "Never have I encountered a woman who I felt would suit me so well. Your wit and vivacity—indeed, your spirit—are ..." He swallowed hard and glanced at the fireplace. "To be honest, words fail me. I am a soldier, not an orator. But should you honor me with your hand, I will do everything in my power to make you happy."

In truth, Elizabeth had not allowed herself to consider him as a potential husband. An earl's son, no matter how impoverished he believed himself, was considerably beyond her expectations. But now that she reflected on their, albeit brief, association she recognized he was one of the most amiable men of her acquaintance. He was unfailingly charming and affable, polite to his aunt and cousins, even when they were at their most vexing.

When all Mr. Darcy would do was stare at Elizabeth in disapproval, Colonel Fitzwilliam would talk to her with great animation, eager to learn about her family and the country around Longbourn. Despite their short acquaintance, she was aware they shared remarkably similar tastes in books and music—and always anticipated their conversations with great pleasure.

Elizabeth had always expected to marry for love, but she fully recognized the precariousness of her family's situation. Someone in her family must marry well, or their circumstances would be dire indeed when Mr. Collins inherited Longbourn. Jane seemed so out of spirits over Mr. Bingley's rejection that Elizabeth wondered if she would ever wish to attract another man's attention. And Elizabeth was loathe to trust her family's future to the whims of her younger sisters. Goodness knows what type of husband Kitty or Lydia would bring home!

She did not love Colonel Fitzwilliam, but she believed she *could* love him upon greater acquaintance. No other man had so provoked her interest since the early days of her acquaintance with Mr. Wickham. And, she realized with no little surprise, she was rather more disposed to the colonel than she had ever been to Wickham. There was a certain openness in the colonel's character, a selflessness, which she very much admired.

He provoked laughter from her far more than any other man she had ever encountered, which she considered quite a recommendation. Surely laughter was an excellent basis for friendship, and friendship a good start for a marriage, she reasoned. She could live a long time and never meet a man who suited her as well as the colonel.

"Miss Bennet?" Colonel Fitzwilliam's eyebrows had drawn together, creating a crease in the middle of his forehead. He must have been awaiting her response for some time.

"Forgive me, Colonel, you have given me much to think about."

He stood. "I should leave you to your thoughts. I have no desire to rush your decision."

At the sight of the colonel moving toward the door, Elizabeth realized what her decision would be. In fact, the decision had already been made.

She rushed across the room, wishing to intercept the colonel before he reached the door. "No, please do not leave. Richard, stay."

At the sound of his Christian name on her lips, the colonel turned to face her. His eyes sought hers, alight with hope.

"Yes." She smiled gently at him. "My answer is yes."

Richard's face broke into a wide smile. "Ah, Elizabeth, you have made me the happiest man in England! Nay, the whole world!"

She laughed softly. He caught her hand in his, and she realized with a shock that neither of them was wearing gloves. The feeling of his warm flesh against the sensitive skin of her hand felt deliciously forbidden, almost as if they had been caught kissing.

"Darling," he murmured and pulled her gently against his chest. Her head nestled just under his chin, a perfect fit. Yes, she could be quite happy with the Col—Richard. Perhaps she was a fair way to being in love with him already.

After a moment, Richard broke off the embrace, regarding her seriously. "Tomorrow, I must ride to Longbourn and call on your father. When would you like the wedding to take place?" He took her hand and led her over to the settee, sitting daringly close to her.

And so Mr. Darcy discovered them a quarter of an hour later.

Chapter 3

If someone wished to devise a personal hell specifically for him, Darcy mused, they could not possibly create a better one. He stood at the foot of the stairs to Colonel Fitzwilliam's new London townhouse. It was not as grand as Darcy House and the neighborhood was not quite as fashionable, but it was certainly elegant and spacious enough for a second son who, until three weeks ago, had no expectations of aspiring to any accommodations beyond a set of rooms to let.

Darcy regarded the house's impressive neo-Classical façade. He had been anticipating this day with all the joy most people might give a raging fever. Now that he had arrived, somehow his legs had turned to lead and would not obey his instructions to climb the stairs.

Even a simple glance at the townhouse caused dread to curl into a tight knot in his stomach. How would he survive the evening with his dignity intact? No, that was beyond hope. How would he survive the evening at all?

His eyes closed briefly, blocking the view of the offending structure. Darcy had quit Rosings the morning after Fitzwilliam's awful announcement. Fortunately, Darcy's plans had already been fixed, so no one thought his swift departure odd, and Richard apparently perceived no strangeness in Darcy's manner. *Perhaps he should consider a career on the stage.*

Richard's letters had described how he had traveled to Hertfordshire, easily securing Mr. Bennet's consent to the marriage, and then returned to Hunsford where he escorted Elizabeth to her uncle's house in London. In the intervening weeks, Richard had sold his commission and visited his estate, attending to all the urgent matters involved in taking immediate possession. Meanwhile, Elizabeth and her aunt made preparations for a wedding scheduled for some three months hence.

Darcy had tortured himself by quite thoroughly perusing each of Richard's letters, absorbing every detail of his cousin's felicity with Elizabeth. Bizarrely, he almost preferred to hear news of her—even when it concerned her betrothal to another man— than to know nothing of her life, a true sign of how pathetic his obsession had become.

He had tried—oh, how he had tried!—to resume his former indifference toward Elizabeth. However, now he had confessed his feelings to himself, the genie refused to return into the lamp. In a moment of honesty, during one of many nights spent staring at his ceiling, Darcy admitted to himself that he had never been truly indifferent to Elizabeth. When he had thought himself indifferent, he had only been fooling himself.

Darcy could only count one slim success in his favor over the past weeks. Since returning from Hunsford, he had adroitly avoided both Richard and Elizabeth.

Until today.

Richard was hosting a dinner so his family could be better acquainted with Elizabeth's. Darcy could not escape the invitation.

He had considered inventing urgent business at Pemberley. Or a sudden illness. Despite Darcy's abhorrence of disguise, these thoughts held alarming appeal, but finally, he had conceded the necessity of facing the happy couple eventually. Prolonging the inevitable smacked of cowardice—and he had faults enough without adding to them.

Darcy opened his eyes. He might as well be a French nobleman facing the guillotine. Perhaps cowardice had something to recommend it.

His stomach churned sickeningly, and his hands were wet with perspiration inside his gloves. But there was nothing for it. He must go. He willed his feet to climb the steps, one at a time, until he reached the porch, having failed to be struck down by a conveniently timed meteor.

His knock was answered almost immediately by a smartly dressed footman who took Darcy's coat and ushered him into Richard's study. Darcy saw no sign of other guests.

Richard glanced up with a smile when Darcy entered. He was seated behind a massive oaken desk, every inch the industrious landowner. "Darcy, good to see you!" He maneuvered around the desk to shake Darcy's hand and gestured toward to a couple of elegant chairs near the fireplace. "Brandy?" Richard asked. Darcy nodded; spirits could only help him survive the night.

Richard poured two glasses from a crystal decanter and handed one to Darcy before taking his seat. "I am pleased you have the opportunity to see the house," Richard remarked.

Was that a subtle suggestion that Darcy might have visited sooner? Well, Darcy supposed he would have visited more than once by now were it not for his cousin's engagement. "It is an elegant residence," Darcy said. "I hope you are pleased with it."

"Oh, quite," Fitzwilliam said. "It is nothing to Darcy House, of course, but far superior to my set of apartments."

"Indeed." Darcy admired the room's large marble fireplace, happy to have a neutral topic of conversation.

"The furnishings are a bit out of fashion, but Elizabeth will have the opportunity to redecorate as she wishes." *Ah, so much for neutrality.* Darcy suppressed his flinch at the mention of her name but finished his brandy in one gulp. "Where are the other guests?"

"I invited you here early. I wished to speak with you privately."

"Oh?" Without waiting for Richard's assistance, Darcy rose and visited the sideboard to refill his brandy glass.

"About Elizabeth."

Darcy froze in place. *Could his cousin suspect something?* He willed himself to act normally, but his hand shook, and he spilled a small puddle of brandy, cursing under his breath.

Richard peered over. "Never mind. The servants will clean."

Having poured a generous amount of brandy on his second attempt, Darcy gulped, hoping to calm the coil of anxiety in his stomach. He sank back into his seat, regarding his cousin warily.

Richard was rubbing his hands together, gazing absentmindedly at the window. Darcy believed he had been successful in concealing his feelings for Elizabeth, but Richard knew him better than anyone. Perhaps he had guessed.

Darcy stared into the fire. He could do nothing but admit the truth. There was nothing he could say in his own defense, even though such an admission might irreparably damage his friendship with Richard irreparably. Damn! How had they come to this pass? He valued Richard's friendship above all others.

Finally, Richard sighed heavily. "Elizabeth believes you do not like her."

"Pardon?" Darcy's hand jerked, and he almost spilled more brandy. Surely he had not heard aright.

Richard's expression was somewhat apologetic. "She ... believes you do not approve of her family and find fault with her behavior."

Darcy pulled his gaze from his cousin's face and stared at the window next to the fireplace, suppressing the temptation to laugh. Only he was in a position to appreciate the irony. "No... I ...." Darcy's voice was choked. "That is not the case at all."

"So I told her. I said you disapprove of most people, and even those who meet your approval often see you as proud and distant."

Darcy grimaced. "I thank you kindly for that endorsement of my character."

Richard shrugged unapologetically. Darcy rapidly reviewed his carefully stored memories of his conversations with Elizabeth. How had he created such a misimpression?

Unable to look at his cousin, he fixed his eyes on the inch of brandy in his glass. "I do not disapprove of Miss Bennet at all. I believe you have made an excellent choice." God willing, Richard would never know *how* excellent. "Her family's situation is unfortunate and some of her relatives can be ... difficult ..."

Richard chuckled. "I *have* been to Longbourn," he said drily.

Darcy chose each word carefully. "But I believe Miss Bennet to be of superior understanding and excellent conversation. I am often of a taciturn disposition in company, you know this."

His cousin grinned. "Yes. But I have known you my whole life. Elizabeth believes you spent the greater part of your visit at Rosings staring at her disapprovingly."

Thank God Richard remained ignorant of the true reason for those stares. That would make the situation intolerable. Well, more intolerable.

Richard stood and used the poker to idly rearrange the logs in the fireplace. It had been unseasonably cold for April, and the room was cooling rapidly as the fire died. "There is more." Darcy's gut clenched in apprehension. "Elizabeth's opinion of you was influenced by lies provided by Wickham during his time in Meryton."

Darcy let loose an oath, startling his cousin.

He had believed nothing would be worse than the revelation that she thought he disliked her. But now he found that when he thought she flirted and teased him at Rosings, she thought him a blackguard and could not wait to escape his company.

Darcy rubbed his face with one hand. He hated that Elizabeth would give credence to Wickham's opinion on *any* topic, particularly himself. Truth be told, Darcy did not like the idea of Wickham breathing the same air as Elizabeth.

Despite being consumed with jealousy, Darcy reflected that he should be grateful she had chosen Richard, who would treat her honorably. At the Netherfield ball, she had appeared to be partial to Wickham; the thought of that alliance could not be borne.

Perhaps he should be grateful that Richard had proposed before Darcy had the opportunity. Apparently, he had saved Darcy from a very embarrassing situation. Somehow the thought was not comforting.

Richard leaned against the mantel, watching the flames dance in the hearth. "I corrected her misapprehension regarding your father's bequest and Wickham's dissolute ways, but I said nothing about his imposition on Georgiana. I wanted your permission."

"Tell her." Darcy's voice was a growl. "She should know." Richard reacted to his vehemence with raised eyebrows. "I do not wish her to harbor any doubts about my character—or Wickham's perfidy." Although it hardly signified now, Darcy loathed the idea of Elizabeth thinking ill of him.

"Very well. I shall tell her."

Darcy seized the opportunity to voice another thought. "I hope Eliz—Miss Bennet will be a friend to Georgiana. She had been so withdrawn. Miss Bennet may be helpful in encouraging Georgiana to socialize in company. She should fully understand Georgiana's history." Of course, when Darcy had pictured Elizabeth helping Georgiana, he had imagined them as sisters, but cousins must suffice.

A broad smile spread over Richard's face. "An excellent suggestion, William! Georgiana only recently arrived from Pemberley, so they have not met. But I believe the acquaintance would be very beneficial to Georgiana. And to Elizabeth as well. Georgiana is one member of our family who might welcome her."

Darcy nodded his understanding. Fitzwilliam's letters had indicated how his parents had been unhappy at his rather precipitous choice of a "country miss" with no fortune. When Richard had refused their request to end the engagement, they had treated Elizabeth with little welcome.

"I hope you can demonstrate to Elizabeth that some of my family does not disapprove of our match." Richard watched Darcy carefully as he voiced the request.

Darcy suppressed inappropriate laughter; after all, he did disapprove—most strenuously. The irony was so thick it threatened to choke him.

His face must have betrayed this bewildering array of emotions. Richard was regarding him with consternation. "You are my oldest and dearest friend. I hope you can be a friend to my future wife."

Darcy closed his eyes briefly. If only Richard knew *how* friendly Darcy could be with Elizabeth! But apparently, he had given a performance worthy of a master thespian.

"I will do everything in my power to support this marriage." Darcy's vow was rewarded with a smile that almost made all the pain worthwhile. "I never intended to cause Miss Bennet discomfort and will endeavor to amend my behavior." The words sounded stiff and formal in Darcy's ears, but more emotion-laden language might betray too many of his secrets.

Darcy stared at his now-empty glass, wishing he could dare refill it. But there would be wine with dinner and then port after. Getting foxed held some appeal, but he might reveal too much to Richard—or, God forbid, Elizabeth—in an unguarded moment. Instead, he promised himself an evening of dissipation when he was safely home.

"Thank you." Richard's tone was warm as he strode over to his cousin and clapped him on the shoulder. He glanced at the clock on the mantel. "The other guests will arrive soon."

Darcy stood, straightening out his waistcoat and cravat. Despite recent events, he could not break the habit of looking his best for Elizabeth.

He followed his cousin to the door, but Richard turned before opening it. "Oh, I seated Elizabeth beside you at dinner, so you will have an opportunity to correct her misimpressions."

Darcy suppressed a groan. His cousin would have made an excellent medieval torturer. Darcy had anticipated that Elizabeth would sit adjacent to Richard and half a table away from himself. Then Darcy could gaze silently upon his beloved and pretend the smiles she bestowed on his cousin were actually for him.

Richard glanced over his shoulder as they exited the study, expecting a response. Darcy attempted to infuse his tone with enthusiasm. "Excellent."

The closer they drew to the entrance hall, the more Darcy's stomach churned with anxiety. Speaking with Richard alone had not been very difficult since the pattern of their friendship had been established since childhood. But seeing Elizabeth …

They arrived in the entrance hall just as the butler opened the door to admit Charles Bingley and his sister Caroline.

Bingley?

Darcy frowned. To Darcy's knowledge, Richard had never met Bingley. How had this come about?

"Bingley! So glad you could make it!" Richard strode across the entrance hall's stone floor and gave the other man's hand a hearty shake. A little bemused, Darcy followed his example.

"I suppose we are a bit early, but no matter!" Bingley's face had recovered some of the color it had lost over the winter. "Colonel Fitzwilliam, allow me to introduce my sister, Miss Caroline Bingley." Surprisingly, Bingley's manner in addressing his sister was cold and brittle. She ignored it, fluttering her eyelashes at both the colonel and Darcy as she curtsied.

Richard smiled amiably as he bowed. "My pleasure, Miss Bingley."

"Charles said you had become the new master of Hargrave Manor." Miss Bingley's smile was excessively ingratiating. As a wealthy landowner, Richard must now warrant her particular attention. Darcy caught the lady giving him a sidelong glance. Perhaps she intended to provoke Darcy's jealousy, but he was quite pleased to share her attentions.

As Miss Bingley and his cousin spoke, Darcy approached Bingley. "Charles, I was not aware you were acquainted with my cousin."

Bingley smiled widely. "We were not acquainted until a few days ago. I unexpectedly encountered the colonel and Miss Elizabeth out for a stroll near my townhouse."

Darcy suppressed a smile. Unexpected indeed! Elizabeth had cleverly engineered a meeting between the two men, most likely with the aim of inviting Bingley to this very event. He could only admire her inventiveness. Then a thought struck him forcefully.

"Has Miss Jane Bennet been invited for the evening as well?" Darcy asked with a raised eyebrow.

"I believe so," Bingley replied. Then he lowered his voice. "She has been staying with relatives in Cheapside these past weeks. Caroline and Louisa visited her, but they concealed Jane's presence from me." Bingley regarded his sister coolly. "I am quite put out with Caroline. We had a horrid row and have barely spoken two words together since."

"Indeed?" Darcy had never known Bingley to bear a grudge.

Darcy hoped Elizabeth's scheme would repair the damage he himself had wrought to the incipient relationship between Bingley and Jane Bennet. Fortunately, Bingley seemed unaware of Darcy's role in the sordid affair. Perhaps someday he might confess, but tonight would be difficult enough without the revelation.

The sound of Miss Bingley's grating laugh echoed off the marble of the entrance hall, drawing the attention of both Darcy and her brother. Without awaiting an invitation, she linked her arm with Richard's; he appeared startled at the familiarity. "May I say, Mr. Fitzwilliam, it is a delight to spend an evening in company with people of quality and breeding."

Caroline Bingley slanted a look to Darcy and her brother. Were her words meant as a condemnation of Bingley's preference for Jane Bennet or the preference she suspected Darcy to hold for Elizabeth? No matter. The evening promised to hold some unpleasant surprises for her. Despite his discomfort, Darcy was cheered by the prospect of such entertainment.

A knock sounded, and Fitzwilliam's butler glided to the door. The first person through the doorway was Elizabeth. Miss Bingley's mouth dropped open in shock. Apparently, Bingley had not troubled himself to inform her of the guest list for the evening.

Elizabeth wore a rather simple yellow silk dress with small flowers in her hair. Caroline Bingley, in contrast, sported an *au courant* orange gown and a large hat bedecked with many plumes. Nevertheless, in Darcy's eyes, Elizabeth's very presence illuminated the room as if she cast a golden glow. He would need to remind himself there were indeed other people present in the room.

Elizabeth's fine eyes, however, were fixed on only one person. "Richard!" Her mouth curved into a lovely smile. Darcy would sacrifice his right arm to see her fix such a gaze upon him just once.

Richard quickly stepped away from Miss Bingley to embrace Elizabeth and kiss her on the cheek, lingering a little longer than was proper. He then took her hand and led her to Miss Bingley. "Miss Bingley, I believe you are acquainted with my betrothed, Miss Elizabeth Bennet?"

"B-betrothed?" Miss Bingley stammered. Elizabeth smiled serenely at her, and Darcy had no doubt she was relishing Miss Bingley's discomfiture as much as he was. The other woman swallowed visibly. "I had not heard. My congratulations."

"Thank you," Elizabeth said.

Others were entering behind Elizabeth and were divested of coats and hats by Richard's servants. A portly man and his well-dressed wife were likely Elizabeth's aunt and uncle from Cheapside. Miss Bingley's eyes narrowed when Jane Bennet entered, but Bingley was bouncing on his heels with barely contained excitement. The eldest Miss Bennet smiled sweetly in his direction, and with this slight encouragement, he hastened to her side.

Jane Bennet was often considered to be the most beautiful of the Bennet sisters, but Darcy had always found such sentiment incomprehensible. She was pretty enough, but had none of the animation and sparkle that made Elizabeth so utterly irresistible.

Bitterly, he again cursed himself for interfering between Bingley and Elizabeth's sister. If Bingley had married Jane months ago, perhaps Elizabeth would not have accepted Richard's offer. After all, the match may have appealed to Elizabeth since it would provide financial stability to her family. However, the shine in Elizabeth's eyes as she regarded her betrothed suggested she was not motivated solely by concerns about future security. Could she have ever turned such a look in Darcy's direction? He would never know.

As Elizabeth spoke with her uncle, her curls bounced, and her skin glowed softly in the candlelight. Darcy was mesmerized. How would it feel to touch that silken hair or creamy shoulders …?

Darcy became aware that Elizabeth was carefully noting every word exchanged between Bingley and her sister. But then, as if suddenly aware of his scrutiny, she turned her gaze toward Darcy and gave him a challenging glare. He returned a smile, hoping to convey his approval for Bingley's attachment to Jane, but this provoked a look of confusion on Elizabeth's face.

Why would she regard him with such challenge in her eyes? Unless …

With a growing sense of dread, Darcy stepped over to his cousin and drew him away from the others for a private conversation. "Richard, did you perhaps relate to Miss Elizabeth the story of the friend I rescued from an imprudent match?"

His cousin appeared mystified. "Yes, I believe I mentioned it at Rosings one day. Why do you—?" Horrified realization dawned on his features. "Damnation, Darcy, was that Bingley?"

"Yes, and the woman I separated him from was Miss Jane Bennet." No wonder Elizabeth disliked him!

"Blast! I did not know."

"The fault is mine. I should never have told the story." *Or done the deed.* Even to his ears, his voice sounded dull and defeated. Here was another fault for Elizabeth to lay at his doorstep, and unlike Wickham's stories, it was all true.

Richard's brow was furrowed with worry. "I never revealed the friend's identity since I did not know it."

"She could not have failed to discern his identity based on the facts of the story," Darcy replied. Across the room, everyone laughed at some *bon mot* of Bingley's. His friend did indeed seem far happier in Jane's presence.

"So you objected to Bingley's marrying Jane but not Elizabeth's betrothal to me?" Darcy returned his attention to his cousin. Richard's tone was jovial, but it held a hint of hardness.

"I did not believe Miss Bennet held much affection for Bingley and was only attentive to him at her mother's insistence." Darcy glanced away, unable to hold his cousin's eyes during such an uncomfortable discussion. "However," Darcy swallowed, "I believe Miss Elizabeth's affection for you to be genuine. She is not the type to be swayed by mercenary considerations."

No, she is not, whispered a small voice in the back of Darcy's mind. *And yet I assumed she would accept* me *for my fortune!* It was the not the first time Darcy had castigated himself for his blindness toward Elizabeth's true feelings.

Richard smiled. "No, not my Lizzy." Darcy clenched his jaw to prevent any words from emerging. *She should be* my *Lizzy!*

Concentrating his attention on the merry gathering around Jane and Bingley, Darcy regained his composure. "I may have been wrong about Miss Jane Bennet as well."

Richard clapped him on the shoulder. "Mr. Fitzwilliam Darcy admitting to a possible error? Perhaps the apocalypse is nigh!" Darcy scowled at his cousin. It was bad enough he had to endure the consequences of his horrendous misjudgment, but to also endure teasing about it seemed particularly unfair.

Oblivious, Richard merely gave Darcy a sunny smile.

The butler drew Richard away to discuss dining arrangements. Perhaps Darcy could find some brandy. Suddenly, Elizabeth was standing by his side.

"Mr. Darcy." She gave him a polite, reserved smile.

"Miss Bennet. A pleasure." He attempted a smile in return but feared it emerged as more of a grimace.

As he gazed into her fine eyes, the realization struck Darcy that he had not consumed enough brandy. Not nearly enough. Perhaps there was not a sufficient quantity of brandy anywhere to fortify him against this experience.

Elizabeth was indicating the older couple who had arrived with her. "May I present my aunt and uncle, Mr. and Mrs. Gardiner?" The sound of her melodious soprano recalled better days when she had enchanted him with her singing at Rosings. But a challenging light in her eye dared him to object to associating with a merchant from Cheapside. Determined to thwart her worst expectations, Darcy shook Mr. Gardiner's hand and exchanged pleasantries with the couple, who seemed sensible and well-spoken.

By now, Miss Bingley had maneuvered herself into position at Darcy's elbow. He was not surprised when Elizabeth hastily took her relatives in search of Richard. Left alone with Miss Bingley, Darcy sighed, anticipating an evening alternating between fawning compliments and thinly veiled insults. "I suppose your cousin's engagement was a surprise to *you*," she smirked. Darcy understood her insinuation; fortunately, no one else of his acquaintance had guessed of his affection for Elizabeth.

"Indeed. They had not known each other long. I believe it was a surprise even to Richard," Darcy said drily.

Miss Bingley tittered uncertainly. "They seem well-matched," she said. Miss Bingley apparently labored under a delusion that Elizabeth's betrothal would bring her closer to achieving Darcy's regard.

"Yes." Darcy employed a familiar strategy; if he said little to Miss Bingley, she would sometimes quit his company due to a dearth of conversation.

"Such happenings in town since last I saw you!" Miss Bingley continued, apparently not requiring a conversational partner. "I hope we shall be seated near each other at dinner."

Darcy was spared the necessity of a reply by another knock at the door. Everyone in the entrance hall turned to view the new arrival. The butler opened the door to admit ... Mrs. Bennet.

Darcy's eyebrows rose as Caroline Bingley's mouth fell open. Jane Bennet hurried forward to take her mother's hand. "Mama, I thought you were too unwell to join us after the long carriage ride."

"I feel a vast deal better after taking a little wine back at my brother's house. And I just had to see everyone again! Oh! Colonel Fitzwilliam! It is so good to see you. Let me give you a kiss!" Richard smiled and allowed himself to be kissed by his future mother. "And Jane and Lizzy, oh, you girls look just lovely tonight!"

Bingley, Jane, and the Gardiners gave her their patient attention as Mrs. Bennet exclaimed rapturously about the entrance hall's marble floor and the wainscoting on the walls.

A few moments later, Elizabeth approached Darcy and Caroline Bingley. His treacherous heart gave a leap of excitement, but Elizabeth's regard was fixed on Caroline. "Miss Bingley," she said with a smile, "my mother's unexpected arrival necessitates that Richard must make some adjustments to the seating arrangements, and we thought to put her next to you. Since so few people in London are known to my mother, I thought she would find a familiar face at dinner to be of comfort. My uncle will sit on your other side. I believe you have met him."

Miss Bingley's mouth opened as she sought an acceptable means to decline this "honor." She gaped for several moments. "Yes, of course," she said finally. Her expression suggested she would prefer to contract a disfiguring skin disease.

"You are the soul of generosity." Elizabeth smiled sweetly at Miss Bingley, who glared back but did not reply.

Darcy masked his inappropriate laughter with a cough. Elizabeth's eyes briefly met his, and she smiled conspiratorially. He allowed himself a brief smile in return. Perhaps her good opinion of him was not irretrievably lost. But it hardly mattered. His hopes lay scattered in shards at his feet. Nevertheless, besotted as he was, Darcy still cared what she thought of him.

Richard's butler ushered the guests into an elegant drawing room where they could enjoy refreshments before dinner. Seating herself on a loveseat, Elizabeth smiled an invitation for Richard to join her, where, in Darcy's opinion, they sat far too close for propriety's sake. However, there was no denying they both appeared very happy.

Perhaps Elizabeth truly was in love with his cousin.

Ah, yes, here was a new idea with which he could torture himself. Excellent.

Although they had not known each other long when they had become engaged, Richard had later confessed to Darcy how he had formed a strong attachment to Elizabeth from almost the first moment of their acquaintance. Did Elizabeth return some measure of his affection? The thought drove the knife a little deeper into Darcy's heart. Somehow their betrothal was easier to tolerate if he imagined that she primarily sought a secure future, while the thought that she cared for Richard …

Elizabeth's heart should have been mine! She has commanded mine for months.

None of this signifies, he reminded himself. It was done. Richard and Elizabeth would marry. Darcy would see them for holidays and occasional visits—and somehow learn to bear it. What she felt for his cousin and when—these questions were of no consequence.

She could not be Darcy's, and that was the end of it.

Darcy's thoughts were too agitated to participate in ordinary conversation. Turning away from the room at large, he stared through the nearby window to the street outside, wishing he could simply open the window sash and dive out. Somehow the situation had managed to go from uncomfortable to intolerable in a mere quarter of an hour.

The darkened window reflected Elizabeth and Richard, in close proximity to each other on the loveseat, laughing and talking with the Gardiners. Darcy hurriedly switched his gaze to Bingley and Jane Bennet, who were having a low-voiced discussion near the doorway. Miss Bennet wore her customary sweet smile, while Bingley grinned widely. They seemed so happy it made his teeth hurt. Damnation! He wanted to gaze upon someone who was as miserable as he was. Where was Lady Catherine when he needed her?

Although, Darcy considered, Caroline Bingley's face at dinner might suffice.

Darcy had anticipated Bingley's attachment to Jane Bennet would be slight and short-lived. Bingley's misery had demonstrated how badly Darcy had misjudged. Now he was forced to realize he may have been wrong about Miss Bennet's affections as well.

And he had been wildly mistaken about Elizabeth's opinions of him.

Good God, had he ever really known the people surrounding him? Perhaps Lady Catherine de Bourgh was in reality a sweet gentle soul and Mr. Collins a genius!

He was no longer amazed that Elizabeth thought he disliked her. Instead, he was amazed that she managed to be at all

civil to him at Rosings while believing him to be the person who
had ruined Wickham's life and her sister's future with Bingley.

Glancing at the clock on the mantel, Darcy realized he had
only been at Richard's house for half an hour; it seemed an
eternity.

There was a commotion at the drawing room door as the
butler announced the Earl and Countess of Matlock and Georgiana,
who had been visiting them for the day. Richard and Elizabeth
rose to greet the newcomers. Darcy quickly crossed the room to
take Georgiana's hand.

His aunt and uncle greeted Elizabeth with cold civility.
While not as unmannerly as Aunt Catherine, they clearly opposed
Richard's betrothal. Elizabeth chose to ignore their disapproval,
returning their indifference with a sly smile and blithely
introducing the earl and countess to her uncle in trade. Her lips
twitched in amusement while the earl shook Mr. Gardiner's hand
as if the man carried the plague.

Viewing his aunt and uncle through Elizabeth's eyes, he
could understand her levity. The Gardiners were well informed
and of good understanding—the kind of company anyone would
desire. Darcy could only pray his relatives did not have the
opportunity for a lengthy conversation with Mrs. Bennet.

When the earl and countess took Richard away for a private
conversation, Darcy seized the opportunity and escorted Georgiana
over to Elizabeth.

"Miss Elizabeth, may I present my sister, Georgiana, to
you?" The two women curtsied. Elizabeth's smile was warm and
genuine; Richard must have shared the plan to coax Georgiana out
of her shell.

"Richard tells me you like music," Elizabeth said to
Georgiana.

"Yes." Although she seemed eager to converse with
Elizabeth, Georgiana's voice was barely louder than a whisper.
Darcy silently cursed Wickham again. Ever since the incident at
Ramsgate, his sister had retreated into herself. Always shy, she
was now particularly anxious in large gatherings. She resisted any
attempts to have her attend social outings, and Darcy was at a loss
about how he would arrange her coming out. "But please do not
ask me to play in front of all these people," Georgiana murmured.

"Not if you do not wish it!" Elizabeth seemed appalled at the suggestion.

Brushing hair from his eyes, Darcy could not help glancing at his aunt. She often insisted that Georgiana needed to exhibit her talent. Darcy had repeatedly asked his aunt to cease, but she listened to him as well as she listened to anyone—which is to say, not at all.

Elizabeth linked arms with Georgiana. "Why do you not rest here by me and tell me which composers you favor?" Georgiana gave Elizabeth a relieved smile and sank easily onto the loveseat. Soon they were engaged in a quiet, enthusiastic conversation.

Darcy savored the sight of the two women he loved most in the world enjoying each other's company. Perhaps something good would come from this fiasco.

Instinctively, he had known that Elizabeth's liveliness and sportive good humor were exactly what Georgiana needed to heal the wounds Wickham had inflicted. Darcy had done what he could, but his own social talents were meager at best, and Georgiana needed another woman's counsel.

The guests were soon summoned into the dining room for the repast. Darcy was indeed seated with Elizabeth, who took the mistress's place at the foot of the table, with Darcy's aunt on her other side. The countess commenced to instruct Georgiana, seated to her right, about the myriad rules governing the hosting of a dinner party—never mind that such a duty would not fall to Georgiana for many years.

In the middle of the table, Mrs. Bennet was in fine form. Her shrill voice described to Miss Bingley every bump and jolt from the carriage ride from Hertfordshire. "And now I have such tremblings in my hands. Do you see?" She extended a hand, which already contained a half-eaten roll, for Miss Bingley's edification. "And halfway through the journey, I was seized with such flutterings in my chest. I thought we might be obliged to turn back to Longbourn." Miss Bingley's pained expression suggested such an event was devoutly to be wished.

Elizabeth's mother took a bite of her roll; however, it did not staunch the flow of words. "But my devotion to my darling girl would not allow me to abandon the journey. I could never leave her to face the wedding plans alone! And perhaps—," Mrs. Bennet glanced slyly at Bingley and Jane, "there will be *two* weddings to plan! Now there would be cause for rejoicing!" Caught up in her own contemplation of this felicity, she completely failed to note the horror on her dining companion's face.

Naturally, Bingley was seated next to Jane, where they inhabited a world of their own creation. So much so that the footman was compelled to ask Bingley three times if he would like any potatoes. *They might as well announce their engagement by the end of the evening.* Darcy immediately chastised himself for such ungenerous thoughts, knowing they stemmed from his own dissatisfaction. He must, he resolved, simply avoid dwelling on the sight of their happy faces.

However, their felicity evidently gave Elizabeth great pleasure. He admired the gentle, genuine smile the sight provoked. How often had he dreamed of her lips curved in just that way when she gazed at him? A smile of welcome to Pemberley ... or their bed chamber ...

No, he must cease such musings lest he betray himself. She was not, and never would be, his.

Noticing Darcy's regard, Elizabeth blushed slightly and returned her attention to her meal. "Jane and Mr. Bingley seem happy to have renewed their acquaintance," she murmured.

"Yes, perhaps I erred in encouraging him to leave Netherfield last autumn. At the time, I thought it for the best." Elizabeth's head swung upward, and she regarded Darcy with such astonishment that he was tempted to laugh. He had nothing to lose by admitting the truth now. "Surely you do not believe me incapable of admitting to mistakes."

She gave him the kind of arch look he always found irresistible. Gritting his teeth, he forced himself not to react. "No, indeed, I suppose even you might be wrong once every five years," she teased.

Although the rejoinder was a jest, it still rankled. Did she not understand how such words affected him?

He sipped his wine slowly, then lowered the glass, staring at the dark red liquid. "If only you knew how many mistakes I regret only in the past few months." He intended his tone to be teasing, but he feared it might have sounded bitter. Elizabeth appeared perplexed. *At least she will never guess my greatest error was failing to court her properly.*

Making no comment, Elizabeth returned to cutting her meat. Darcy pushed some potatoes around on his plate with little appetite. *Do not be bitter*, he chastised himself. *Now is your opportunity to improve her opinion of your character.* "I will be quite pleased if Bingley's acquaintance with your sister brings them both joy," he said. "They deserve every happiness."

Elizabeth looked up at him sharply as if expecting some hidden meaning. He returned the look steadily.

Finally, she glanced away, taking a sip of her wine. "Be careful with your words, sir!" The teasing tone had returned to her voice. "Should they become engaged, you will not be able to escape acquaintance with the Bennet family—with two of your friends married into it."

Only Elizabeth could wrap such a blunt truth in a jesting tone!

He cut a piece of meat while considering his response. "I would consider myself fortunate to socialize with you and your sister," he said finally. Her eyebrows rose at his words. "But it is doubtful I would see others in your family, except perhaps when visiting Netherfield."

She smiled, recognizing how neatly he had avoided voicing his true opinions about the rest of her family. "Indeed."

Darcy pinched the bridge of his nose, aware he should say more to convince her of his favorable opinion, but he was weary. Weary of the event. Weary of the evening. Generally, he basked in Elizabeth's presence, but this dinner was fraught with too many difficulties, too many reminders of what he had lost.

A headache was forming behind his eyes and he wondered how soon he could depart without being impolite. Drinking more of Richard's fine Burgundy, he longed for the quiet of his study and its bottle of port.

When he and Elizabeth fell silent, Darcy heard Mrs. Bennet declaiming to Miss Bingley about the price of lace in London, while Mr. Gardiner droned on about tariffs and the quality of various textiles. Caroline Bingley stared at her dinner knife as if contemplating plunging it into her own chest simply to escape her dining partners. Darcy frowned. He had found Mr. Gardiner to be an engaging conversationalist, but then he noticed a smirk on Elizabeth's lips. Was her uncle being tedious just to annoy Miss Bingley? Darcy suppressed a smile but winced when he was forcibly reminded of his headache.

"Mr. Darcy?" Elizabeth's voice still sent a thrill of excitement down his spine. "Are you unwell?"

"Only a slight headache. Perhaps brought about by too little sleep."

Elizabeth glanced over at his aunt pedantically lecturing Georgiana, while his uncle vociferously debated politics with Richard. "Or perhaps too many relatives?" she murmured in a low voice.

His chuckle sent pains shooting through his forehead. "Truthfully, I believe the pain originates in an inability to change the past."

Good God! He silently upbraided himself. *Am I already foxed? How could I reveal so much to Elizabeth?* Perhaps he should depart immediately, claiming the headache as an excuse—cowardice be damned.

Elizabeth's eyes widened, but she merely murmured, "I believe many of us suffer from that affliction."

"I cannot imagine you experience many regrets." Darcy wanted to clap his hand over his mouth. *Damnation! What will I say next?*

Some of this internal battle must have appeared on his face; Elizabeth tilted her head and regarded him with concern. "Are you quite all right? Your skin is very pale."

No, I am quite ill. I am a lovesick fool. Darcy was struck with a most inappropriate impulse to laugh and hastily wiped his mouth with his napkin.

Elizabeth appeared most alarmed by the state of his health. Fortunately, before she could form another inquiry, their attention was drawn by the penetrating tones of his aunt addressing Georgiana. "You are a Darcy! You must relinquish these silly reservations and live up to your name!"

Darcy recognized belatedly that he should have been paying more heed to Georgiana's conversation with their aunt so he might protect his sister from inappropriate badgering.

"I am sorry, Aunt." Georgiana's face was pale and strained, her eyes watery with the effort to hold back tears.

"Aunt Rachel?" Darcy infused his tone with enough authority to command her attention.

The countess leaned back in her chair and speared a small potato with her fork, feigning unconcern. "Your sister believes she does not wish to make her come out next year."

Georgiana said nothing, but her eyes pleaded with Darcy for understanding. "We have discussed the possibility of delaying it until the following Season," he said calmly.

"Ridiculous!" his aunt cried, the potato poised halfway to her mouth. "Why delay? Georgiana does not have older sisters yet to be married! The younger she enters the marriage market, the more eligible suitors she will attract!" The countess jabbed the potato in the air for emphasis. "Her beauty will only fade with time." Her eyes slid sideways to glance at Elizabeth. Darcy bristled. At twenty, Elizabeth was hardly on the shelf.

The blood pulsed in his temples, compounding the pain in his head. His aunt and uncle had a remarkable ability to provoke his temper, particularly when questioning his decisions regarding Georgiana.

Darcy understood all too well her reservations about presenting herself to strangers. Georgiana's coming out ball would necessarily be one of the high points of the Season, with hundreds in attendance. He himself would not relish being the center of such a maelstrom.

Coming out a year from now would be an exercise in torture for Georgiana. Darcy could only hope that someday when she was older, she could tolerate it—even if she would never enjoy it.

"There is no rush." Darcy attempted to keep his voice level. "I have discussed this with Richard, since he is Georgiana's other guardian." He emphasized the last two words, reminding his aunt who held the authority in this situation. "If she is more comfortable waiting a year for her come out, then we will accommodate her wishes." Georgiana bestowed on him a small, grateful smile.

"I am certain she will only grow in beauty," Richard added. "And she will be much sought after, no matter when she comes out."

Her dowry guarantees that, Darcy thought. *Even if she had a face like a horse.*

Opposed on all sides, the countess harrumphed and commenced to dictate to Georgiana on the subject of hats.

Satisfied with his victory, Darcy took another sip of wine, only then noticing Elizabeth's wide, approving smile—directed at him. He was caught unprepared, unaccustomed to experiencing her approbation. For a moment, he indulged the fantasy that she smiled at him with love and returned the smile.

Abruptly, Elizabeth colored and dropped her eyes to her plate. *Good God! I have been staring at her lips! Get a hold of yourself, man!* At this juncture, the best he could hope was that she would attribute his behavior to excessive imbibing. *Have I been brought so low?*

Blast! How else would he betray himself after a few more minutes in her presence? Closing his eyes, he massaged his forehead again.

Only then did he realize his aunt was once more talking about Georgiana's debut. "William, I declare, you do have some peculiar notions. And, Georgiana, every girl loves to make her bow. Just think of the beautiful gowns you will have and all the suitors who will send you flowers!"

Georgiana said nothing as she hunched over her plate, picking at her food and trying to render herself invisible.

"I do not believe, madam, such occasions hold much appeal for my sister," Darcy said firmly.

The countess sniffed in disdain. "Singular. Most singular."

"Yes," Darcy said. "Many people have described the Darcys thus."

A smile quirked at the edges of Elizabeth's lips. "So I have heard as well," she murmured, her fine eyes sparkling.

Perhaps the evening was not a complete loss after all.

Chapter 4

The weeks since the betrothal dinner at Richard's townhouse had been dull ones for Elizabeth. After receiving word from his steward of problems with some tenants, Richard had departed for Hargrave. The difficulties had proved to be quite serious, owing to his aunt's long neglect of her estate, and Richard had already delayed his return twice. In her daily letters, Elizabeth assured him that she understood the need for his continued absence, but she dearly missed his liveliness and wit. In a short time, she had grown accustomed to his company and amiable conversation.

If only she could have accompanied him to Hargrave! But they were not yet married, so traveling together would be impossible.

Elizabeth's excitement at her impending nuptials was doubled by the not unexpected news of Jane's engagement to Mr. Bingley. The day following the betrothal dinner, he had called on Jane at the Gardiners' house and promptly asked for her hand. The news of a second daughter engaged had set Mrs. Bennet into a frenzy of lace purchasing and visits to silk merchants. However, she had demanded the wedding be held at Longbourn, so she and Jane, being of a more tractable disposition than Elizabeth, had returned to Hertfordshire to make plans for the wedding.

Although Richard's mother did not approve of Elizabeth, the countess had insisted that their ceremony take place at their home parish in London. Elizabeth had agreed as a means of keeping the peace. Who she married was of far greater import to her than where.

The dullness of weeks without Richard—or even Jane—for company was alleviated by frequent visits to Darcy House. Much to her surprise, Elizabeth had received an invitation to visit Georgiana two days following the betrothal dinner. Although she had enjoyed making Georgiana's acquaintance, she had expected Mr. Darcy to discourage his sister's association with a woman of low connections and "tolerable" appearance.

On further reflection, Elizabeth concluded that Mr. Darcy had conceded the necessity of the women's acquaintance based on his sister's fondness for Richard. Perhaps he saw Elizabeth's presence in their lives as unavoidable.

The first invitation was followed by others, and soon Elizabeth was visiting Darcy House almost every day. Mrs. Gardiner also invited Georgiana for tea on numerous occasions, and she accepted quite graciously.

Mr. Darcy was in London but appeared to make it a practice to never be at home when Elizabeth visited. So she was spared his cryptic remarks and disapproving glares. Richard maintained that Darcy did not dislike her, and Elizabeth conceded that he seemed to approve of her at the betrothal dinner—although she could not say he actually enjoyed her company.

However, he went to some trouble to avoid her at Darcy House, and upon the rare occasions she encountered him, his manner was proud and distant.

Before his departure for Hargrave, Richard had acquainted Elizabeth with the particulars of Georgiana's sad history with Wickham. Elizabeth had been horrified at the story and disgusted with herself for believing any words the man spoke.

Georgiana herself later confessed the story to Elizabeth and appeared quite eager for a confidante. Having herself been deceived by Wickham, Elizabeth was quite capable of sympathizing with Georgiana's sense of shame, and the two women had many long talks on the subject.

They also amused themselves for many hours playing the pianoforte. Georgiana was a far more accomplished player than Elizabeth, but lacked any confidence in her abilities. Elizabeth encouraged her to practice performing before an audience, using Mrs. Annesley and servants who were diverted from their daily tasks as listeners.

On other occasions, Elizabeth would entertain Georgiana with satirical performances. One day, about three weeks into her acquaintance with Georgiana, Elizabeth was performing a particularly silly imitation of an instructor who had taught the pianoforte to her sister, Mary. Elizabeth pounded on the keys with stiff, straight arms, while simultaneously expostulating in Italian-accented English. After a few minutes, both women dissolved into giggles.

Just then, Elizabeth recognized they were not alone in the music room. She raised her gaze from the pianoforte to see Mr. Darcy standing in the doorway and observing them with a very serious air. No doubt he disapproved of such frivolities, but Elizabeth was not prepared to desist. Darcy's sister required more levity in her life, and Elizabeth had undertaken this mission. She raised her chin a fraction, daring Mr. Darcy to disapprove.

"William!" Georgiana strolled across the room and took her brother's hands. He kissed her warmly on the cheek. Whatever his other faults, Elizabeth thought, Mr. Darcy was an excellent brother. Georgiana would sing his praises at every opportunity.

Even following the disaster at Ramsgate, Mr. Darcy had apparently treated his sister gently and with great consideration for her feelings. Elizabeth could imagine many brothers or fathers flying into a rage over such behavior.

"Miss Bennet." Darcy bowed slightly, and she gave him a small curtsey in response.

"If you have come to frighten us into seriousness of purpose, I am afraid you will fail with me, although I cannot vouch for your sister," Elizabeth teased.

Georgiana's eyes sparkled as she laughed at the sportive way her friend spoke with her brother.

"Indeed, you mistake me," Mr. Darcy said. "The sound of your laughter was a most pleasant welcome home. I pray you, continue." He settled himself into a chair and regarded her with a small, challenging smile.

Georgiana's eyes widened in alarm at the prospect of exhibiting such merriment before her very proper older brother.

Elizabeth lifted her head a little higher. "My courage rises with every attempt to intimidate me. Come, Georgiana, shall we play our duet for him?"

Georgiana bit her lip nervously—she understood which duet Elizabeth meant—but she seated herself on the bench beside her friend.

This particular bit of silliness had been inspired by a performance Elizabeth had observed once in Meryton, where two sisters in the Hamilton family had been determined to outperform each other—even when performing a duet. Each had attempted to play with more flourish and louder than the other until the entire piece dissolved into a cacophonous mess.

As they played, Elizabeth and Georgiana deliberately bumped each other and pushed each other's hands out of the way, placing arms on top of hands and striking the keys more and more forcefully. Only halfway through the piece, both women were laughing too much to continue.

Elizabeth caught Mr. Darcy smiling, without any evident sign of disapproval. "Have we assaulted your ears long enough?" she asked pertly.

He lifted an eyebrow and considered before responding. "While I would not say the listening experience was precisely pleasurable, there is enjoyment to be had in observing others enjoying themselves."

Expecting censure, Elizabeth was confused by Mr. Darcy's reaction. Perhaps he was simply happy to observe his sister laughing. Richard had said his cousin was concerned about her lack of spirits.

Elizabeth rose from the bench. "I should allow you time alone with your sister."

"No stay, Elizabeth!" Georgiana insisted. "I shall ring for tea."

Darcy's eyes caught and held hers with an unnerving intensity. "Yes, stay for refreshments." Elizabeth glanced away, her body tingling with that vague unsettling sense she always felt in his presence. Did he truly wish for her company, or was he only inviting her for his sister's sake?

"Of course," she murmured. "If you wish."

"Miss Bennet." Something in his voice compelled her to meet his eyes. "I do wish it. Most ardently."

***

For how long had he been staring at nothing? Darcy once again concentrated his attention on the letter from his steward at Pemberley. Blast! He must have read this passage three times. He could blame exhaustion; he had not slept well in the past weeks. Truth be told, it had been months—since his ill-fated visit to Rosings—since he had experienced a complete night of rest. Brandy or port before bed helped him to drop off, but he frequently awakened in the middle of the night.

However, if he were honest with himself, he would admit the true reason for his inattention this night was straining his ears for the sounds of Elizabeth's arrival. His study was near the back of Darcy House, and activities at the front were often muffled.

It is of no matter when she arrives, he reminded himself. *She is Georgiana's guest, not mine.* Despite delivering stern lectures to himself all morning, he knew he would be helpless to resist the sounds of Elizabeth's voice singing or gently teasing his sister.

It was pathetic. A grown man. The master of Pemberley. And he could not stay away from a woman any more than a small boy could resist an illicit sweet.

Perhaps he should resume his routine of repairing to his club when she was due for a visit. But that was almost worse. He would wonder where she had sat, what she had said, which dress she had worn, and what she had eaten. He worried anxiously whether she was happy. If Richard had returned from his estate. If he had kissed her….

Darcy attempted to keep his visits to the music room short. He said little and addressed as few comments to Elizabeth as possible. But he had an overwhelming need to simply share her presence and bask in her essence. He wanted to observe the power of her fine eyes and see where their gaze alighted. He wanted to provoke that arch smile and teasing glance. Above all, he wanted to remove her to Pemberley and make love to her.

Darcy shook his head sharply. He must suppress such thinking. Richard's prolonged absence was both a blessing and a curse— for it permitted him to fantasize that Elizabeth was his.

Darcy pushed himself out of his desk chair, hoping some movement would help. At Pemberley, he would often use a long ride to clear his thoughts, but it was impossible in London. He loathed the forced inactivity.

He poured himself another brandy, despite knowing he should not indulge so early in the day, but he could not discover a different means of quieting his roiling thoughts. At least each glass of brandy rendered his feelings a little more distant.

The crystal clinked, and the liquid splashed into the glass as he poured. Darcy heard no sounds of girlish laughter or quick feminine footsteps in the hall. Elizabeth had been engaged to visit

Georgiana and stay for dinner the previous day but had sent a note delaying by a day. What if she was ill? Fear gripped Darcy, and he was seized with a desire to burst through the study door and seek out Elizabeth immediately.

Get a hold of yourself!

Darcy clutched the almost empty glass and forced his leaden limbs into the chair. Georgiana would inform him if Elizabeth were sick.

But would the Gardiners know the best doctors in London? He knew Elizabeth's aunt had several children. Would she have time to adequately nurse a sick niece? What if the Gardiners themselves were sick?

Darcy rose again with the intention of seeking out Georgiana when he heard the front door knocker sound. He sank again into his chair, relieved and a bit foolish.

However, he did not hear Elizabeth. The muffled voice sounded like a man's. Was he to have no relief from his worries over Elizabeth? Darcy scowled at the paper spread on the desk before him as if it were responsible for his confusion.

A moment later, a footman opened the door and announced, "Colonel Fitzwilliam, sir."

Richard strode in, rumpled and travel-worn. His mouth was set, and worry lines were carved around his eyes. Darcy's anxiety about Elizabeth's health returned twofold.

Darcy clasped his cousin's hand. "When did you return to London?"

His cousin ignored the chair Darcy indicated but grabbed its back hard enough that his knuckles turned white. "Just now. I only stopped at the Gardiners before coming here."

Darcy's eyebrows rose. Richard had not taken the time to return to his own house? There *was* a problem with Elizabeth! He felt as if a hand were squeezing his lungs, making breathing difficult. "What has occurred? Is Elizabeth ill?"

"No, thank God, nothing like that." Richard sighed, running his hand over his jaw. "It is Wickham."

Anger surged through Darcy. He believed he had managed to banish the blackguard from their lives. Had he somehow imposed himself on Elizabeth? Darcy's hands itched to wring Wickham's neck.

"Wickham has run off with Elizabeth's youngest sister, Lydia." Richard's tone was bitter. "She was visiting a friend at Brighton, where Wickham's regiment was stationed. They escaped under cover of darkness—three days ago. Mr. Bennet is here; he believes they are in London, but he and Mr. Gardiner have been unable to locate her. I returned as soon as I received word."

The enormity of Fitzwilliam's words washed over Darcy. What Elizabeth must be suffering with such scandal having befallen her family! If only he could be at the house on Gracechurch Street to comfort her. But it was not his place. He could not so much as touch her hand.

Why had the Gardiners not notified Darcy of the matter immediately? But, no, they had no reason to believe he had particular interest in Wickham or assisting Elizabeth. Damn the need for discretion!

And damn Wickham! Richard raised an eyebrow, and Darcy realized he had spoken the words aloud.

"Indeed," Richard agreed. "I knew I would regret not shooting him after Ramsgate."

"You would regret Newgate as well." But his cousin waved thoughts of imprisonment away.

"Tell me everything." Darcy gestured Richard to a seat and poured some of his best French brandy for his cousin, who accepted it gratefully. Then he obtained another brandy for himself, noting that the level in the decanter was getting low. A broken heart was expensive.

After seating himself, Darcy swirled the caramel colored liquid in his glass. "Poor Elizabeth. She does not deserve such scandal."

Richard regarded Darcy strangely, and only then did he recognize he had used her Christian name. He set the brandy down on the desk and said the first thing that came to mind. "Is she very distressed?"

Richard's free hand clenched into a fist. "Yes, very." He frowned at Darcy. Did he suspect something? Feigning a nonchalance he did not feel, Darcy sipped the brandy but barely tasted the liquid on his tongue. Richard continued. "She is concerned about the family's loss of reputation. She even offered to release me from the engagement."

How like Elizabeth! Darcy was ashamed at his surge of hope.

"Naturally, I declined."

Darcy nodded. "I would never let her go either." Richard frowned again, and Darcy cursed his loose tongue.

Darcy needed to divert the other man's attention. "What has been done to recover them?" he asked.

Richard shook his head and leaned forward in his chair. "I know not. Elizabeth's father and uncle were out when I called. They were traced as far as London, and we have no reason to think they have left. Lydia appears to believe Wickham would marry her, but we know his character too well—he would need monetary inducement."

Darcy nodded a grim assent.

Full of restless energy, Richard pushed away from the chair and prowled about the room like a caged animal. Finally, he stopped at the window and gazed out at the street. "I hoped you might know of some of his old acquaintances in London, someone he might contact."

"I have some ideas."

"Good." Richard regarded Darcy intently. "If you give me those names, I—"

"No."

His cousin blinked in surprise. "I beg your pardon?"

"I will not give you the names. The fault is mine, so must the remedy be."

Richard sighed in exasperation. "The fault is Wickham's."

"If I had not been so hesitant to lay out my private business before the world, he could not have imposed himself on an innocent girl like Miss Lydia."

Richard rolled his eyes. "You take too much on yourself."

"Nevertheless, allow me to be of service to Eliz—Miss Elizabeth—and to you." He chuckled mirthlessly. "It will be your wedding gift."

Richard gave Darcy a long look. "Very well. But let me be the one to pay Wickham. Elizabeth is my family, or will be shortly. You must not lay out funds for this."

"Your desire to care for your fiancée's family is commendable," Darcy said neutrally.

Richard shook his hand, apparently not noticing that Darcy had not agreed to his terms. "Thank you. I knew I could count on you."

Darcy gave an inward sigh of relief. He had no intention of allowing his cousin to pay a penny. If Darcy could not marry Elizabeth, at least he could be of some service to her in this matter. "My pleasure."

"I shall retire to my townhouse for some clean clothing and then visit the Gardiners to learn if they have made progress. Send word when you have news."

"I will."

***

Darcy handed his hat to the footman and strode toward the ballroom without waiting for the man to announce him. He was certain he had actually declined the invitation to this ball celebrating Lady Howard's birthday; he declined most invitations. He was equally certain that Lord and Lady Howard would be delighted at his presence. Enticing the "elusive" Mr. Darcy to a ball was considered a social coup.

Not that he planned to linger.

It had taken him two days to locate Wickham and arrange for a satisfactory agreement with the scoundrel. But when he had visited his cousin's townhouse to share the news, Darcy had been told Fitzwilliam was at the Howards' ball. Darcy very much doubted Richard had wished to attend a celebration under the current circumstances, but perhaps his mother had applied her unique persuasive powers to insist on it.

These affairs could drag on into the small hours of the morning, and Darcy wished to immediately inform Richard of the recent developments. So he had returned home, donned suitable attire, and rushed to Howard House.

Standing at the entrance to the ballroom, Darcy scanned the crowd. If only Fitzwilliam still wore his uniform! The red would render him far more noticeable.

It was quite a crush of glittering jewels, silk dresses, and fluttering fans. Matrons gossiped along the edges of the dance floor, while the young people danced and flirted. Most of the older men would be in the card rooms. Perhaps he should seek his cousin there. Darcy espied his Aunt Rachel but discarded the idea of soliciting her assistance. Richard likely was avoiding his parents.

Darcy's eye was drawn to one of the dancers, a light and pleasing figure he would recognize anywhere. Elizabeth wore an elegant gown of light blue silk and flowers in her hair that complimented it perfectly. Since she was unaware of his regard, Darcy indulged his desire to gaze upon her. The force of her personality shone in every step as she moved in perfect harmony with the music. However, knowing her as he did, Darcy discerned how her smile was a bit forced and her spirits rather subdued. Her sister's scandal had taken its toll.

The dance came to a close, and only then did Darcy notice that Elizabeth was partnered with Richard. The countess must have convinced her son it was a perfect opportunity to introduce his betrothed to the society of the *ton*. Darcy pushed through the crush toward his cousin, but his progress was slow. Revelers around him noted his presence, staring and remarking on it behind their hands. No doubt matchmaking mothers and simpering society misses were already planning their strategies.

Darcy increased his pace, fearing he would lose his cousin in the crowd. Finally, he found the couple near the lemonade table. "Cousin!" Richard exclaimed. "I never expected you here." But Darcy's eyes fixed on Elizabeth and would not waver. She was as beautiful as ever, but her fine eyes were shadowed by dark circles, and her complexion was pale. *Thank God it is within my power to relieve her suffering!*

"I had no plans on attending this ball. I came seeking you." His cousin's eyes widened, and Elizabeth seemed alarmed. "The news is good." Elizabeth relaxed visibly.

Darcy took his cousin by the elbow. "Let us repair to the veranda. I pray you, excuse us, Miss Bennet." Richard murmured something to Elizabeth, then turned and followed Darcy through a pair of French doors.

The night was warm, but there was a breeze, which rendered the outside slightly more tolerable than the ballroom. There were several trysting couples on the veranda; Darcy led his cousin to a deserted location cast in shadows by the leaves of a weeping cherry tree.

"What is it?" his cousin asked in a low, urgent voice. "Do not leave me in suspense."

"I found Wickham and Lydia," Darcy said. "They are in London, as yet unmarried." His cousin frowned at this revelation. "But I was able to persuade Wickham to it. An announcement of their engagement has been placed in tomorrow's paper, and Lydia arrived at the Gardiners' house three hours ago. They will be married within the week."

"Damn it! You have left nothing for me to do!" Fitzwilliam scowled and turned away, leaning his elbows on the marble balustrade of the veranda.

Darcy had anticipated his cousin's dissatisfaction. "I feared that only immediate monetary incentive would prevent Wickham's flight."

Richard gave a derisive snort. "I made my wishes clear. I did not wish you to take on the expense!"

Darcy ignored the outburst. "There is much still to be accomplished, which I am happy to leave in your hands." His interest piqued, Richard glanced over his shoulder at Darcy. "The agreement with Wickham will need Mr. Bennet's approval." His cousin regarded him with narrowed eyes. "I do not wish anyone to know of my involvement. Wickham is sworn to secrecy, and Lydia is unaware of my role."

Realization dawned on Richard's face. "So you have accomplished all the work, and I am to take all the credit!"

Darcy nodded. "It is fitting. I have no desire to explain my history with Wickham to the Bennets, and they will be grateful for your assistance." Darcy grimaced. "*I* do not need their gratitude—and would prefer they never know."

Richard regarded him soberly. "Only *you* would prefer to conceal the best of yourself from others." He sighed heavily. "Very well, I will abide by your wishes, but you must allow me to reimburse your expenses."

"No," Darcy spoke firmly. "You are rehabilitating a neglected estate. Wickham is my responsibility, and I will bear the expense."

Richard slammed his fist on the balustrade. "Darcy!" There was no mistaking the tone of exasperation.

"I will not be moved in this."

"Always so damned high-handed!" Darcy said nothing; this was a complaint he heard before from his cousin. Richard stared into the night. After a minute, he finally grumbled, "Very well. But you should know I will be seeking an opportunity to return the favor."

"As you wish." Darcy cleared his throat. "Above all, do not reveal my involvement to Miss Elizabeth. If you must say anything, tell her I only acted as your emissary to Wickham." Richard frowned, but Darcy held up a hand to forestall any protest. "I ask much of you, old friend. But I do not wish her to ever feel beholden to me." Richard regarded him with narrowed eyes for a long moment, and Darcy feared he had betrayed himself. Finally, his cousin nodded.

Darcy leaned on the balustrade beside Richard. "I think it best if you inform Miss Elizabeth this night. She will see the announcement in the morning's paper."

Richard sighed. "Just as well. She only attended this ball at my insistence, and *I* only attended at my mother's insistence. But I had hoped it would divert her attention from her sister."

As if conjured by the mention of her name, Elizabeth's voice floated through the air, calling for her fiancé. Both men turned to see her rushing toward them.

"I apologize for interrupting your pressing business, but I heard your mother asking, 'Where is my son hiding now?'" Elizabeth imitated his aunt's stentorian tones so perfectly that Darcy could not help but laugh. "She has arranged for you to dance with someone named Honoria Pigeon."

Richard groaned. "She laughs like a horse and jabs my ribs with her elbow when we dance." He regarded Elizabeth with chagrin. "If Mama hopes to persuade me to break our betrothal, Honoria Pigeon is not the means to accomplish it."

Darcy laughed. "Perhaps you should make good your escape."

Richard gave him a knowing look. "Indeed. As soon as I tell Elizabeth your news, I shall call for the carriage."

Darcy bowed, said his farewells, and strode toward the French doors, now open to receive the evening breezes. Once inside the ballroom, however, Darcy hesitated. Some impulse toward self-torture caused him to turn back toward the veranda.

Partially concealed by the draperies, Darcy could view Elizabeth and Richard quite clearly but not hear the words they exchanged.

Such covert actions were beneath him, but he felt compelled to it. Although he did not have the luxury of claiming the credit for helping Elizabeth's family, he selfishly wished to witness her reaction to the news.

Richard spoke earnestly to her, clasping both her hands in his. Her eyes fixed on him anxiously as her teeth worried her lower lip. Then suddenly, her face transformed with joy, and she flung her arms around her betrothed's neck. The relief and happiness etched on her features made Darcy's every action worthwhile. She would never be his, but at least he had given her this gift.

He told himself sternly that it was time to depart, but he could not bring his body to move. He might as well have been carved from marble. Elizabeth's slim body was clinging to Richard's as she gazed at him, full of adoration. He did nothing to discourage the embrace, despite the public location. In fact, his hands tenderly caressed her back.

And then, his head descended toward hers, and he kissed her.

It was a brief brushing of the lips but enough to excite Darcy's imagination. How would he feel to be the one kissing her? How would her body feel, pressed to his? Would her heart beat faster? Would Richard have gone further in a less public venue? *Had he kissed her before? With greater passion?* Richard gazed down at Elizabeth as if she were the air he needed to breathe. And Elizabeth, her fine eyes shining, clung to front of his coat, almost begging him to kiss her again.

Darcy could not pull himself away from the sight, even as it drove knives, one by one, excruciatingly slowly, into his heart. His eyes would not even close to shut away the view. He could only watch, transfixed, as the torture continued.

Richard kissed her again, more slowly and with more passion, drinking in the taste of her lips. One hand cradled her head and kept it pressed to his.

Darcy had kissed women. Enough to know something about the process. However, he had never known the kind of physical passion that approached what his cousin was experiencing at that moment—with the woman Darcy loved.

Richard ended the kiss after a matter of mere seconds and contented himself with gazing into her adoring eyes. *What a fool,* Darcy thought scornfully. *She would have allowed him more liberties!* He would have kissed her until she was gasping for breath. He would have touched her everywhere propriety would permit—and a few places it would not.

A black beast of jealousy descended over Darcy. He clutched at the velvet draperies with trembling hands so his body would not yield to the temptation to race onto the veranda and rip them from each other's arms, demanding that Elizabeth accept him instead. He could challenge Richard to a duel, a time-honored method for ridding oneself of rivals. Then he could claim her for his own.

Darcy stood there for several long moments, attempting to control his racing heart and trembling body. He was a man, not a savage. He was Fitzwilliam Darcy, master of Pemberley. He could master jealousy, not let it provoke him into destructive and rash actions.

Darcy was disgusted with himself, falling prey to these baser emotions. Lusting after his own cousin's fiancée.

Finally, the happy couple broke apart and made their way toward the ballroom. Darcy was released to stumble away from the window. Staggering out of the ballroom, he no doubt convinced many guests he was in his cups. Within minutes, he had achieved the safety of his coach and was clattering back to Darcy House.

Choked and sickened, Darcy tore savagely at his cravat. He could not continue in this manner. He had believed his feelings to be under control, but tonight had demonstrated how thoroughly he had deceived himself.

He desperately needed a different solution. A more radical solution. And he needed it immediately.

***

Darcy was writing last-minute letters in his study, while Tucker packed away estate records into a trunk on the far side of the room. Without any warning, Richard burst through the door.

Darcy did not glance up. "You must have received my note."

Richard brandished the paper at him. "Is this a joke?"

Darcy stood, folded his letter, and handed it to Tucker for posting. He waited until Tucker had departed to take the trunk up to the attic. "No," he responded shortly.

"It must be," Richard insisted.

"Look around you." Darcy's voice was calm.

His cousin glanced around. Covers had already been draped over most of the furniture. With one night remaining at Darcy House, only the bedrooms, dining room, and drawing room were still fully available for the family's use.

"I do not understand!" Richard sputtered. Under other circumstances, Darcy might have found it amusing.

"I am closing up Darcy House," Darcy patiently repeated what he had written in the note. "It will run on a skeleton staff. The remaining staff will travel to Pemberley. After staying at Pemberley for a week, we shall close it up as well. Then Georgiana and I will take a ship for America."

Richard shoved his fingers through his already unruly brown hair. "Just like that?"

"Indeed."

"But why?" Richard was watching Darcy's face a little too intently for his comfort.

"My father's brother, my Uncle Clive, has invited us to visit him in Philadelphia."

"Yes, yes, so you said in your note. But why now?"

If he only knew the true reason, he would happily purchase my passage himself.

Darcy shrugged. "I have always desired to see it, and Georgiana never had many opportunities to travel, since she was so young when our parents died." Fitzwilliam was still frowning at Darcy, and he found himself staring down at his desk, rearranging the ink bottle and papers. His cousin's gaze weighed upon him.

He struggled to keep his face blank. "It is also a good excuse for delaying Georgiana's coming out. The idea of a debut frightens her. Time away from the concerns of the *ton* and the marriage market will be beneficial to her." Richard's shoulders relaxed fractionally, and some of his frown lines smoothed out.

Darcy had hoped Georgiana's debut was a reason his cousin would understand.

"But America is so far away!" Richard exclaimed.

And that is why it appeals. "Indeed. It *was* inconsiderate of them to put the country on another continent. But we shall not be gone long."

Richard regarded him suspiciously. "How long is 'not long?'"

-"We have no fixed departure date. A couple months, maybe. We will see how we like it and whether they have anything that resembles decent tea."

"Months!" Richard cried. "You will miss the wedding."

"I am afraid so," Darcy murmured.

"Elizabeth will be disappointed."

Darcy noticed his cousin carefully scrutinizing him. Had he flinched at the mention of her name? "You *did* change the wedding date," Darcy observed.

Although Lydia and Wickham's marriage had served to quell the worst of the scandal, rumors still circulated, and Richard's parents had insisted that he and Elizabeth delay their wedding a few more months until the scandal abated. Darcy thought his cousin a fool for acquiescing. If Elizabeth agreed to marry *him*, Darcy would not rest until he had dragged her before an altar.

"You will miss Bingley's wedding as well!"

Darcy experienced a twinge of guilt. "I penned a letter of apology to Bingley."

Richard sank into a dustcloth-covered chair. "This is ridiculous! When did you become so impulsive? It must be Bingley's influence."

Darcy laughed, although it sounded hollow to his ears. "I have wished to visit America for some time. My business affairs are stable. The opportunity presented itself."

"I have never heard you express a desire to visit America," Richard observed. Darcy merely shrugged. "What about Georgiana? Will she be safe in such a savage country?"

"It is not darkest Africa." Darcy grinned. "I am fairly certain they have cooked food and draperies and banks – among other trappings of civilization." Richard merely folded his arms over his chest. "I will write to you. Mail is regular—every two weeks or so depending on the winds. If any tricky estate issues arise, I am happy to advise you by letter."

Richard snorted. "Hang the estate!" He stood and looked Darcy directly in the eye. Did he suspect Darcy was hiding something? God willing, he would never guess what.

Richard finally shook his head and walked restlessly to the window. "I-I will miss you, William." Darcy was touched. He knew that removing himself from England—and temptation—was the best course, but he would miss his cousin's company.

"I will miss you as well." Darcy crossed the room to rest his hand on his cousin's shoulder. "But we will return before you have had a chance to notice we are gone."

Chapter 5

"I cannot believe it has been nearly a year!" Georgiana exclaimed.

"It did pass quickly," Darcy agreed. They had viewed many corners of the new country of America and met many interesting people. They had not intended to remain so long, but the promise of some new wonder or intriguing place would always entice them. And in truth, both Darcy and Georgiana had reasons to delay their return to England.

In fact, if Darcy had not been concerned about growing tensions between England and America over naval issues, they might have remained longer. But if the two countries went to war, crossing the Atlantic would be fraught with danger.

It had been almost a year since Darcy had stood on the deck of a ship crossing the Atlantic Ocean to the New World. Now he crossed in the other direction, pleased that a thin, gray band of English coastline was within sight. Darcy experienced an unexpected swell of emotion. Despite the attendant anxiety, he was very happy to be home.

Georgiana stood beside him, one hand on her bonnet lest it blow away. Darcy had dispensed with his hat altogether while up on deck. Darcy glanced down at her. "Well, dear heart, are you happy to be back?"

"Oh, yes!" she breathed. "I shall miss all the friends we made during our travels—and I do hope Uncle Clive comes for a visit—but America is not home. I cannot wait to see Pemberley again!"

Darcy smiled indulgently. "I missed Pemberley as well." Traveling had been beneficial for Georgiana. Away from the pressures and snares of the *ton*, she had blossomed as a mature young woman and grown in confidence.

"But mostly, I cannot wait to see everyone! Mrs. Reynolds and Cook and Mary at Darcy House. And Gwendolyn and Cecily." During their travels, Georgiana had maintained correspondences with many school friends. "And even Uncle and Aunt Fitzwilliam. But especially Elizabeth and Richard!"

America had been a refuge for Darcy. It was a relief to know he would not encounter Elizabeth at a dinner party or a stroll in Hyde Park. The entire continent had been blessedly free of Elizabeth.

Unfortunately, Elizabeth was not equally absent from Darcy's dreams—waking and sleeping. Everywhere there were little reminders. He would see a dress that reminded him of one she wore, discover a book they had discussed, or hear a piece of music she had played. Such incidents would often provoke black moods, which he endeavored to conceal from Georgiana.

These occurrences had decreased in frequency, however, and Darcy hoped that seeing her married to his cousin would allow him to banish this obsession forever.

If not … no, it did not bear thinking on. Friendship with Elizabeth and Richard was important to Georgiana—and to Darcy himself. The thought of permanent exile was insupportable. Darcy would simply have to further hone his thespian abilities.

"Oh, may we visit them first?" Georgiana asked. "I wish to see Elizabeth's wedding dress, and she has a duet to learn with me."

Darcy hugged his sister close to his side. "They should be in town, unless they are still on their wedding trip."

Letters to Darcy and Georgiana had described how Richard and Elizabeth had delayed the wedding because of the scandal surrounding Lydia's marriage. Then came the news that Lydia was with child and too ill to travel for the wedding. Softhearted Elizabeth had agreed to delay the event until Lydia was well enough to travel. Tragically, Lydia had delivered a stillborn child too early and then had followed him into death.

The entire Bennet family thus entered into a period of mourning, during which it was unthinkable to conduct a wedding ceremony. Just as the mourning period was drawing to a close, Mr. Bennet had fallen ill, and Elizabeth had been needed at Longbourn to help care for him.

In a letter to Darcy, Richard had joked that the entire Bennet family seemed to conspire to prevent their marriage. The last letter from his cousin had been four weeks ago—just before Darcy and Georgiana had departed for a two-week tour of New England prior to boarding a ship in Boston. Richard had written the letter two days before the wedding date, so by now the couple would have been wed several weeks.

Selfishly, Darcy was relieved to be spared attendance at the wedding ceremony. Although Georgiana would have loved to witness the event, Darcy could not imagine calmly sitting in a pew while his heart shattered.

"William! I see church spires!" Georgiana exclaimed joyfully. "We are so close. Will we see Richard and Elizabeth first? I have missed them so!"

More than a year of practice helped Darcy conceal the anxiety flooding his body. "Naturally, dear one. I can deny you nothing." He even produced a smile for his sister.

***

As they walked down the street, drawing ever closer to Fitzwilliam's townhouse, Darcy breathed deeply, attempting to quiet the agitation in his chest. This visit reminded him uncomfortably of the awful betrothal dinner. Desperately, he prayed that time apart and the sight of Elizabeth as a married woman would break her hold on him.

As they drew closer to the house, Darcy espied a dark figure on the porch, closing the door and walking slowly down the steps to the sidewalk.

Forgetting herself, Georgiana rushed the remaining distance, calling, "Elizabeth!"

Elizabeth looked up at them, her mouth slightly open in surprise. Her eyes were wide, a rich dark blue, and her glossy dark hair hung in curls around her face. She was so beautiful it stole the breath from his body.

In that moment, he knew all of his efforts had been for naught. Hundreds of miles and a year's worth of days—and it came to nothing. He was still as much in love with Elizabeth as he had ever been.

And he always would be.

Elizabeth gave a small smile as Georgiana nearly collided with her and then wrapped her in an enthusiastic embrace. Darcy could not stifle his grin. It was a rare occasion indeed when Georgiana was the more exuberant of the two women.

Only after Georgiana released Elizabeth did Darcy realized she was dressed in black. From her hat to her shoes. Mourning!

But for whom? Had her father passed away? Had the wedding been further delayed?

Darcy gave her a small bow. This close, he noticed how thin she was; had she neglected to eat while nursing her father? Her skin was pale and tight. Yes, she was beautiful, but he felt a chill of alarm at her pallor and the haunted look in her eyes. Something was very wrong.

"Mr. Darcy." Her slight smile did not reach her eyes. "How long have you been in Town?"

"We only arrived today!" Georgiana announced. "We changed clothes at Darcy House—which is all in an uproar because they never received William's letter informing them we were returning—and then we ventured out again to see you and Richard!"

Elizabeth started. Her eyes darted from Georgiana to Darcy. "Did you not receive the last letters I sent you?" Darcy shook his head mutely, a deep sense of alarm forming in his chest. "I sent you several letters—beginning four weeks ago." Elizabeth had written directly to *him*? What could have prompted it?

"We were visiting New England for two weeks before we sailed; it would have been difficult for any letter to reach us," Darcy explained.

"Oh." Elizabeth's stricken face further stoked Darcy's anxiety. *Elizabeth* would not have written to inform him of her father's death or a similar Bennet family crisis. She would have left that to Richard.

"What is it?" he demanded, anxiety making his voice rough. "What has happened?"

He saw tears gather in her eyes. She looked wildly about her as if hoping someone else would take this unpleasant task from her.

"Oh, Georgiana, Mr. Darcy, I am so sorry to have to tell you. Richard is dead."

Chapter 6

Tears spilled down Elizabeth's cheeks as she said the words, but she kept her gaze fixed on them.

Darcy had known awful news was coming, but he had not been truly prepared for the full horror. His mind wanted to reject her words.

Not Richard.

Not Richard!

It must be a mistake. A ghastly joke.

No. No.

But the truth was written on Elizabeth's face.

The ground seemed to shift beneath his feet, a huge sinkhole sucking him down into the earth where no light or air could penetrate. He felt his heart beating at a galloping pace, and his breathing emerged in great constricted gasps.

"I-I believed you had—" Elizabeth's voice was constricted with emotion. "I t-thought my letters about Richard had prompted your return."

Darcy simply shook his head, unable to form a response.

Without a word or sound, Georgiana collapsed on the cobblestones beside him.

"Georgiana!" Darcy's cry was almost as a scream. *I cannot lose her as well!*

He gathered her into his arms, grateful that she had not struck her head. His sister moaned and rolled her head from side to side. Reason reasserted itself. She was not suffering from an awful disease but had crumbled under the weight of this sudden shock.

Elizabeth stroked Georgiana's hand. "Oh, my poor girl. She was not prepared for such news. Perhaps I should have waited."

"One can never be prepared for news of that nature." Darcy was pleased his voice did not tremble too much. "Nor could you have concealed the truth for long."

Elizabeth regarded Georgiana sadly. "I suppose not." She gestured to the door of the townhouse. "Bring her inside. She must rest."

As Darcy carried Georgiana through the door and into the drawing room, he realized dully that this house no longer belonged to Richard. It would now be the property of Richard's younger brother, Thomas, whom Darcy knew only slightly.

Darcy laid Georgiana on a couch. His sister sighed and turned her head but did not seem truly awake. Elizabeth directed the servants to obtain water and blankets for Georgiana, appearing to be quite at home. Of course, she had spent a year preparing to become the mistress of this house.

Had Richard's death occurred before or after the wedding? Darcy supposed it was of little import now, but a voice at the back of his mind would not let the matter rest.

As he watched her press handkerchiefs into Georgiana's hand, Darcy realized that as much pain as he was experiencing, Elizabeth's loss must have been even more wrenching. Darcy had lost a cousin, but she had lost the love of her life. And now *she* was lending comfort to Richard's wayward relatives!

Elizabeth knelt by Georgiana and roused the other woman enough to drink some water. Georgiana would have stood, but Elizabeth encouraged her to lie down as she recovered from the shock.

"You seem to be managing very well," Georgiana whispered hoarsely.

Elizabeth retreated to a chair near Georgiana's couch. "I have had three weeks to accustom myself to the loss. At first, I confess I did not cope well at all." She glanced down at her hands.

Darcy strode to the sideboard and poured himself a generous portion of brandy, not caring whose decanter it now was. Thus fortified, he seated himself and asked, "Will you tell us how this dreadful event came to pass?"

Elizabeth swallowed, still gazing at her hands twisted together in her lap. "Richard fell while he was riding—here in London. He was not even riding fast, but the horse shied and lost its footing. Richard fell onto a wrought iron fence and sustained an injury to his side. It was the day before we were to be wed." Elizabeth's voice was calm and level as she recited the events, but her hands twisted over and over, fingers tangled, while her eyes seemed to focus on nothing.

"At first, he seemed all right. The doctor said he detected no internal damage, and they stitched him up. But then—" She closed her eyes. "The wound became infected." Darcy inhaled a harsh breath through his teeth. Georgiana might not understand what that meant, but he certainly did.

Elizabeth opened her eyes, staring at the floor. "They tried everything but could do nothing to help him." Tears were now spilling freely down Elizabeth's cheeks; she wiped them away with the back of her hand. "Richard was so strong. Up until the very last, he was joking and telling everyone we would be better off without him." Elizabeth gave a watery smile and met Darcy's eyes for the first time.

He attempted to return her smile. "That sounds like Richard."

"Yes." Elizabeth dabbed at her eyes with a handkerchief. "He knew he was dying, but his only thoughts were about those he was leaving behind. He rewrote his will and spent hours telling Thomas about Hargrave Manor. He wrote you a letter, Mr. Darcy, a long one. I do not know what it contained, but I posted it to America."

Darcy cursed the impulse that had brought him back to England both too soon and too late. "My uncle will forward our post."

Elizabeth nodded. "He was so strong for so long and then—" A sob escaped her throat.

Darcy leaned forward and covered her hand with his. "You need not share every detail now."

She met his gaze. "In the end, he did not feel much pain. The doctor gave him laudanum."

He savored the warmth of her hand; it felt so right in his. Disgusted with himself, he pulled his hand away. The woman had just lost everything.

Georgiana was freely sobbing, having soaked the handkerchiefs Elizabeth had supplied. Darcy moved to sit beside her on the couch, wrapping his arm around her and murmuring words of comfort. His relationship with Elizabeth might be fraught, but at least he could provide help to his sister.

Elizabeth recovered her composure quickly. She rang for tea and served it, remembering how both guests preferred theirs prepared. Although her eyes were puffy and red, she concentrated her efforts on improving Georgiana's spirits. Effortlessly, Elizabeth steered the conversation to happy memories and persuaded Georgiana to relate a story about Richard from her childhood. Darcy was full of admiration of Elizabeth's skill at assuaging his sister's grief.

Within an hour, Georgiana's tears had ceased, but she was very sleepy.

"I should return her to Darcy House," Darcy said, dreading the trip in a jolting carriage to a house ill-prepared for their arrival. The cook did not have sufficient food, and none of the maids had been summoned from Pemberley, so Georgiana would only have the assistance of the housekeeper.

"Would you like to remain here for the night?" Elizabeth asked softly, watching Georgiana drowse against the back of the couch. "We can send for some clothing for you and Georgiana."

Darcy hesitated, uncertain how to respond. How did Elizabeth come to be acting as a hostess in a house that now belonged to Thomas Fitzwilliam? Was she no longer living with the Gardiners? Surely she was not authorized to issue invitations?

"Is—" Darcy cleared his throat. "Is Thomas here?"

Elizabeth knitted her brows in confusion. "No. He is at Hargrave." Then her expression cleared. "Oh, I should explain. Richard wrote a will before he died. In it, he bequeathed this house and a sum of money to me." She blinked rapidly to hold back tears. "He was so good to me. He said these were the terms written into our marriage contract. Of course, we were never married ..." Her voice choked up, and she rubbed her hand over her mouth. "But he wanted me to have the house and some means of support."

Richard had accomplished all this while he was in pain and sick with a fever. Elizabeth had been right to accept his offer of marriage. Here was proof yet again that his cousin was the far better man. "That was very good of him." Elizabeth merely nodded, her lips pressed tightly together, holding in grief and pain. "But we should not impose on your privacy."

"No, please!" Her plea seemed too spontaneous to be other than genuine. "I have been quite alone here since taking residence two weeks ago. Some company would be very welcome." Her smile was merely the ghost of the arch smile he remembered so well. Darcy would, of course, agree to stay. He could deny her nothing, no matter the cost to him.

She made an attempt at her old teasing tone. "And if it is not too much trouble, I was hoping you might favor me with stories about the 'savage' lands of America."

***

The following morning, Elizabeth awoke at her usual time and descended for breakfast. Living in this house without Richard still felt wrong in many subtle ways. With so many memories of visiting him here, she found it difficult to remember he would not simply walk through the door one day. For the most part, she found it comforting to be surrounded by such memories, but upon occasion, they grew to be too much, and she needed a brisk walk or visit to the Gardiners.

Richard had not related to her the alterations to his will, so his bequest had been a revelation when the solicitor had notified her. Her first thought had been to refuse the house and the income, which was unnecessarily generous. She understood his reasoning about the marriage contract, but they had not actually been married—although there were times she felt like his widow— and she did not believe herself to be entitled to his money or property.

Her Aunt and Uncle Gardiner had spent many hours persuading Elizabeth of the difficulties inherent in refusing the bequest. Ultimately, Elizabeth had been swayed by her knowledge that, on his deathbed, Richard's concerns had been about her future. Refusing the bequest would be refusing his wishes for her.

The Gardiners had also advised that possessing an income might be necessary to her family. Although her father's health had stabilized, he was still weak, and Mr. Collins would not hesitate to claim Longbourn once her father passed on.

Her mother fretted about their future and had relied on Mr. Bingley to care for her and the unmarried Bennet sisters. Jane, however, had confided to Elizabeth that Mr. Bingley's business interests had suffered a setback, and Caroline's spendthrift ways were costing him dearly. In fact, the Bingleys had recently sold their London house, and Jane had told Elizabeth that they might give up Netherfield in favor of a smaller house.

While the Bingleys' situation was by no means dire, Elizabeth recognized that she could not in good conscience refuse an income that could support her family without imposing a burden on Charles and Jane. The money Richard had settled on her was comfortable but not extravagant; however, the townhouse was a valuable property, and Elizabeth could sell it should her family need assistance.

In the short term, the townhouse had provided a valuable refuge during this trying time. Peace and quiet were often in short supply in the bustling Gardiner household, but Elizabeth had desperately needed both to grieve and plan for her future. Over the past year, her aunt and uncle had repeatedly reassured her that she was not a burden to their household, but she was pleased to relieve them of their responsibility toward her.

Nevertheless, she was very conscious that she was in an odd position. At one and twenty, never married, she now owned and managed her own household. More than one person had insisted she needed a chaperone to live with her, but Elizabeth had demurred. She had no relatives to fulfil the role and did not wish to incur the expense of hiring someone.

As she strolled toward the dining room, she wondered what Mr. Darcy thought of her situation. The previous day, his demeanor had been grave and distant, but she could not imagine he approved of all her choices. Did he believe Thomas should have the townhouse? Did he think it was improper for a young woman to live alone in London? He observed rules of propriety and felt his family pride strongly. Yes, he probably disapproved of almost everything.

Elizabeth reminded herself to make allowances for Mr. Darcy's feelings. His grief was fresh, while Elizabeth's had been a daily companion for three weeks. Although Mr. Darcy was often difficult and unpleasant, he had always been a good friend to Richard, who had thought very highly of his cousin. At the very least, Mr. Darcy did not appear to treat her with the same degree of disdain as Richard's parents or brothers.

Truth be told, Elizabeth was pleased to have the Darcys staying. Their presence was a reminder of happier times, and having visitors was a welcome distraction from the melancholy that sometimes threatened to weigh down her days.

Mr. Darcy was already seated at the breakfast table, a plate of food in front of him and a folded newspaper next to it. However, he was neither eating nor reading but was staring at nothing, apparently absorbed in his own thoughts.

"Mr. Darcy?" Elizabeth asked gently. He started out of his reverie. "I am sorry to startle you."

"No, I ... um ..." He blinked rapidly, only slowly focusing his eyes on her. "That is ... I fear I am not at my best this morning." He peered down at his plate as if surprised to find food before him.

"Indeed. It is quite understandable," she said softly. "I have experienced many such days lately."

Mr. Darcy looked up from his food, and his blue eyes caught and held hers in a mesmerizing gaze. "Miss Elizabeth, I apologize if I did not adequately convey this sentiment yesterday, but I am sorrier than I can express. To lose someone you love is grievous. But to lose a fiancé before you even had an opportunity to wed ..." He seemed at a loss for words and instead shook his head, massaging his forehead with one hand.

"Thank you for your kind words." Elizabeth was uncertain how to respond to this more sensitive version of Mr. Darcy. How long until he reverted to his haughty, difficult demeanor?

He did not seem to require further response, so Elizabeth filled her plate from the sideboard and seated herself at the table. Across the table sat the empty chair Richard had favored. She blinked back tears and took a bite of her eggs, hoping Mr. Darcy did not notice her melancholy spirits.

It had grown no easier over the past three weeks to live without Richard. He had been her best friend, her confidante. Aside from Jane, there was no one in the world with whom she had felt so comfortable. Together, they had laughed at many of the foibles of the society of London. Richard had helped her navigate the sometimes treacherous societal waters, but he had never regarded the world of the *ton* very seriously, as the rest of his family was wont to do.

She found Mr. Darcy's stern profile more than a little intimidating and wished she had Richard's reassuring smile to encourage her. Mr. Darcy was an eternal conundrum to Elizabeth but had been an open book to Richard. He would have ably interpreted the man's current mood and teased him out of any ill humor.

Elizabeth took a sip of coffee for strength. Richard was not here, but he would not wish her to shirk her duty as a hostess. Besides, Mr. Darcy might be a mystery, but at least solving the mystery would give her wits focus and distraction. "How is Georgiana?" she asked.

Mr. Darcy appeared to be pushing the food around on his plate rather than consuming it. "She was still asleep when I checked on her, and I thought it best not to awaken her. Unless of course, you need us to depart."

"No, no. She is welcome to stay as long as she likes—and you as well." Elizabeth silently castigated herself for sounding as if Mr. Darcy was an afterthought. Why did she always misspeak to the man? Fortunately, he appeared to take no notice.

Darcy swallowed some coffee and cleared his throat. "Last night, you said you felt alone in the house. Surely someone from your family could stay with you during this difficult time."

Would Mr. Darcy never stop surprising her? With the dreadful news she had imparted the previous day, why had he given her living arrangements any consideration at all? "Unfortunately, no one can be spared. My mother and sister Mary are occupied with helping my father during his convalescence. Jane would have visited, but she is close to her confinement, and I did not think it wise for her to travel."

"What of Mrs. Collins?"

Elizabeth gave a wan smile. "Lady Catherine objected most strenuously to my engagement to her nephew, so Mr. Collins has forbidden his wife to visit me." Mr. Darcy made a noise which sounded disapproving. "My sister, Kitty, offered to come, but I declined. She would be less of a help than a hindrance. But of course, my Aunt and Uncle Gardiner live nearby. They are excellent people."

Darcy frowned. Had she provoked his disdain already? "But they must be occupied with their own children."

How did he even remember the Gardiners' children? His unexpected concern was touching but also somewhat disconcerting. "Yes. Still, they have been most generous with their time and assistance." Darcy still frowned. Did he think her family should do more for her? Did he believe she should not live alone? Perhaps he would rather she had not taken possession of his cousin's house.

Mr. Darcy did not seem inclined to speak again. Elizabeth swallowed some coffee as she considered what to say next. "To be honest, some quiet time for reflection has been welcome. The days of Richard's illness were ... frantic and difficult." Mr. Darcy was silent, so she returned her attention to her plate. Oh, what could she say to him? He was always so inscrutable!

Perhaps a change of subject ... "But, I am pleased you and Georgiana are returned. It will be good to have your company." *Oh dear, did that sound as if I expect Mr. Darcy to bear me company?* Not that his visits were precisely unwelcome, but he was so unsettling and ... *How does he always manage to unnerve me so?*

Mr. Darcy gave her a guarded look, then returned his gaze to his plate. "Yes, Georgiana will undoubtedly be a frequent visitor, and you will be a great comfort to each other."

Apparently he did not anticipate visiting often, Elizabeth thought with relief. *Very well, I can bear the deprivation.*

However, she could not help wondering *why* he was not planning to visit. Perhaps he would seize this opportunity to sever his family's association with a woman of such low connections. But, no, then he would discourage Georgiana from visiting her. Oh, he was such a vexing man!

Elizabeth was startled by a knock at the front door, followed by the sounds of Grayson, her butler, opening it and a chorus of male voices she immediately recognized. Ah, another welcome distraction! She smiled despite herself.

Chapter 7

Darcy scowled. Whoever the visitors in the entrance hall were, they were too early and too loud to be intruding on a house in mourning. *Not to mention, too male.* Certain Elizabeth would resent the discourtesy, he was surprised to see a slight smile playing about her lips. Clearly she recognized the intruders' identities.

An all-too-familiar sensation pressed against his chest, speeding his heartbeat. Why were *men* visiting Elizabeth? The previous night, as he tossed unsleeping in his bed, Darcy had sorted through the emotions provoked by Richard's death and come to a painful realization. He might have expected shock and grief to destroy—or at least lessen—his desire for Elizabeth, but it had not. His heart still contracted when he heard her voice, and now he ached with the need to alleviate her pain.

Thus was his guilt doubled and re-doubled. It made his stomach churn with nausea. Darcy not only lusted after his cousin's fiancée, he lusted after his *dead* cousin's fiancée, practically his widow. He should be comforting her, not desiring her, and certainly not reacting like a jealous beast at the thought of other men visiting her home. There must be a special level of hell reserved for his particular kind of betrayal.

The butler entered with a small smile. "Forgive me, Miss Bennet, but you may have surmised who is calling."

Darcy suppressed a sigh. Only Elizabeth would have her servants addressing her with such familiarity after being the head of household for only a few weeks.

Elizabeth's smile was more than tolerant. "Yes, Grayson. Please show them to the blue drawing room. I will be there directly." Grayson left, closing the doors behind him, and Elizabeth looked back to Darcy. "Some of Richard's friends have come to visit, as is their wont over the past weeks. But you must have pressing business matters and should not feel obligated to remain on my account."

After nearly a year's absence, Darcy did indeed have numerous matters of business that required immediate attention, but Napoleon's army could not have prevented him from accompanying Elizabeth as she received an unknown number of male visitors. "I would be pleased to join you. I will remain until Georgiana is ready to depart in any event."

Her eyebrows rose in surprise, but Elizabeth merely nodded and led the way out of the breakfast room. As they crossed the entrance hall, Darcy's entire body tensed as if he were preparing to defend Elizabeth from these other men. The savage side of his nature was asserting itself. Despite loathing the sensation, Darcy was helpless to stem the tide of jealousy.

Full of visitors, the blue drawing room appeared far smaller than Darcy recalled from his previous visit. He recognized most of the men as friends of Richard's, although he knew none of them well. Lieutenant Johnson and Colonel Grant had served with his cousin on the continent; Richard had thought highly of both men. Gregory North, a friend of Richard's from school, had the decency to bring his wife, a petite woman with dull brown hair. At least Elizabeth was not the only woman.

However, he had a difficult time not frowning at the fourth man, Lord Michael Kirkwood, the son and heir of a viscount in Surrey. Darcy knew Kirkwood the best since they often traveled in the same circles. He was tall and handsome, with a quick wit and pleasing manners.

Greetings were exchanged, and everyone settled into chairs or settees. A maid entered with refreshments. The conversation was amiable but in subdued tones and of little consequence. Nevertheless, Darcy noticed how the visit buoyed Elizabeth's spirits; she smiled at little jokes, and some of the color returned to her face. No doubt Elizabeth had spent much time in the company of these men during her engagement to Richard.

Darcy distracted himself by marveling again at how similar Richard and Elizabeth had been in temperament, interests, and amiability! What could Darcy offer by comparison but a resentful temperament, taciturn disposition, and jealous heart? True, he could provide far more material advantage, but he now understood Elizabeth well enough to know fortune meant nothing to her. No, all he could have offered was a desperate, pathetic love—and that she did not need.

He would have preferred to believe his distaste for the visitors sprung from loyalty to Richard, but he must be honest with himself. Her fiancé, his cousin and best friend, was hardly dead a fortnight, and he still wanted her passionately, desperately. He disgusted himself. But his heart, treacherous organ, refused his command at every turn and insisted on beating only for Elizabeth.

Perhaps this time I will need to visit India. For two years.

Darcy forced his attention back to the conversation. The men were relating a story about a prank some years ago involving an acquaintance who raced horses. Kirkwood had taken over the narrative. "And Livingston never suspected a thing! Fitzwilliam had arranged it—" Kirkwood's voice faltered as he glanced warily at Elizabeth.

Elizabeth's head was tilted slightly to one side, and she regarded the man with a soft, open expression. "Pray, continue. If we attempt to avoid Richard's name, I fear our conversation will be extremely stilted." The accompanying smile was designed to set her visitors at ease. "I love to hear stories of his misspent youth."

"Youth?" Colonel Grant said. "I believe Fitzwilliam was six and twenty at the time!" Subdued laughter followed this pronouncement. As Lord Kirkwood finished his story, Darcy wondered if the others recognized how neatly Elizabeth had rescued the situation. And, did they know what it cost her?

Mr. North launched into a tale about Fitzwilliam and a Latin instructor, which kept everyone amused for several minutes. The animation in Elizabeth's face was not completely feigned and prevented Darcy from fully resenting the men's presence. Accustomed to being surrounded by family, she was coping with a devastating loss all alone and must sometimes welcome company.

The visitors also fed her hunger for stories about her lost fiancé. She did not wish to forget Richard but to collect more memories of him to last the rest of her life. Darcy would give his entire fortune to inspire such love in a woman like Elizabeth!

As the visit drew to a close, Darcy scrutinized Elizabeth's visitors. She valued them for their connection to her lost love, but it did not necessarily follow that the other visitors' motivations were likewise honorable. Whatever fortune Richard had bequeathed to Elizabeth was likely sufficient to make her the target of fortune hunters. The very thought made him want to stand at her doorway with a loaded pistol.

Colonel Grant was a second son, like Richard, and needed to marry well. Darcy knew nothing of Lieutenant Johnson's finances but intended to have them investigated. Kirkwood dressed well, and his lineage was impeccable, but rumors suggested his father had incurred large gambling debts. At least Mr. North could be acquitted of ulterior motives, unless he planned to do away with his wife. Darcy's lips twitched at the thought. Clearly, he was becoming excessively suspicious.

Whatever the visitors' potential matrimonial hopes, Elizabeth demonstrated no particular interest in any of the men. Indeed, the visitors had roused smiles from her, but her merriment was a dim shadow of her former vivacity. Her face was strained; sadness blurred her eyes. Others might not notice, but he knew her grief ran deep.

Perhaps she might never overcome the pain of losing Richard. At least if she did not accept another offer of marriage, Darcy would be spared a repetition of that agony. That thought spurred an immediate sensation of guilt; he should wish her to be happy, no matter the personal cost to him.

The visitors did not stay overly long. After their departure, Darcy hoped to discover if Elizabeth evidenced any particular feelings toward one of them, but she immediately retired, pleading a headache. After worrying fruitlessly about Elizabeth's health for some minutes, Darcy climbed the stairs to find Georgiana.

***

Elizabeth read again the letter which had appeared in that day's post. It was from an unfamiliar solicitor. "Dear Miss Bennet … represent the interests of the Earl and Countess of Matlock … the estate of their late son …" With a growing sense of urgency, she finished the letter; unfortunately, she discovered she had accurately grasped its import on her first perusal.

From the doorway, Grayson cleared his throat, startling her. "Mr. and Miss Darcy," he intoned. Elizabeth stifled a cry of dismay. Now was not the moment to encounter Mr. Darcy!

Since the Darcys' return three weeks ago, Georgiana had been almost a daily visitor, but Mr. Darcy had been absent.

Georgiana had credited urgent estate business, but Elizabeth thought it just as likely he was avoiding her.

Elizabeth placed the letter on the end table gingerly as if it had bitten her. She gritted her teeth. *I will not weep!* Blindly, she felt in her pocket for a handkerchief with which to dab her eyes. Only then did she realize she was not alone in the drawing room. In the doorway, two pairs of eyes were regarding her with concern.

"Elizabeth?" Georgiana said gently.

"Miss Bennet, did we arrive at a disadvantageous time?" Mr. Darcy said at almost the same moment.

"No, no." Elizabeth gestured for them to sit. "I am delighted to see you. Please be seated." She rang for Grayson. Ordering tea gave her time to compose her spirits. If it had only been Georgiana, she might have managed tolerably well, but coping with Mr. Darcy ... Why must he choose *today* for a visit?

A maid delivered the tea, and Elizabeth busied herself with serving. She and Georgiana discussed the weather and new hat styles. Mr. Darcy watched them silently.

More accurately, Mr. Darcy watched *her*, Elizabeth realized. Was he awaiting some error in her etiquette or speech? Generally, she would laugh at such attempts at intimidation, but today, she did not feel equal to the challenge.

There was a break in the conversation. Elizabeth nibbled one of Cook's lemon biscuits, her favorite. But she had no taste for it. Mr. Darcy asked, "Miss Bennet, was there something particularly distressing in this morning's post?"

Why did he have to arrive at just that moment? Why must he be so observant? And why could he not pretend—as anyone else would have—that he had not noticed her distress?

She brushed nonexistent crumbs from her skirt. "It is of no matter."

"I hope your family is well?" His concern sounded genuine.

"Yes, very well."

"And Mrs. Bingley?"

"Her confinement is proceeding smoothly."

She glanced up and met dark eyes, regarding her with unnerving intensity, eyebrows raised in inquiry. He would not rest until he knew the cause of her distress. The thought sparked her sense of mischief. Well, he has asked for it. *If the information makes him uncomfortable, so be it.*

She sighed. "The letter was from a solicitor."

Darcy's face darkened. "Regarding Richard's estate?"

"Indirectly." Elizabeth wished for some embroidery to occupy her hands and focus her attention. Instead, she stared at the wall beyond Mr. Darcy's shoulder. "The solicitor was hired by Richard's parents and brother. They wish to challenge his will regarding the possession of this townhouse on the grounds that it is part of the Hargrave estate and cannot be separated from it."

"Oh, Elizabeth!" Georgiana's cry was shrill. "This cannot be allowed!" She looked beseechingly at her brother, whose expression had not altered. "Thomas has more than sufficient funds to purchase another townhouse."

In the ensuing silence, it occurred to Elizabeth that perhaps Mr. Darcy had been aware of his uncle's plan to recover the townhouse; perhaps he had even encouraged the scheme. The thought caused a wave of sadness she knew to be completely unwarranted. Would she really expect Mr. Darcy to take her part against his own family?

"It is of no matter," Elizabeth told Georgiana softly, hoping they could hastily dispense with this subject. "My solicitor will investigate the issue and advise me." She cleared her throat. "It is a fine day. Perhaps we should go for a walk." At least as they walked, she would not constantly feel the weight of Mr. Darcy's stare.

Georgiana's face was set in an uncharacteristic frown. "Uncle Fitzwilliam is being most unfair to you in your time of grief!" She rose from her seat and came to sit next to Elizabeth, taking her hand. But then she looked expectantly at her brother. "William, is there nothing you can do?"

Elizabeth groaned inwardly. If only Georgiana had agreed to a walk! She had no desire to have Georgiana force her brother into a favor he did not wish to perform. "I can hardly ask you or your brother to intervene in a matter between me and your family," Elizabeth said hastily. "I do not wish to cause any difficulties."

Before Georgiana could reply, Mr. Darcy surged to his feet. His eyes were stormy, and his hand brushed through his hair in agitation, disarranging it. "Indeed, madam, I must disagree with you most strenuously." He paced to the fireplace, empty in the mild weather, and stared into the dark grate. *Would he enumerate the reasons she should vacate the house?* Elizabeth did not wish to debate this topic, particularly in Georgiana's presence.

"Mr. Darcy—"

His voice overrode hers. "I believe my uncle's actions are most inappropriate. I will speak with him about it."

Shock rendered Elizabeth speechless for a moment. She swallowed. "You were not aware of their plans?"

Mr. Darcy looked startled. "No, they did not see fit to inform me. They knew how I would respond." His grimace was directed at the fireplace.

Oh, goodness. Was he implying that he had defended her to the earl and countess previously? Mr. Darcy had tolerated her as Richard's betrothed, but Elizabeth always suspected he had attempted to talk Richard out of the engagement.

"I will visit them this afternoon and attempt to persuade them against this course of action." Next to Elizabeth, Georgiana sank back into her settee with a smile of satisfaction.

"I do not need you to fight my battles. I have a solicitor for that." Elizabeth's voice was firm.

For the first time in the conversation, he regarded her directly, startling her with the ferocity of her gaze. "Will your solicitor wish to cross the Earl of Matlock? It could destroy his career."

Elizabeth opened her mouth and closed it. That had not occurred to her. She took a sip of tea to calm her nerves. "I do not wish to be the cause of a breach between you and your family—a breach which could extend to Georgiana. It would grieve me deeply."

Darcy's gaze was cool. "Your feelings do you credit. However, you are not requesting anything of me. I proceed as my conscience dictates, regardless of your desires."

Elizabeth blinked in surprise, at a loss of what to say. She was pleased he wished to defend her, but he implied that his motives were quite impersonal. She could not make out his character at all. What a vexing man!

Georgiana had no such reservations. She clapped her hands together. "There! William will have the difficulty resolved in no time at all."

Elizabeth made a firm resolution to cease any attempts to understand Mr. Darcy's character.

***

"What a lovely surprise!" Darcy's Aunt Rachel marched into the drawing room of Matlock House. She frequently complained how Darcy did not visit enough; however, he was uncertain how pleased she would be once she learned the impetus behind this visit.

Darcy stood when she entered the room. "This is not a social visit, but business. Is my uncle at home?"

"Yes," the countess gestured vaguely down the hallway with the lacy handkerchief she always seemed to have in one hand. "But I believe he is quite busy."

Darcy's blood boiled, and he suppressed an urge to yell. "It is a matter of some urgency."

His aunt sighed dramatically but rang for a footman to summon the earl. While they waited, the countess questioned him about Georgiana's health. Darcy responded in as few words as possible, instead concentrating his efforts on restraining his angry impulses. A maid brought in tea, but Darcy declined his aunt's offer of a cup.

His uncle finally strode into the room. "So, Nephew, what is this urgent business that cannot be delayed?" he demanded gruffly, grabbing two chocolate biscuits and seating himself.

"I understand you are challenging the terms of Richard's will regarding the townhouse he gifted to Miss Bennet." Darcy kept his voice level with great effort.

The countess stared at Darcy in surprise, but the earl merely waved his hand. "Is true!" he said through a mouthful of biscuit. "She's an upstart country miss," he finally swallowed, "who never married our son. Our family should not have to finance her social ambitions."

Darcy's stomach clenched at this description of Elizabeth. Every cell in his body tingled with the desire to leap to her defense.

He took a deep breath before formulating a reply. "Thomas has wealth enough; he does not need the house. And he has never visited the place—there is no sentimental attachment. Elizabeth did not ask for the house or the bequest. It was Richard's wish to provide for her."

Aunt Rachel waved her handkerchief disdainfully. "*His* wish? Who knows what arts and allurements she used to take him in!"

"I was present when they met, madam," Darcy said through clenched teeth. "She did nothing save delight him with interesting conversation."

"Yes, but who knows what occurred when you were not present. Some women are quite crafty." The countess took a sip of tea as if she had said the last word.

This aspersion on Elizabeth's honor stoked Darcy's anger further. "Do you believe Richard so easily deceived? He was a man of the world."

Before his aunt had a chance to reply, Darcy turned to the earl. "I had a pleasant conversation with Richard's solicitor. If they had been married—even without children—the marriage contract Richard had signed with Elizabeth's father would have provided the exact benefit he stipulated in his will."

"But they were *not* married!" the earl thundered, banging his hand on the arm of the chair for emphasis. "This is the material point!"

His aunt took a more conciliatory tone. "If they had married and perhaps had a child by now, her position would be quite different."

Unable to remain seated, Darcy pushed himself to his feet and paced toward the fireplace. "And *why* were they not married?" His aunt and uncle both looked so shocked at this question that he almost laughed. "Do you not recall demanding that they delay the wedding following Mr. and Mrs. Wickham's marriage?"

His aunt spoke immediately. "Yes, of course. The scandal—"

Darcy did not allow her to finish. "If they had married then, her sister's death or her father's illness would not have caused further delays."

Aunt Rachel shrugged. "It matters not—"

Darcy's gaze caught and held his aunt's. "Elizabeth's sister and her husband delayed their nuptials only a fortnight following the scandal, and she is nearing the end of her confinement." Darcy's eyes bore into the countess's, refusing to allow her to look away. "Had you not interfered, you might now have a grandchild—even if you still suffered the loss of your son."

His aunt gaped at him. Obviously, such a thought had never occurred to her. Finally, she closed her jaw with a snap and lowered her eyes to the floor. "I – I –" Now the handkerchief was employed to dry her eyes. "I would have liked a grandchild...."

The earl's face was red with consternation, and he was leaning forward in his chair. "Now see here! No need to upset your aunt! The will, the house—it is strictly business. We bear Miss Bennet no ill will."

Darcy snorted in disbelief. "Business? You only have one reason for incurring the cost of a solicitor's fees: you wish to punish Miss Bennet for having the audacity to love your son!"

"Love!" His uncle huffed and shoved another biscuit into his mouth.

However, his aunt appeared intrigued. "Do you believe she loved him?" Her hands were worrying the hem of her handkerchief.

"Yes. And she loves him still. I thank God he knew such love before he died." Elizabeth had made Richard's last year on earth a happy one.

The countess had a faraway expression on her face. "He did seem quite happy with her."

Darcy nodded. *What a fool I was for heeding my fear of my family's reaction to Elizabeth! If I had made the decision to propose earlier ...* No, he could not afford to think such thoughts. She had been, and always would be, Richard's.

His aunt turned to her husband with a troubled mien. "Perhaps we *should* abandon this business with Miss Bennet. I do not wish to cause difficulties within the family. Thomas does not truly care about the townhouse. He can buy another property."

"There are no difficulties within the family," the earl said gruffly. "She is not a member of the family."

"No, but William is."

The earl looked at his wife in consternation. "He would not cause trouble within the family over so trifling a matter." His eyes then focused on Darcy. "Would you?"

Darcy held his uncle's gaze steadily. "Without a second thought."

Uncle John blinked and then blinked again, as if he could not believe his nephew had actually uttered those words. "What is Miss Bennet that you would value her fortune over your own flesh and blood?"

Darcy closed his eyes briefly, praying to find words that would not reveal too much. Then he opened his eyes, pacing restlessly to the other side of the room. "She is the woman who loved my cousin with her whole heart and has suffered grievously for his loss. She deserves our support, not our censure."

The earl shook his head as he stared at his tea. "No. She is nothing but a fortune hunter, and you will never convince me otherwise." He cleared his throat. "However, I will halt my efforts to challenge Richard's will, if you wish."

Darcy released a relieved breath. "I do."

The earl sighed heavily. "Very well."

Darcy stood, eager to quit a room so thick with tension and distrust. "I thank you, sir."

Aunt Rachel stood as well. "I will walk you out, William." Darcy's breath caught. Had she guessed his feelings for Elizabeth?

They reached the elegant, marble-clad entrance hall, and a footman handed Darcy his hat. His aunt regarded him steadily. Fortunately, his aunt's words put him at ease. "We should make preparations for Georgiana's come out."

Darcy donned his hat. "She has matured over the past year, and I believe the prospect is not as frightening to her as it once was."

His aunt's expression suggested she was not interested in considering Georgiana's fears. "If we begin preparations soon," the countess observed, "we should be ready for the start of the Season."

"Very well." Darcy sighed. Georgiana would loathe the preparations, which would require much time in Aunt Rachel's company. The woman was overbearing and unsympathetic to Georgiana's shyness. His sister had difficulty asserting herself, so their aunt would discount Georgiana's preferences, making his sister miserable. Although Darcy might occasionally accompany her, he could not be present for every visit to the *modiste* or decision about the invitation list.

However, an idea occurred to him. Perhaps there was someone who *could* help Georgiana …

"—important Season for you as well." Darcy realized he had not been giving his aunt's words the least attention.

A response seemed to be required from him. "Indeed?"

"You must find a wife." She said it with an air of stating the obvious. "You are eight and twenty. I understand how young gallants wish to sow their wild oats." Darcy rolled his eyes; his aunt knew him little if she thought this description applied to him. "But it is past time for you to seriously apply yourself to this task." He had heard this speech before, but today, it provoked greater heat in him than previously. "With Georgiana making her debut, it will be an ideal time to meet the most eligible young ladies of the *ton*. I could write a list of those who would suit—"

"No!" Good Lord! He had practically shouted at his aunt, and she took a couple of steps away from him. Carefully modulating his tone, Darcy continued. "You will not seek a wife for me. I am capable of conducting my own domestic arrangements."

Aunt Rachel seemed almost bewildered. "But you have had no success! Obviously, you need help!"

Darcy turned and strode toward the entrance; the sooner he departed, the less likely he was to say something he would regret. "Madam, my marital status is not your concern."

His aunt followed him so closely Darcy almost stepped on her toes. "You cannot leave Pemberley without an heir!"

Darcy stopped, his hand on the door knob, breathing deeply and reminding himself that the countess could not understand how the subject of marriage and heirs haunted him day and night. "Pemberley is not entailed. If I never marry, Georgiana and her children will inherit it."

"But you must wish to—"

Darcy regarded her over his shoulder. "At the present moment, I have *no* plans to marry. I think it highly likely I will *never* marry. And I will thank you to never mention the subject again."

His aunt's mouth opened, but no words emerged. Darcy turned the door knob with a shaking hand and escaped the house.

Chapter 8

Elizabeth pored over the housekeeper's neat columns of numbers recording the expenditures for the month, a task she actually did not mind performing. The daily activity of running a household provided a focus for her energy and a welcome distraction. "Mr. Darcy is here, ma'am."

Grayson's voice startled her out of her reverie.

But he visited just yesterday! "Did Miss Darcy accompany him?" she asked.

"No, ma'am."

"Very well. Show him to the blue drawing room." Elizabeth glanced about the study; with its dark wood and leather chairs, it was a handsome room, which reminded her poignantly of Richard. Undoubtedly, he had often met Mr. Darcy in this room. But it was far too intimate a setting to receive an unmarried man, particularly one who unsettled her so.

Her entrance to the blue drawing room was followed by the usual inquiries about her health and her family's wellbeing. After a long silence, Mr. Darcy cleared his throat, appearing decidedly uncomfortable. "I have spoken with my uncle, and he has agreed to cease any attempts to challenge Richard's will."

A great weight was lifted from Elizabeth's body, and she immediately felt far lighter. "I thank you, Mr. Darcy. It was very good of you." She tried to convey her gratitude with her eyes, wishing she understood *why* he had interceded. Elizabeth had asked him not to, but now she was too relieved to care that he had ignored her wishes. Had he intervened because Georgiana was so distressed? "I hope your uncle is not angry with you."

"Not in the least." Mr. Darcy shifted in his chair, looking away.

Elizabeth had the uneasy feeling he was concealing something. "I am happy to hear it," she said nonetheless.

There was a long pause. Words eluded her. Elizabeth wished to express her appreciation, but Mr. Darcy seemed uncomfortable enough. Should she speak about the weather or inquire after Georgiana?

Mr. Darcy fiddled with the end of his walking stick, drawing Elizabeth's eyes to his hands, which seemed to betray some kind of nervousness. "I had a favor to ask of you if you are willing to undertake it," Mr. Darcy said finally. A favor? She was almost too shocked to speak. Instead, she nodded for him to continue.

Mr. Darcy took a deep breath and went on. "You know my sister will be making her debut at the start of this Season. She is quite nervous about the process—well, 'terrified' might be a more apt description. My aunt, while an excellent judge of fabrics and a wonderful hostess, does not always understand Georgiana's reservations. I think Georgiana would benefit during this time from the assistance of a friend closer to her age. I was hoping you would be willing to be that friend." His eyes rose from the walking stick to meet hers with an almost pleading look.

It was quite the longest speech Elizabeth had ever heard from Mr. Darcy; to say she was astonished would be an understatement. She believed he disapproved of her, if not actively disliked her. Now, in the space of five minutes, he had given her two incontrovertible indications that he did not disapprove of her. In fact, he appeared to hold her in some esteem.

Elizabeth felt a little dizzy as she struggled to reorient herself to this new understanding of the world. It was like suddenly discovering the sky was green.

Mr. Darcy was watching her intently, awaiting her response. The intensity of his gaze made her blush, and she needed to look at the wall to regain her composure. "I thank you. You honor me with your trust." She took a deep breath and turned to face him again. "However, I did not have much thought of remaining in London very long." Did his face seem to fall at her words?

"Not in London?" he echoed, as if he could not quite comprehend her meaning.

"London is not my home, after all." Mr. Darcy almost seemed to wince. How odd! "I have been living here awaiting my wedding to Richard." She hastily swallowed the lump in her throat. "By all rights, I should have returned to Longbourn immediately after his p-passing, but I had matters of business." She blinked rapidly to keep tears from falling. "And truthfully, I needed time to grieve apart from the uproar my family sometimes creates."

"But surely you will not return to Longbourn permanently!" He seemed appalled at the suggestion.

She gave him a small smile, which helped to fend off the threatened tears. "I miss my family, and Jane's time draws near. I will certainly return to Hertfordshire soon. Jane has invited me to live permanently at Netherfield with her and Charles." A deep furrow appeared between Mr. Darcy's eyebrows. "I confess the idea has its appeal. I can be the maiden aunt—giving her children their lessons and teaching them to play the pianoforte very ill."

She smiled at her jest, but Mr. Darcy did not. He actually appeared stunned by this vision of her future. "You do not plan to return to London?" His voice was rather strangled.

She shrugged. "I do not particularly care for London. I always enjoy its diversions for a time, but soon I long for the fresh air and fields of the country." Then she recognized the origin of his distress. "This does not lessen the value of your efforts on my behalf! The house will be of great use. Should my father pass away soon ,… my mother will need assistance. The townhouse will fetch a good price…"

Her words petered out as she noticed the thunderous look on Mr. Darcy's face. Did he disapprove of a plan to sell the house? "You take excellent care of your family." His words were complimentary, but his tone was severe.

"I do what a daughter must," she said lightly.

"No, there are many who do not fulfill their family obligations nearly so well. Your parents are most fortunate."

"Thank you," she murmured, thinking she must add this conversation to her list of things she did not understand about Mr. Darcy.

"I hope you will not entirely deny yourself the pleasures of London." Mr. Darcy's voice was strained, almost pleading. "If you find yourself in Town in the coming months, I hope you will consider assisting Georgiana in her preparations."

"Indeed, there are few things which would give me more pleasure, but I cannot make a promise under the circumstances." Elizabeth almost felt guilty for disappointing the man, a most odd sensation.

"If you are here at the start of the Season, you must at least attend Georgiana's come out ball." He said this most insistently; this was a man who was accustomed to being obeyed.

"I cannot imagine the earl and countess would welcome me to that event," Elizabeth demurred. This was another good reason not to participate in Georgiana's coming out preparations, but Elizabeth had been reluctant to share it.

"Georgiana and I would, and that is enough." Darcy's mouth was set in a firm line.

"I thank you for the honor of the invitation. I will attend if it is possible."

"That is all I can ask." With this cryptic remark, Mr. Darcy stood, made a small bow, wished her well, and quit her company.

Elizabeth sat alone for a moment, reviewing all that had passed between them. "Whenever I believe I understand the man, he confounds me once again!" Elizabeth said to the empty room. "It is most vexing!"

**

By the time Darcy had arrived at his townhouse, his thoughts were in a frenzy. "Leave London! Live at Netherfield?" he muttered to himself as he strode into the Darcy House entrance hall. He ignored a sidelong glance from his footman and stalked toward his study.

When Darcy had conceived the scheme to ask Elizabeth's help with Georgiana's debut, he had recognized how it would benefit his sister. However, he was not unaware of the advantages of having Elizabeth as a regular guest at Darcy House. Despite vowing to avoid her company, he could not resist the comfort of seeing her frequently and knowing she was well. And if he should sometimes encounter her at tea or dinner … well, that was simply an accident of fate.

It had never occurred to him that Elizabeth would return to Hertfordshire at all, let alone that she would leave so soon. "You are a fool." he muttered to himself as he threw his body into a chair by the fireplace. He ran both hands through his hair, disordering it completely. "A fool!"

Darcy had known her father was ill and her sister was expecting, yet somehow the inevitable conclusion had escaped him. He could never expect more than friendship from Elizabeth, but he had allowed himself to envision a future in which she was a frequent presence in their lives. Such a future would not come about if she resided with the Bingleys—living like a poor relation when she had the means to maintain her own household. Darcy pounded his fist on the arm of the chair. "Netherfield!" It emerged like an oath.

If she lived at Netherfield, he would only see her once a year, if that. The thought made his chest tight.

Yes, Elizabeth would need to be with Mrs. Bingley for the birth of her child. But surely she could return to London after a month or so? Darcy's teeth ground together as he envisioned Elizabeth's future devoted to sacrifice and caring for others' needs.

Standing, Darcy paced the length of the room. He must entice her back to London for her own sake. At least here she was free from her family's demands. If he could have her return for at least part of Georgiana's preparations … perhaps she would change her mind about London.

But how to entice her? He had pressed the point as much as propriety permitted. Any further words on the subject would risk revealing too much.

However … a corner of Darcy's mouth curved upward. Elizabeth might listen to pleas from another quarter. In fact, she might find another's arguments more difficult to refuse. He had not yet mentioned the possibility of Elizabeth's assistance to his sister, but he knew she would welcome the idea.

He rang for a footman. When Jenkins opened the door, Darcy commanded, "Please ask Georgiana to join me."

Chapter 9

Darcy lifted the brandy decanter and started pouring before realizing it was empty. With an oath, he slammed the decanter down and grabbed the bottle of port beside it. He eyed the liquid suspiciously. Would there be enough?

He poured a healthy measure of port into his glass and took a swallow, relishing the burn at the back of his throat. Ah, that was what he needed. He staggered to the chair next to the fireplace and slumped into it. The damn cravat was choking him, so he tugged at the knot until the strip of cloth hung loosely around his neck. He had already divested himself of his waistcoat. The London weather was unseasonably warm for November, and the brandy had warmed him further.

The port slid smoothly over his tongue. Perhaps only a little more was necessary to achieve his goal: oblivion. And oblivion was essential. This morning at breakfast, Georgiana had announced that Elizabeth was in town and would be arriving for a visit in the afternoon.

Darcy had not seen Elizabeth since that awful visit in July when she had informed him of her plans to return to Hertfordshire. He still shuddered at the memory. With Darcy's prompting, Georgiana *had* secured Elizabeth's promise to assist with some of the preparations for the come out. He had known Elizabeth would be unable to refuse his sister when the debut so clearly frightened her. Of course, the preparations had only recently begun in earnest.

During Elizabeth's first visit to London in October, Darcy had managed to visit Pemberley, but now business required him to remain in the city. An encounter with Elizabeth was inevitable—if not tonight, then soon. But he was unprepared. He had exerted great effort to ensure Elizabeth's continued contact with his family … and he longed to see her but knew he should not. For months, the day when he would again see Elizabeth had loomed large in his imagination, creating a sickening combination of desire and dread.

Each time he had pictured their reunion, he experienced again the fear that he would not be strong enough to restrain his desire. Then he would be overcome by the self-loathing that accompanied lusting after his dead cousin's fiancée. The cycle was depressingly familiar to him.

Darcy snorted at that thought and drank deeply.

Now, deep in his cups, he realized *lust* was not an accurate description. Lust would be simple; the needs of the body he could control. His dilemma was that he was *in love with* his dead cousin's fiancée. If he would own the problem, he should at least own the enormity of it.

Darcy had survived three months without careening off to Longbourn to kneel at Elizabeth's feet and declare his love. But it had been a near thing once or twice. Occasionally, he had permitted himself the fantasy.

However, even if—by some miracle—she agreed to accept his hand, he would be betraying Richard's memory in the most fundamental way imaginable. While it was simple to picture Elizabeth in his bed and as mistress of Pemberley—in fact, he had difficulty banishing such visions—he could not possibly envision living with the guilt. No, it was impossible. Richard would forever stand between them.

Ironically, it was at such times that Darcy missed his cousin most acutely. Richard had been the only one to whom Darcy had ever confided his deepest thoughts and feelings. At every turning point in his life, Darcy had relied on his cousin's advice. Darcy could easily picture himself discussing his dilemma with his cousin, if the source of his troubles were anyone other than Richard's betrothed. Richard's absence felt as if someone had cut off one of Darcy's limbs. In the back of his mind, he was aware that something was missing every minute of every day.

Darcy tossed off the remaining port and staggered to his desk to refill his glass. The drinking was a short-term solution at best. He had repaired to his study for the purpose of avoiding Elizabeth. At least in *this* condition, he would never surrender to the voice reminding him Elizabeth was in *his* drawing room visiting *his* sister—and urging him to stride down the hall to join them. No impulse was stronger than his fear of saying something to make a fool of himself.

Like suggesting that he was in love with her.

No, better that she believed he avoided her because he disliked her.

Unbidden, he recalled a conversation he had overheard between Georgiana and his Aunt Rachel two days previous. His harsh words over the summer had prevented his aunt from attempting matchmaking again. But he had heard her asking Georgiana if her brother had a mistress, something no one should be discussing with a girl of that age. His aunt must be desperate. Far from being shocked, Georgiana had merely responded thoughtfully that she did not believe so.

Then his aunt had the impertinence to inquire if Darcy was in love with a married woman! Apparently, she was exceedingly determined to ferret out the reason he had declared he would never marry. Georgiana had denied that supposition as well. Darcy supposed he should be grateful that neither woman suspected the truth, but the conversation had not improved his present mood.

Despite his defiant words to his aunt, Darcy did wish to marry. He had always imagined bringing a wife home to Pemberley and raising a family. However, he could not envision marrying anyone other than Elizabeth. Nor could he envision marrying Elizabeth.

Damned if you do, damned if you do not.

Just damned.

However, either he or Georgiana needed to produce heirs for Pemberley. He could not stomach the thought of it falling into the hands of a distant cousin he barely knew. If Georgiana were disinclined to marry, Darcy would not require it of her. Should it come to that, perhaps he could find a respectable woman who would understand he was incapable of loving her. They could lead separate lives and rarely see each other.

The thought threatened to make him vomit.

Or perhaps it was the port.

The room spun in lazy circles around him while his arms and legs felt unusually heavy. At least now he was sufficiently foxed. Even if he could walk without falling, his pride would forbid him from allowing anyone, even Georgiana, from observing him in this state. He was safe from any foolish impulses to visit Elizabeth.

He stared out the window at the rapidly descending dusk and the rain pounding against the glass. At least he had accomplished his mission for the day. With that thought, he rested his head on his desk and fell asleep.

***

Upon awaking, he noticed that the unconsumed port had spilled and stained the right sleeve of his shirt, so he smelled even more like a distillery than before. Outside the window, the day had turned to night, and rain was pounding against the glass. He had slept longer than he expected.

He stood cautiously, holding onto the desk for support. The room was no longer spinning, but it still swayed like the deck of a ship during a storm.

Experimentally, he released the desk and was inordinately pleased he could stand without support. Perhaps he could walk under his own power as well. At least he had slept through the danger of Elizabeth's visit. Georgiana had undoubtedly already retired for the night as well. No one would be about, except perhaps a few servants, whom he could easily avoid.

He stepped carefully to the study door, placing each foot precisely in front of the other to increase his chances of remaining upright. As he opened the door, he reflected on the need for a different strategy to handle Elizabeth's presence in London. While daily drinking held a certain appeal, it would create many other problems. Avoidance was the best solution but would be almost impossible if Elizabeth were a daily visitor.

Perhaps he could suggest to Georgiana that they meet at Elizabeth's townhouse—or even Matlock House. Or maybe he could devise a reason to visit Pemberley, although with Georgiana's coming out ball approaching, he could not stay away for long.

One hand trailing along the wall for balance, Darcy struggled down the corridor that led to the back stairs and the blessed sanctuary of his bed chamber.

Too late Darcy, discerned the whisper of light footsteps on the back stairs, the sound of leather soles too fine to be servants' boots. Georgiana! He drew back from the foot of the stairs, hoping she would be too distracted by her own thoughts to notice his current disordered state. His cheeks flushed with shame; he never wanted her to see him like this.

He did not look up until she was nearing the bottom step. "Geor—"

The words died of dismay on his lips. It was Elizabeth!

Despite his horror, his eyes drank in the sight of her like a man needing water in the desert. Her dark curls framed the porcelain skin of her face, which had a bit more color and fullness than three months previous. Although still quite slender, she appeared to have gained back some of the weight she had lost following Richard's death. In the dimness, her blue eyes were nearly black and bottomless, capable of uncovering his every secret and fault.

Unfortunately, many of his faults were on display.

He might as well be naked. With no coat or waistcoat and his cravat hanging around his neck, he resembled a wastrel returning from a night at the pub. Darcy swallowed, trying to think of something to say which might save this situation. But his thoughts had turned to mud, and his tongue was thick and unresponsive in his mouth.

Elizabeth appeared slightly less shocked to see him, but one could reasonably expect the master of the house to traverse his own corridors. Her eyes widened as she noticed his disheveled state. She nodded a greeting. "Mr. Darcy." Was she smirking at him?

His brain and tongue immediately had a disagreement about how to address her. "Eliza—Mish--Elizamish Bennet Miss!"

Good Lord! What a disaster. He should give up speaking altogether. Yes, a vow of silence! That would save his dignity.

Panic stricken, his eyes shot to Elizabeth's face. She appeared bemused but not horrified.

The silence dragged on between them. *Say something, anything!*

"Is it still … that is … raining?" His tongue was thick and uncoordinated.

She appeared perplexed by this odd choice of subject. "I believe so. I was caught in a sudden downpour on my way here, and Georgiana generously lent me some dry clothing."

Of their own volition, his eyes traveled over her form, noticing how Georgiana's dress was a little tight on Elizabeth, outlining her legs and drawing attention to her bosom, framed by the lace of the dress's neckline…. The bodice revealed more cleavage than Darcy usually saw on Elizabeth. So much creamy skin … the gentle swell of her breasts … His eyes feasted on the sight.

Elizabeth cleared her throat. Damnation! Did she think he was leering? Had he been leering? Good Lord, perhaps he *had* been leering!

He jerked his eyes up to her face. Correct though it may be, he must disabuse her of that notion. "The color suits you." He tried to remember the color without looking down again but quickly gave up. "And t-the—" He gestured wildly with his hands. "The lace frames your—" he caught himself at the last moment, "face to great effect."

"Yes, I daresay if I should wear this dress to the park, all the young men would be admiring my *face*." Even foxed, Darcy could hear the mocking edge in her voice.

Damn! Now he had offended her!

His thoughts were sluggish. *I must say something to lessen her contempt!* "Y-you are in hood gealth—good health?" Darcy winced. *Oh yes*, he told himself, *she will be* very *impressed*.

A smile twitched at the corners of her mouth. "I am, thank you. And you?"

"I am well." He nodded vigorously, hoping to demonstrate his lack of inebriation. Unfortunately, the sudden movement caused an attack of dizziness, and he grabbed the wall for balance.

Elizabeth's eyebrows rose as she watched him. "I did not see you at dinner. Were you at your club?"

Ah, she wonders where I came to be so intoxicated, not to mention disheveled. No doubt she wonders if I carouse regularly. Certainly it was not unusual behavior for many other men of Darcy's class.

"No," Darcy asserted firmly. Elizabeth tilted her head to the side and regarded him questioningly. *Good Lord, does she believe I visited a public house or, even worse, a mistress?* "I have been here—in my study—*alone*." She nodded quickly as though his statement made sense when, in fact, he knew drinking alone in his study was hardly less pathetic. "I had many matters of business to attend to." The moment the words were out of his mouth, he wished them back. Only a fool would believe he had been *working* in his study, and Elizabeth was not a fool.

"I see," she said solemnly, but her lips twitched as if she suppressed a smile.

He must escape before further mortifying himself. But it was difficult to pull himself away when his whole body felt so alive near her. The thought of leaving was like plunging into a cold lake after enjoying a warm bath. Just breathing the same air was a tonic to him. How could he tear himself away from such bliss?

Then he gazed into the fine eyes he knew so well and saw ... pity.

I must escape! Darcy removed his hand from the wall experimentally, but immediately, his whole body began to sway.

Elizabeth reached out an arm as if to steady him. "Forgive me, but you do not seem well. Will you not sit down?" Her eyes were dark with concern.

Darcy closed his eyes, willing away the vertigo. *I must concentrate all my energy on one single, essential purpose: do not look like a fool.* "I thank you, no. I ... have not been sleeping well these past days." Well, that was true enough.

"Perhaps you should lie down. I could summon a footman to help you—"

His first impulse was to avoid sharing the moment with anyone else, even a servant. "No! No footmen." Instantly, he realized he sounded peevish and ridiculous. "I do not need their help. Sometimes they are just in the way, you know." Elizabeth made no response, but her expression was dubious. "Always everywhere ... in the way ... with their feet ..." *For the love of God, man, will you just close your mouth!*

With a quick glimpse at Elizabeth's face, he saw she was carefully not laughing at him, but her expression was too purposefully blank. *I must get out of this situation however I can!*

Concentrating his energies on balancing, Darcy pushed away from the wall and staggered for the stairs. Once upstairs and out of Elizabeth's sight, he could collapse.

He carefully placed one foot in front of the other. *One ... two ...* Elizabeth watched his progress with concern in her fine eyes, not realizing how her presence made this operation all the more difficult…

Good. Almost there …

He had almost reached the bottom step when he lost his balance. Flailing, he missed the banister by inches, and his legs slid out from underneath him. He was falling!

Then he felt something—Elizabeth's shoulder—under his arm, holding him up. Her hand slid around his waist so her arm could further steady him. Darcy was grateful for the rescue, but it created a new dilemma. Perhaps it would have been easier to fall on the floor.

Elizabeth's body pressed along the entire length of his side, sending tiny electric shivers up and down his spine. Instinctively, his body quickened with desire, demanding that he embrace her and draw her closer.

He was mortified that he required Elizabeth's help simply to stand upright. He was humiliated by nearly every word that had emerged from his mouth that evening.

And he wished she would never release him.

Her slender body felt so right beside his, a perfect fit. He heard her rapid breathing, enjoyed the warmth of her skin through the thin muslin of her dress, and smelled the rosewater scent he had long associated with her.

And *he* smelled like a distillery.

How could he find any pleasure in her presence when he had abased himself so thoroughly?

He pulled away. "I thank you for your … assistance, Eliz—Miss Bennet."

Refusing to release him completely, Elizabeth helped him hobble to a bench under the stairs, placed there, no doubt, for the servants' use. "Perhaps you should sit here for a while." Her hand was trembling as she removed it from his arm. Dare he believe she was not unaffected by his touch? He chanced a glance into her eyes, dark and fathomless, but could not decipher the expression he saw there.

Blushing, Elizabeth turned away quickly and strode toward the entrance hall, her heels clicking on the corridor's wooden floor. "I shall fetch a footman to help you."

Before she disappeared, however, Darcy's brain perceived a detail which he had not noticed before.

She was wearing gray. Half mourning. Of course. She was still mourning Richard. It had not been so long since his death.

Darcy rested his head in his hands. What a fool. And more. The worst kind of blackguard. A little port, and all his inhibitions were overcome, all his resolutions of gentlemanly behavior dissolved. With her body pressing against his, he had been a heartbeat away from declaring his feelings. Or, God forbid, kissing her!

The fact that he had not was only a small consolation. How much had he inadvertently revealed to her? Had she guessed how her touch had affected him? Did he disgust her?

He rubbed his face with one hand. Even if she had not guessed, now that she had seen him as a drunken sot, her opinion of him would fall even further. After tonight's disgraceful behavior, he would not be surprised if she quitted the house and broke off their association.

At least then he would not have to worry she would someday guess his feelings.

But he would be responsible for Georgiana losing Elizabeth's friendship.

However, maybe all was not lost—yet.

If by some miracle she did not sever all ties to the Darcy family, he would take whatever steps were necessary to redeem himself.

Even if it meant staying away from her.

***

"I have some lovely cream silk which I believe may suit." The *modiste* and her assistant bustled about, laying down a bolt of cloth next to one of the dress patterns the Countess of Matlock had selected for her niece.

Elizabeth had expected Georgiana's coming out to be extravagant, but she had been unprepared for the sheer magnitude of the event. Georgiana's aunt was outfitting her niece with no fewer than 12 ball gowns, as well as countless day dresses, riding habits, gloves, hats, pelisses, reticules, and other necessities. Some days Georgiana might change her clothing four or five times! She even required a special dress, never to be worn again, for her presentation at Court.

The process was rather interesting, but Elizabeth felt grateful not to be the focus of the countess's attention. Being more interested in fashion than Elizabeth, Georgiana enjoyed visiting the shops, but some days she simply became overwhelmed by how many people would constantly solicit her opinion. At such moments, Elizabeth would try to intervene, suggesting a trip to Gunter's for some ices or simply an end to the day's expedition. While the countess barely tolerated Elizabeth's interruptions, Georgiana always appeared grateful.

Elizabeth observed Georgiana and her aunt examining different bolts of silk in great detail but did not participate. She simply did not possess the patience for discussions about the minutiae of fabrics.

Her thoughts drifted back to the previous evening's encounter with Mr. Darcy. The sight of the normally fastidious man so disheveled had been so alarming that she had first believed illness or emotional distress to be the cause. Despite the overwhelming aroma of port, she had been slow to realize his uncharacteristic behavior was the result of inebriation.

She did not believe he regularly imbibed so excessively, but what did she truly know of the man? It would not be so shocking. Many men of the *ton* drank and gambled to excess at their clubs. But she had never thought Mr. Darcy to be that kind of man, and he had been in his study all evening. Did he habitually drink alone? Would she not have noticed it before now?

No, his behavior simply seemed out of character. Perhaps something had distressed him, and he had sought escape in drink. She found this thought rather disturbing and wished she could do something to help him. But she could do little for Mr. Darcy within the bounds of propriety.

The women had agreed on an ivory damask silk, and now the countess was negotiating a price with the *modiste* for the various gowns they had selected. Aware the negotiations could take some time, Elizabeth wandered to the shop window, where she could watch the activity on the street. Georgiana joined her, sitting on the window seat while Elizabeth stood.

Naturally, Elizabeth had not whispered a word to Georgiana about her evening encounter with Mr. Darcy, but the younger woman might know the cause of his distress. "How has your brother's health been?" Elizabeth kept her voice casual and disinterested.

"He is in excellent health, I thank you," Georgiana replied promptly, but then she frowned. "I should say, rather, he *appears* well ... but I worry about him. He is so quiet and sober...Oh, he is the best brother, and he is always good to me, but there are times I do not believe he is...very happy."

Elizabeth was not surprised at Georgiana's insights. Quietly observing others' behavior, Georgiana understood far more than most people credited. "Have you asked him about his melancholy?"

Georgiana's lips pressed together before she responded. "Yes, but he denies there is a problem."

"Is it perhaps because of Richard's death?" Elizabeth asked.

Georgiana looked down, playing pensively with a ribbon that trimmed her dress. "We all miss Richard exceedingly. He was dear to us and William's best friend. But these moods began before—he has not been himself for more than a year. Visiting America helped, but even there ... I wish I knew what disturbed him, but he always says it is nothing." As she plucked at it, the ribbon tore off the dress, but Georgiana did not notice; she was looking fiercely up at Elizabeth. "As if I cannot see for myself! I know there is some trouble, but he will not share it with me!"

Elizabeth sat beside Georgiana on the window seat and took her friend's hand gently in both of hers. "Perhaps he is trying to spare you the worry."

Georgiana gazed at the street outside the shop, but she was blinking back tears. "I wish he would confide in *someone*, but Richard was the only one he would talk with. He feels our cousin's loss most keenly."

Elizabeth nodded. "Has anyone else noticed his melancholy disposition?"

Georgiana gave a quick laugh. "Aunt Rachel believes he simply needs a wife, but she fears his temper if she speaks of it."

Marry! Mr. Darcy? Elizabeth found the idea surprising and slightly alarming, but she could not fathom why. He was eminently eligible and of an age when many men settle down. No doubt he had been pursued by many women—beyond Miss Bingley.

Yet somehow she could not picture him with a wife.

Despite his vexing behavior—and occasional drunken fall—she enjoyed his company. However, if he married a well-bred lady of the *ton*, she would rearrange his life and might not tolerate social interactions with his cousin's former betrothed. Why did the prospect sadden her?

She realized Georgiana awaited a response. How long had she been lost in reverie? "Does your aunt have anyone particular in mind?" *Why did I ask that? I do not actually wish to know who he might marry.* For some reason, the thought made her uncomfortable.

"I do not believe so. He has told her not to play matchmaker, but I know she will throw every well-bred lady of the *ton* his way during the Season. Aunt Rachel is determined we shall both be wed this year!" Georgiana bit her lip pensively and glanced away.

Elizabeth gave her hand a reassuring squeeze. "Your brother will not force you to marry before you find the right man." Georgiana nodded quickly. Then she turned back to Elizabeth, lowering her voice to a whisper. "But William told Aunt Rachel he has no intention of marrying!"

Elizabeth felt shock and another, more difficult to identify, emotion at this news. Was it relief? Of course, she reasoned. She did not wish to disturb her comfortable friendship with the Darcys, since they helped her cope with losing Richard.

"Why would he say such a thing?" Georgiana asked, her brow creased with worry.

"Perhaps he simply dislikes your aunt's matchmaking," Elizabeth suggested.

Georgiana considered this. "It is true he attends few social events, and he complains about the women of the *ton*, so false and languid. He has never demonstrated any particular interest in a specific lady." Georgiana brought her lips close to Elizabeth's ear and breathed, "Aunt Rachel speculated he has a mistress!"

"Georgiana!" Elizabeth attempted a chastising tone, but she could not stifle a laugh, which provoked a giggle from her friend. "You should not know such women exist!"

This prodded Georgiana into more fits of laughter. "What do you think girls talk about at school?"

Elizabeth smiled indulgently. "Indeed. I have sisters. No doubt some gentlemen would be shocked at some of the topics we have discussed!" She lowered her voice, drawing closer to her friend. "Do you think he does have a mistress?" Why did the thought unsettle her so much?

"No! He would never—I know many men of the *ton* have them, but William would not." Georgiana's whisper hissed with her vehemence. Elizabeth decided the feeling of relief she experienced was for the sake of her friend's propriety.

Georgiana tugged the sleeve of her dress into place. "If he never marries it would be a shame. He would be an excellent husband."

Elizabeth nodded agreement and then stopped, amazed. Not too long ago, she would have believed he was the last man in the world who would be a good husband. Had her view of Mr. Darcy undergone such an alteration, or had his behavior itself changed?

Why was everything about the man so confusing?

The door to the shop opened, revealing a well-dressed, plump, older woman. Her eyes lit on Georgiana. The smile that settled over her face made Elizabeth think about Mr. Darcy's dislike for false women.

"Miss Darcy! What an unexpected delight!" Ingratiating mask in place, the woman bustled over to Georgiana.

"Mrs. Greenlow." Georgiana dutifully stood and curtsied. "This is my friend, Miss Bennet."

Mrs. Greenlow barely acknowledged Elizabeth before returning her attention to Georgiana. "You are making your debut this year?" Georgiana nodded. "I suppose your brother will escort you to most of the events of the Season?"

The older woman may not have heard Georgiana's small sigh, but Elizabeth did. This was the third time Georgiana had been asked about her brother just today. "At least some of them. My aunt and uncle will escort me as well," Georgiana replied.

Mrs. Greenlow regarded the younger woman for a moment, mouth slightly open. Perhaps she was about to ask for a list of which events Mr. Darcy would attend. Elizabeth smothered a laugh at the thought. Finally, the older woman nodded briskly. "It will be a pleasure to see you then!" She hurried over to the counter, where she engaged the countess and the *modiste* in a conversation about the price of silk.

Georgiana tipped her head close to Elizabeth's and murmured, "She has two marriageable daughters and a husband with gambling debts." Elizabeth's eyes widened a little at this frank assessment, provoking a cynical laugh from Georgiana. "Did you believe she has a sincere interest in my friendship? Her son is already married, so at least *I* am safe from her." She watched the feather on the woman's hat bob as she spoke to the *modiste*. "Poor William."

"Poor Georgiana," Elizabeth observed, "to be valued primarily for your connection to your brother."

Georgiana assumed an expression of indignation. "Do not be so severe upon the *ton*. Many people value my connection to my fortune." Both women dissolved into laughter, earning a disapproving look from the countess.

Mrs. Greenlow soon rushed out of the shop, and Georgiana was required to consult about lace. Elizabeth wandered about the shop, examining ribbons and fabrics, but her thoughts were far away.

Her conversation with Georgiana had prompted a revelation: she and Mr. Darcy had both been deprived of their primary confidante by Richard's death. At least Elizabeth had Jane or her Aunt Gardiner to occasionally confide in during the months following Richard's death, but Mr. Darcy appeared to have no one at all. Perhaps Mr. Bingley, but he was in Hertfordshire and preoccupied with his new daughter. Elizabeth's heart grew heavy as she imagined his loneliness.

It was an odd sensation—to feel sorry for a man like Mr. Darcy. When Jane had married Charles Bingley, Mrs. Bennet's demeanor had suggested a secure income would solve all their problems. However, Mr. Darcy did not appear to be carefree but just the opposite. The anguish she saw in his eyes the night before? She might not know its source, but it was real enough.

Feeling sorry for Mr. Darcy. An event she never believed would come to pass. Perhaps the sun would rise in the west tomorrow, and pigs would fly. Elizabeth laughed a little at her own sense of whimsy.

Idly admiring some gloves, Elizabeth recalled when she almost lost Richard's townhouse. Mr. Darcy had come to her rescue. If only there were some way she could help him!

How silly! What could Elizabeth Bennet from Longbourn do to help the master of Pemberley? But still, was it not incumbent on her to make the attempt? At least she could be a friend to him—just as she was to his sister.

Even as the thought occurred to her, Elizabeth rejected it. Being friends with another woman was a simple matter. For an unmarried woman to be friends with an unmarried man … the rules of propriety would make it very difficult.

Still …

Elizabeth could not forget the idea that she must somehow help Mr. Darcy. The idea of being his friend was strangely appealing. He was often complicated and vexing, but recently, he had seemed to value her opinion and enjoy her company.

Yes. She was resolved, despite the obstacles. To the extent propriety allowed, she would show Mr. Darcy her friendship and endeavor to help him through this difficult period in his life.

When she visited Georgiana throughout the upcoming months, Elizabeth would see Mr. Darcy— and would do what she could to demonstrate her friendship.

***

In preparation for tonight's dinner, Darcy had taken exquisite care with his attire, even though it was a simple evening at home. Georgiana had invited Elizabeth; he would see her for the first time since he had made a drunken fool of himself three nights ago. He held little hope of redeeming himself in her eyes, but he must be a model of self-control and rectitude.

Indeed, he was pleased Elizabeth seemed willing to still associate with Georgiana at all; if she was unsettled by his presence, Darcy was prepared to simply quit the room for the sake of her comfort. But the thought sent cold chills through his heart. Without the aid of large quantities of brandy, how would he survive another visit hiding from her? Even a temporary exile would be the worst punishment imaginable.

You should have considered that before you got foxed, commented an angry voice at the back of his mind. He could offer no excuse. Despite knowing the possible consequences, he had indulged in self-pity and inebriation. He deserved any punishment he suffered.

Except exile from Elizabeth.

He adjusted his cravat, hoping the damn thing was still even. Fussing with it earlier had nearly driven his valet to distraction.

No wine, no brandy, and particularly no port, he admonished himself as he strode down the hallway to the drawing room. Before reaching for the door knob, he braced himself. What would he find inside? Would she ignore him? Act cold and distant? Cutting? Swallowing hard, he opened the door.

Elizabeth and Georgiana were seated together on a settee, their heads—dark and light—bent over a book. They looked up in unison as Darcy entered. His eyes darted directly to Elizabeth, fearing his reception. "Miss Bennet." He nodded a greeting.

"Mr. Darcy." Her smile was warm enough to melt the dread surrounding his heart. Darcy released a relieved breath. Perhaps she had forgiven the incident in the hallway.

"Elizabeth brought me a novel as a present!" Eyes shining with excitement, Georgiana held up the small brown book. "It is one of her favorites, but an author I have never read."

Relief swept through his body, making his knees weak. *She does not hate us!* "That is very thoughtful of you." He attempted to convey his gratitude for her forgiveness in the warm look he returned to Elizabeth but feared he merely appeared pained.

As he approached the settee, Elizabeth rose, watching him steadily. "The bookseller also had the latest volume of Mr. Wordsworth's poetry. I remembered our lively conversations about his verses at Rosings, so I purchased it for you." She held out a book that had been resting in her lap.

Darcy extended his hand automatically to take the volume. His fingers closed about the book's spine, savoring the texture and weight. *She has given me a gift!* "I-I thank you, Miss Bennet." He was entirely too stunned to frame another response.

Her eyes regarded him uncertainly. "You do not already own it?"

"No, indeed. It is a most welcome addition to my library." He stared in wonder at the slim blue book, feeling as if he held a miracle in his hand.

"Very good." She shot him another uncertain smile and settled herself once more beside Georgiana.

Darcy got himself into a chair, only staggering slightly. He was utterly nonplussed. He had prepared for coldness and disdain, not warmth and generosity—as if he had braced himself for a blow that had never come.

By the strict rules of propriety, he should decline a gift from an unmarried woman, but he had never been less inclined to follow the dictates of propriety. Refusing the gift would embarrass Elizabeth, and he had mortified her sufficiently for the week. Besides, the unassuming blue book had already become his favorite, and he had yet to open it.

Elizabeth knew how improper her gesture was, yet here she had flaunted the accepted rules. Why? What was he to think? Could Elizabeth possibly be flirting with him?

The thought caused his heart to beat a fast, relentless rhythm.

However, as she discussed the novel with his sister, Elizabeth seemed only slightly aware of his presence. Hardly the behavior of a flirt. And the smile she had bestowed on him had been gentle, not at all coy or enticing.

No, it would be presumptuous to think he had won her regard. He turned the book over in his hands, telling himself it was simply a friendly gesture. Elizabeth had purchased a book for Georgiana and had bought one for him as an afterthought. Darcy must not presume any other meaning.

Elizabeth and Georgiana were no longer conversing; his sister was drinking her tea. Darcy seized the opportunity. "You are too kind to us, Miss Bennet."

She smiled at him, but her eyes quickly dropped to her lap. "It is you who have been kind to me. The friendship you and Georgiana have shown over these few months has been of immeasurable benefit during a difficult time." Of course. She was speaking of Richard's death. Darcy had almost managed to forget about Richard and his role in her life. How was that possible? "It is unfortunate that we did not have the opportunity to become cousins in truth," Elizabeth said as she patted Georgiana's hand. "You and Georgiana feel like members of my family—almost as if we *are* cousins."

Georgiana clasped Elizabeth's hand. "Yes, indeed! We are quite like cousins, are we not William?" Unable to utter a word, Darcy merely nodded.

The two women continued to speak, but Darcy did not attend to the conversation. Elizabeth viewed him as a cousin, akin to an older brother. The message could not be clearer, despite being unintentionally delivered.

It was for the best. Nothing had changed. Although he still loved Elizabeth, he could never act on it. He would satisfy himself with being her honorary cousin. Compared to the fear that she would refuse the acquaintance, this was a delight, he reminded himself.

Yes, honorary cousin was a great prize.

Why did some part of him remained unconvinced?

Chapter 10

Darcy resisted the impulse to fuss with his cravat or yank at his cuffs. His ensemble was perfect; his valet had fussed over it for an hour. But his hands must be occupied; he pushed his fingers through his hair. Had he had disordered his valet's careful arrangement? Guiltily, Darcy smoothed the locks into place. Next his fingers worried the edge of his hat where it rested on his knee.

There was no helping it. His hands could not bear to be idle.

In the seat across, Georgiana remained stiffly erect, barely moving despite the swaying of the carriage. Her face was devoid of color; her hands twisted in endless circles in her lap. She was too terrified to fidget with her clothing or her hair, but she watched Darcy as if she longed to follow his example.

The Darcys did not perform well to strangers.

Tonight was the grandest performance of all: Georgiana's coming out ball. The last few weeks had been a flurry of invitation lists, menu selections, and dress fittings. Georgiana had borne it without complaint, but with all the enthusiasm of a child presented with a plate of cold gruel. She relished the opportunities to purchase the latest fashions, but all other tasks were a burden.

At least it would soon be behind them.

Noticing his eyes on her, Georgiana gave him a tight smile, recognizing they were partners in anxiety. However, she did not know that Darcy's anxiety did not spring at all from the ball itself. He was confident in his aunt's arrangements; the event was bound to be a success.

He was equally certain that Georgiana would perform very well. Although she did not share the easy manners and flirtatiousness of many girls her age, she was gracious and proper. She had practiced her dancing until it was flawless. Her conversation was appropriate, if a bit sparse. No one would find her lacking.

No, Darcy's mind fixated on Miss Elizabeth Bennet. Just today, she had put off her half-mourning colors. For the first time since his long ago visit to Meryton, Darcy could dance with her. The memory of their dance at Netherfield still haunted him, and he was determined to have another—or perhaps even two. Although he would never win her heart, he would allow himself this small pleasure.

For one night, he would permit himself the fantasy that Miss Elizabeth Bennet was a woman he could pursue.

Reality would reassert itself soon enough.

Georgiana shivered, and Darcy chastised himself for neglecting his only sister. He leaned forward and wrapped his hand around both of hers. "Do not worry, dear heart. You will be brilliant." Her smile was so brief he almost failed to note it. "Everyone will be charmed with your beauty and poise."

One side of her mouth quirked up. "I would be satisfied with not embarrassing myself by doing something like spilling lemonade on my dress or stepping on the Duke of Lennox's toes." Darcy laughed at this unexpected show of spirit. Elizabeth had helped her grow more confident in her own opinions.

The carriage lurched to a stop. Any remaining color drained out of Georgiana's face. Darcy gave her hand a reassuring squeeze before releasing it.

"Courage, dear heart," he murmured. She nodded stiffly, but as Darcy climbed out of the carriage he wondered if his words were really intended for her—or for himself.

***

The room was bursting with women wearing silks or satins and dripping with jewels. The men wore the finest, best-cut suits Elizabeth had ever seen. She had attended a few balls with Richard, but nothing that could truly have been considered *haute ton*. This was, the Countess of Matlock had assured her, the premiere event of the Season—the occasion no one would dare miss. The size of the crowd suggested the countess had not been exaggerating. Most of the London *ton* seemed to be packed into the ballroom.

The noise was quite deafening. The music was faint here, nearer the ballroom entrance, but the cacophony of conversation was overwhelming. Elizabeth and her Aunt Gardiner had withdrawn to a corner near the entrance, while her uncle fetched some lemonade. However, given the crush, she feared he might not return before the end of the week.

"You were right," she said as they surveyed the scene. Mr. Darcy had caused a minor row with the countess when he had insisted on inviting Elizabeth's aunt and uncle, but he had prevailed.

"Naturally!" Aunt Madeline said with a playful smile. "About what in particular?"

"The gown. It was not an unnecessary extravagance."

"You look lovely," her aunt said, raising her voice to be heard over the din. Elizabeth had not wished to spend extra money for the shop's most expensive silk or lace. Although Richard had left Elizabeth a comfortable sum, she felt the need to be frugal.

However, Elizabeth's aunt had insisted the extravagance of the event required the best the shop had to offer. If Elizabeth had chosen a lesser fabric, she would have felt out of place in this august assembly.

"That color becomes you," Mrs. Gardiner observed. The gown was a pale yellow, which set off Elizabeth's coloring. Having cast off her half-mourning only a week ago, she was still self-conscious about wearing any color. "I am sure many young men will be vying for your attention."

Elizabeth smoothed the curls over her forehead. "I fear you gravely overestimate my appeal." Although her dress had cost an extraordinary amount, it was rather simple and plain compared to many of the extravagant creations worn by the other women in attendance. She pressed on a piece of lace at her neckline which refused to lie flat. It hardly signifies, she reminded herself. *I am here because Georgiana invited me, not to impress anyone in attendance.*

"You do not believe any young men would be interested?" The tone of her aunt's voice suggested she would not let this matter rest until Elizabeth had responded to her satisfaction.

Elizabeth sighed, preferring to avoid the subject. The size of her dowry had always been an impediment to marriage, but Richard's bequest had improved her financial situation greatly. Now that she was forced to think on the matter, she conceded that she might be considered a more desirable marital prospect.

"You are a beautiful young woman," her aunt continued.

"I would not mind dancing, but I am not at all interested in entertaining suitors." Elizabeth stared down at her gloved hands.

Surely no one would expect her to seriously consider marriage so soon after Richard's death, would they?

"I understand, my dear." Aunt Madeline's voice was gentle and compassionate. "But you must contemplate it someday."

"Must I?" She swallowed the lump in her throat. "Now that I have a measure of security ... I do not know. Lately, the thought of living at Netherfield has held appeal."

"But, my dear, what about love?" Her aunt's eyes were full of concern. "At such a young age, will you give up on finding love?"

Elizabeth bit her lip, continuing to gaze at her hands. "Richard was such a dear companion. We were so alike, so well suited. I could never find another like him."

Her aunt considered this as she watched throngs of people jostle against and weave among one another. "Of course, you will not find another like him, but you might find another man you might love in a different way."

Elizabeth said nothing, not wishing to contradict her aunt. Instead, she allowed herself to be mesmerized by the dancers, whirling in a complicated pattern. She sighed a little. She did dearly love to dance.

"Someone will ask you to dance, Lizzy," her aunt said. "I am certain."

"I am acquainted with very few people here."

"At least you can dance with your uncle."

"Of course." Elizabeth thought of her uncle's indifferent dancing skills.

"Miss Bennet!"

Elizabeth turned at the unexpected sound of her name. Mr. Darcy had pushed his way through the crush to reach them. Had he actually braved the crowds to seek her out?

She curtsied, and he bowed. However, now that he stood before her, he seemed to have forgotten why he had hailed her. He was regarding her seriously, his mouth slightly open. "Did you require my assistance, Mr. Darcy?" she prompted.

"Yes, yes. Of course!" Mr. Darcy shook himself from his reverie. "Georgiana has been asking after you every five minutes. I finally undertook the commission to discover your whereabouts."

She suppressed an inexplicable sense of disappointment he had not sought her out to ask her to dance. "I did not think Georgiana would need me here! I cannot assist in the selection of dance partners. Your aunt—"

Mr. Darcy interrupted with a smile. "Georgiana wishes your help with those things my aunt *cannot* assist her with. The countess can be … insistent. And of course, the ball itself is overwhelming."

"Of course. I did not realize!" Elizabeth was mortified. Did he believe she had abandoned her friend in her time of need? Was he angry?

"I understand. So, I sought you out." His tone was conciliatory. "May I escort you to my sister?" He waved his hand toward the front of the room.

"Yes, of course."

Mr. Darcy extended the invitation to her Aunt Gardiner, but she decided to wait for her husband's return before joining her niece. Darcy offered his arm, and together they made slow progress through the crowd.

Perhaps it was Darcy's height or his forbidding manner— or simply because many guests recognized him—but he fought through the crush far more easily than Elizabeth had earlier. Soon they reached their destination. Standing with their niece, the earl and countess had also put off their half-mourning and were resplendent in their finery. However, they could not outshine Georgiana, who wore a lovely white silk gown embroidered with small pink roses.

Elizabeth smiled at Georgiana, proud of how beautiful and poised she appeared. Embracing the younger woman, she kissed her cheeks and exclaimed over her dress. Georgiana immediately commenced a long soliloquy about the ball and her dance partners. The gleam in Georgiana's eye warmed Elizabeth's heart; although Darcy's sister was obviously nervous, she was also finding pleasure in the event. In fact, Elizabeth's primary usefulness seemed to be lending an ear to Georgiana's concerns and effusions.

Georgiana was soon carried away by her next dance partner. Elizabeth noticed someone standing at her elbow. Turning, she discovered Lord Kirkwood, Richard's friend. "Lord

Kirkwood!" she exclaimed happily. He had been a tremendous help to her in the days following Richard's death.

He kissed Elizabeth's hand, holding it a fraction longer than was expected. "Miss Bennet. May I tell you how love you are tonight?"

Elizabeth smiled at the dashing young lord. "Thank you. You are too kind."

"On the contrary," he said smoothly. "I speak only the truth. I cannot say enough how well that color sets off your eyes."

Elizabeth's cheeks heated. "Thank you." Out of the corner of her eye, she noticed Mr. Darcy stalking toward them.

"Are you engaged for the next set?" Lord Kirkwood asked her.

"Yes," Mr. Darcy said before Elizabeth could open her mouth. "She is dancing it with me."

Elizabeth opened her mouth and then closed it with a snap, regarding Mr. Darcy in confusion. He had said nothing about dancing with him! But she could not embarrass him by contradicting him in public.

Lord Kirkwood nodded easily, holding Elizabeth's eyes rather than focusing on Mr. Darcy. "Then would you honor me with the following set?"

"Yes, of course," Elizabeth responded before Mr. Darcy could speak. No one should answer for her!

Darcy said nothing but looked as if he had chewed on something unpleasant. Lord Kirkwood merely nodded to them both and departed. Elizabeth glared at Mr. Darcy. "We are to dance? It must have slipped my mind."

He had the grace to color. "I was planning to request the next set."

"And you were so certain I would accept that an actual invitation was rendered unnecessary. How efficient of you," she said archly.

His color deepened. "Naturally, if you do not wish to dance with me, I will understand."

Elizabeth was immediately contrite. She wished to act as his friend, not cause him additional distress. "Forgive my teasing. I would be very pleased to dance the next set with you." Her reward was a relieved smile. Did a dance with her mean so much?

"Do you find something objectionable about Lord Kirkwood?" she asked, wondering if perhaps he saw her dancing as disloyal to his cousin.

Darcy glanced briefly at the man in question where he stood a short distance away. "There are rumors his father left him with many gambling debts."

"And therefore, I should not *dance* with him? You are very severe, sir."

"He may be seeking a wife of some fortune." Mr. Darcy addressed his remarks to the space above her left ear.

It took a moment before Elizabeth comprehended his meaning. "While my finances have improved, I am hardly a temptation to a fortune hunter!"

Mr. Darcy scowled at the floor but did not respond. Upon reflection, she realized with some surprise that her fortune might be considered large enough to interest a desperate man, but she would never believe such motives of Lord Kirkwood. He was merely acting as a friend in Richard's memory. *You promised to be better friends with Mr. Darcy*, she reminded herself.

"But I thank you for your concern," she added, somewhat stiffly. Mr. Darcy's eyes darted to her face, regarding her in surprise, but he said nothing. Silence descended on them.

Being his friend was more difficult than she had anticipated!

Couples were moving into position for the next set. "I believe the next set is forming," she observed with relief.

Mr. Darcy seemed to be recalled from a reverie, although she had the odd impression he had been staring at the flowers in her hair. *Nonsense! You do have a vivid imagination, Lizzy!*

He took her gloved hand in his and led her into position for the set. As they waited opposite each other, they were silent. He did not smile at her—as almost any other dance partner would have—but his attention was wholly fixed on her face as if he would memorize her features. After a moment, she felt unequal to meeting the intensity of his gaze and had to glance away. It was a relief when the music commenced.

The dance at Netherfield had demonstrated that Mr. Darcy was an excellent dancer. He was quite light on his feet, and they were well-matched as partners.

Unlike at Netherfield, he made an effort at speech, particularly as they waited to take their turn in the figure. He commented on the progress of the ball and how Georgiana seemed to be faring. Was it possible he attended to her earlier reproofs about his taciturn demeanor? No, most likely he had entirely forgotten that conversation. Perhaps he was simply more at ease with her now that they were better acquainted.

When the set was complete, Elizabeth felt it had been too short. Dancing with Mr. Darcy had actually been quite enjoyable, and she would have been pleased to stand up with him again. However, as they left the dance floor, he was holding her hand rather tightly, and his mouth was set in a stern line. Perhaps he had not enjoyed the dancing as well.

Lord Kirkwood emerged from the crowd to claim her hand for the next set. Mr. Darcy must have noticed the other man but ignored him. Mr. Darcy focused all the power of his penetrating gaze on Elizabeth, taking her hand in both of his. "I thank you for the dance. Rarely has anything given me more pleasure."

Elizabeth's breath caught, and her heart suddenly pounded very loudly. Why was her mouth so dry she was unable to speak? *So he* had *enjoyed the dancing,* she thought inanely, but was unable to account for why his simple compliment had such an effect on her. "Would you do me the honor of reserving the final set for me?" His expression suggested her response was of the greatest urgency.

She swallowed. "I-I thought you would dance it with Georgiana."

Mr. Darcy's expression darkened, and she thought he might actually utter an oath. "Yes, you are quite right. The penultimate set then."

Elizabeth nodded, a little stunned. "Of course."

With another deep, penetrating look into her eyes, he turned and melted away into the crowd, never acknowledging Lord Kirkwood, standing only a few feet away. The other man watched Darcy's retreating back with a frown. "I do not understand Mr. Darcy's behavior at times."

Elizabeth sighed. *Neither do I.* Nevertheless, she could not help bristling at the implied criticism. "He was always a good friend to Richard."

"Yes, yes." Lord Kirkwood seemed eager to clear up any misimpression. "Richard always spoke very highly of his cousin. I do not know him well, but I am certain he is an excellent man."

"He is indeed." *Why does it trouble me if Lord Kirkwood is less than complimentary of Mr. Darcy? I have voiced far less kind thoughts about the man in the past.*

In fact, two years ago, she would have been his severest critic. As they took their places in the figure, Elizabeth remembered with shame how she had allowed her opinion of him to be founded on misunderstandings and a credulous belief of Wickham's lies. God forbid Mr. Darcy ever learned the extent of her previous dislike!

The music started, and she and Lord Kirkwood moved through the figures. She responded automatically to his conversation about the size of the crowd and the weather, but her thoughts seemed fixed on Mr. Darcy. His behavior had altered considerably, she realized.

The Mr. Darcy she knew today would not describe anyone as "tolerable" or "not pretty enough to tempt me." When had he changed? And why? Had he been in a particularly foul humor in Meryton so that she formed an erroneous impression of his character? Or had he made an effort since then to become more agreeable?

And why do I care so much?

With a shake of her head, Elizabeth attempted to clear her mind of such unproductive thinking. Decorum demanded that she devote her full attention to Lord Kirkwood. Fortunately, he was involved in a long description of a recently purchased horse, so nothing had been lost to her inattention.

However, his monologue unfortunately allowed her to obsess about a new and more disturbing question.

Why can I not banish Mr. Darcy from my thoughts?

***

He was pathetic. Darcy had dozens of details to address and many guests he was obligated to greet. He must placate his aunt and uncle while ensuring that Georgiana was reasonably happy and not overwhelmed. He was performing most of these tasks at least adequately.

And yet some part of his mind still managed to follow Elizabeth's whereabouts in the enormous ballroom and catalogue in painful detail the names and attractiveness of her every dance partner. No matter where she was in the vast, crowded room, he somehow knew her location every minute.

Unfortunately, after dancing with him and Lord Kirkwood, Elizabeth had become quite popular as a partner. And naturally, all her partners would be enchanted by her wit and vivacity. They would be thoroughly charmed and would form plans to court her. Who would not want to marry her? If Darcy had foreseen this eventuality, he might not have postponed the pleasure of a set with her until later in the evening. Or perhaps he could have locked her in a sitting room.

Damnation! If only propriety allowed him to dance more than two sets with her! He would dance his feet raw just to keep those vultures away. Not that dancing with Elizabeth was ever a chore.

Surely these predators would know that she was still grieving, despite her clothing. Did they not recognize she would never love another man? Did they have no respect for his cousin?

Darcy pulled on his stiffly starched cravat; the damn thing was choking him. Thank God the night was nearly at an end. The whole event had been exhausting, and he was heartily sick of smiling at people he barely recognized.

The current set was drawing to completion. Darcy could now claim Elizabeth as his partner. His entire body tingled with anticipation, longing for the moment when he could again touch her.

Elizabeth had barely departed the dance floor with her current partner, a second or third son of a duke who had been friendly with Richard, when Darcy intercepted them.

A little startled at his sudden appearance, Elizabeth nonetheless performed introductions perfectly. Darcy gave the other man a stiff nod and a perfunctory glance. Elizabeth was his for only a brief time; he would not waste it speaking with a total stranger. Taking her hand, he hastily led her away from her previous dance partner and onto the dance floor.

Once they arrived at the edge of the dance floor, however, Darcy realized his mistake. The musicians were playing the opening bars of a waltz!

How could he have forgotten? His aunt had insisted on a waltz as the next-to-last dance. This new style of dance was becoming fashionable and was considered somewhat daring. Of course, it was incumbent on the earl and countess to demonstrate they were at the forefront of every style.

However, the waltz—with its placement of hands on other's bodies— was considered too intimate for unmarried couples to perform. Georgiana would sit it out, and naturally, Darcy had planned to avoid it as well, but he would then lose his opportunity to dance with Elizabeth. He muttered a curse under his breath.

"Mr. Darcy?" Elizabeth asked.

"I apologize, Miss Bennet, but I had forgotten that this dance would be a waltz." He regarded her with dismay. He must dance the last set with Georgiana. He had a reckless impulse to dance the waltz with her anyway, propriety be damned. But he could not expose her to that kind of gossip. A small voice at the back of his mind reminded him that a lost dance was hardly a tragedy, but anger and despair drowned it out. Her presence was the only thing that had made that evening endurable for him.

Elizabeth was watching him closely, apparently noticing his disappointment. She tilted her head to the side, regarding him archly. "I *do* know how to waltz."

"You do?" Had Richard taught her? Jealousy of his cousin flared in his chest.

"Yes. Jane taught me, since she is a married woman. Naturally, I have never danced it in public."

Darcy suppressed a groan at the thought of dancing with Elizabeth, his hand on her waist, separated from her body by a thin layer of silk. He would be able to feel the warmth of her skin under his fingers ...

Desperation sparked an idea. "Would you like to dance it?" he asked her.

"Yes. I find it extremely diverting," she answered immediately. "But we cannot—"

Darcy knew he would act on this impulse, even though it was a dangerous and quite possibly ruinous idea. Once the thought had taken root, he could not let it go. "We cannot dance it in the ballroom, but ..." Without another word, Darcy took Elizabeth by the hand and led her to the far side of the ballroom, where a door emptied out onto a little-used corridor. From there, he opened another door into a darkened parlor.

As he pulled her behind him, he was too anxious to glance back and notice her expression. He could only hope she trusted he did not have improper intentions.

The parlor had French doors that opened onto a rather large balcony. Once through the doors, Elizabeth and Darcy could hear the waltz music quite clearly and could see swirling figures illuminated by the hundreds of candles in the ballroom's chandeliers. The balcony, in contrast, was swathed in the deep shadows cast by the house, and Darcy doubted anyone in the ballroom could perceive them. The world outside was bathed in the cool light of a full moon, rendering it beautiful and foreign at the same time.

He now chanced a glimpse of Elizabeth's expression. Would she be horrified at the liberties he had taken? But he was relieved to see a mischievous grin on her face. She was enjoying the adventure. Then as she looked around, her face glowed with wonder at the beauty of the setting.

He bowed briefly to Elizabeth. "May I have this dance, Miss Bennet?"

She curtsied. "It would be my pleasure, Mr. Darcy."

Darcy took one of her hands in his and carefully placed his other hand on her waist. Touching her was unlike touching any other woman. His hands trembled with the realization that they had come into contact—so long denied—with the object of his affections. Electric shocks fired all of his senses and compelled thoughts about where else he might touch her.

In part to forestall these completely inappropriate musings, Darcy launched them into the circular patterns of the waltz.

The experience was hypnotic, transcendent. The cool, crisp night air rushing past, the warmth of her body in his arms, the slight rosewater scent of Elizabeth's skin, and the gentle, insistent rhythms of the music. She fit perfectly into his arms and followed his lead effortlessly, as if they were made to be together—two halves of a whole. Why had he never danced a waltz with her before? What a fool he had been!

He could easily lose himself in these sensations. With the entire balcony at their disposal, Darcy could maneuver them in a circular pattern as they twirled on their own axis.

A delighted laugh bubbled out of Elizabeth, provoking a swell of joy and pride in her companion. Nothing could please him more than to know he had given her pleasure. "Mr. Darcy," her tone was playful, "I believe *you* have waltzed before with someone not your wife."

Darcy was delighted to be teased by her. "Indeed, madam." He nodded solemnly.

"Oh?" She arched a brow at him.

"Yes. With my Aunt Fitzwilliam and Georgiana and—upon one memorable occasion—my Aunt Catherine." Elizabeth's brows rose at this revelation. "And, I can assure you that although my aunt may appreciate music more than most, you are far more adept at keeping a beat."

He was rewarded with Elizabeth's ringing laughter. Warmth spread through his chest. *So this is how pure happiness feels.*

Instinctively, he drew her closer so they could more easily move in harmony. Briefly, he closed his eyes, savoring the sensations ... her warmth, her soft skin, the silky slide of her dress. When he opened them again, he drank in the sight of her radiant smile, the flush in her cheeks, the bright shine of excitement in her eyes. He must catalog these sights and sensations to remember at a later date.

She is happy. I have made her happy, he marveled. He was seized by a strong impulse to want to make her happy again—to find ways to make her happy for the rest of her life. *This could become an addiction.* But firmly, he put worries of the future aside and focused on the moment here before him.

Finally, the music came to an end, the last notes of the violin dying on a breeze wafting through the ballroom's windows. Darcy did not want it to end. How could he bear to release Elizabeth's hand?

Glancing down at the positions of their bodies, he realized he was holding Elizabeth quite close indeed. They had started with enough distance between them to fit a third person, but now ...

Mere inches.

Good Lord! The distance between them would be considered inappropriate in public even for a married couple. If anyone were to see them ... he could be justly accused of compromising her reputation. Darcy was appalled at himself, in part because his first reaction was not nearly as horrified as it should have been. Despite the gross impropriety, part of him wished to remain like this forever.

He should release her immediately.

Yes. Let her go... and gently push her from him....

And yet ... her luminous eyes were looking up at him. She did not seem alarmed at his proximity, but he could not read her expression. She was breathing hard from the exertion, her lips slightly open, soft and pink. The dance had affected her as well. Even across the inches that separated them, he could feel the heat radiating from her body.

He was lost.

His gaze was again pulled to her lips, full and enticing ...

How could he be expected to resist?

He tilted his head down, preparing to kiss her—imagining how her lips would taste. How would she respond? In the back of his mind, he wondered if Richard had ever held her thus ... had ever kissed her with such passion ...

Oh, Good Lord, Richard!

Darcy whipped his head away and staggered backward, practically thrusting Elizabeth from him.

How could he have—? What was wrong with him? He had lost all control!

His heart beat double time, and his chest heaved, his breath coming in gasps as he tried to master himself.

Elizabeth's expression held utter bewilderment. Her mouth opened in shock, but she seemed to be at a loss for words. His wildly inappropriate behavior must have elicited her deepest disgust.

He owed her an abject apology. He opened his mouth to deliver it, but all he could imagine was blurting out a confession and a declaration of the deepest, most enduring love.

No! It would not do!

He could not chance it. He must not say anything.

He met her eyes, recognizing the confusion and hurt he saw there. Silently, he pleaded that she would understand his dilemma. Someday. Then he turned and disappeared through the French doors, leaving her alone on the balcony.

Chapter 11

Elizabeth was unsure what to expect when she arrived at Darcy House. Mr. Darcy's behavior at the ball the previous evening had been confusing—and a little alarming. For a moment, she had thought he meant to kiss her.

But in the light of the next day, she knew that to be a silly illusion conjured by moonlight and the proximity created by the waltz. She was not the princess in a fairy tale—and Mr. Darcy was certainly not Prince Charming. Why, in the very next moment, he had pushed her away as if she intended to poison him!

They *had* been standing daringly close, although she had not noticed until the dance ended. Did Mr. Darcy believe she had somehow contrived that intimacy in the hopes of encouraging a romance? Was that why he had thrust her away so violently? No, surely he knew her better than that.

She was uncertain how they had come to be so close. Had Mr. Darcy drawn her toward him without realizing it? Fervently, Elizabeth hoped that *she* had not unintentionally moved closer as they danced. What would he think of her? The very thought provoked a blush.

No, she must not assume the worst. It was most probable that Mr. Darcy had simply recognized the impropriety of how close they were standing and left abruptly because of his embarrassment. He was not always skillful at articulating his thoughts.

That must be the explanation. He would never consider kissing her. It was unclear if he even truly liked her! He could marry any number of women and would have no desire to favor a country miss with no connections—particularly his cousin's betrothed. It was a foolish mistake. A trick of shadows and moonlight. *It is not as though I wish him to kiss me!*

She now deeply regretted consenting to the waltz. His actions had skirted the boundaries of propriety, but she had voiced no reservations. If Mr. Darcy's opinion of her had suffered as a result, she could blame no one but herself.

After exiting the balcony, Elizabeth had seen him at a distance as he danced the last set with Georgiana, but they had not spoken again. She had hastily found the Gardiners, and they had made an expeditious exit from the ball.

Perhaps he would be at tea with Georgiana. Naturally, he would not mention the incident, but his demeanor might reveal something of his thinking. Only now did she realize how sad she would be to lose his friendship

The butler escorted her into the drawing room, where Georgiana was sitting with her embroidery. The first thing Elizabeth noted was that the room was full of flowers; arrangements of different sizes and many different varieties covered nearly every available surface.

"Elizabeth!" Georgiana exclaimed. "I am so happy you have come!"

"Have you resolved on opening a flower shop?" Elizabeth asked.

Georgiana laughed as she gestured her friend to a seat. "I very well could! These flowers are from gentlemen who attended the ball last night." She blushed a deep crimson.

Elizabeth had guessed as much. "I can see you made quite an impression."

"I suppose." Georgiana's hands twisted in her lap, and her eyes were downcast.

"I thought the ball went very well," Elizabeth said, trying to catch her friend's eye.

Georgiana looked up. "Yes. It was ever so much better than I feared. People were so kind, and I never missed a step while dancing. I even enjoyed myself—some of the time."

"So it is the flowers themselves you find displeasing?" Elizabeth teased. "They are perhaps too fragrant?"

Georgiana giggled. "No, indeed!" Darcy's sister stood and pensively examined a delicate pink rose. "I just wish … I knew which gentlemen admire me and which only admire my dowry."

Elizabeth leaned toward her friend. "I can see why that would trouble you. Fortunately, there is no need for haste. In time, I have no doubt you will find a gentleman who is worthy of you."

Georgiana's mouth was a thin line. "I hope so. I do hope to marry for love." She wandered among other arrangements, admiring the flowers.

"I am certain you shall." Elizabeth considered ways to keep the conversation amusing. "So now I understand why I had to fight through a jungle of blossoms, but how is it you escaped a corresponding throng of admirers for afternoon visits?" She would have expected many of these interested young gentlemen to commence their courtship of Georgiana immediately.

The younger woman smiled gently. "William left strict instructions that I am not to receive any gentlemen callers without him—or most ladies either, since most of them would be pressing the suits of brothers or sons. As a result, I am not at home to anyone except you or my aunt. I confess myself relieved. I would not be equal to a day of receiving visitors after such a night."

A maid brought in a tray with tea and biscuits. Georgiana poured a cup for Elizabeth, adding a little cream and sugar, just as she liked.

So, Mr. Darcy was not at home? "Did your brother go to his club?" Elizabeth sipped her tea, attempting to appear disinterested.

Once again seated, Georgiana paused with her cup halfway to her lips. "Oh no! I forgot to tell you. He has gone to Pemberley."

"Pemberley? So soon after the ball?"

"Yes, apparently, there is crop blight in some of the fields. They have had prodigious amounts of rain this year."

While crop blight sounded serious, Elizabeth wondered how the master of Pemberley could help. "But to leave the day after your ball ... Had he planned this trip?" Elizabeth selected a biscuit and took a bite.

"No. It is all rather puzzling. He only mentioned it this morning—when his trunks were packed and he was ready to depart." Frowning, Georgiana took another sip of tea.

"How long will he be away?"

"At least a week." Georgiana shook her head. "Aunt Rachel will be extremely vexed if I cannot receive any callers for a full seven days."

Elizabeth drained the last of her tea and gazed into the empty cup. Gypsies were rumored to read tea leaves. If only someone could read her leaves and help explain Mr. Darcy's behavior.

A voice in the back of her head whispered that his hasty departure was connected to the agitation he displayed on the balcony, but she pushed the idea away. It was the height of arrogance to believe that Mr. Darcy's actions had anything to do with her.

In all likelihood, he had not spared her a thought since the previous night.

***

If only he could rid his thoughts of Elizabeth as easily as he had removed his person from her vicinity …

Darcy tried to focus his thoughts again on the estate records before him.

He had come within seconds of kissing Elizabeth! Not the best way to conceal his feelings, Darcy reflected wryly. He crumpled a blank sheet of paper into a ball and threw it to the floor, where it joined many others. Nearly two years of hiding his love, and he almost undid it all in an unguarded moment! Truly, he could not be trusted alone with her.

Fleeing London the day after Georgiana's ball had been an act of pure cowardice, but he had feared another encounter with Elizabeth would provoke an uncontrollable need to confess his feelings. Even now, there were moments when he felt the impulse to order his horse saddled for a hasty trip to London to lay all he had to offer at her feet. But then he pictured the expression on Elizabeth's face following such a declaration. What if she evinced horror or disgust? Or worse: pity.

No. Every time he mused about Elizabeth's dark curls or the charming turn of her head when she laughed, he recalled that Elizabeth belonged to Richard. To think otherwise was sacrilege.

Yes, he may have been a coward, but better cowardice than risking the ruin of their friendship—and her good opinion— through unseemly revelations. *It is probably too late anyway*, he thought bleakly. His shameful behavior at the ball had undoubtedly killed any fond sentiments Elizabeth might have possessed.

He owed her an apology—an abject apology— but could not deliver it as of yet.

Elizabeth had spoken of returning to Longbourn not long after Georgiana's ball; she had never intended to remain for the entire Season. Darcy planned to wait at Pemberley until Georgiana's letters informed him that Elizabeth had departed. Undoubtedly, they would meet again in London or Netherfield. Indeed, despite his appalling breach of decorum, he could not imagine enduring the pain of a lengthy separation.

But with the benefit of distance, perhaps Darcy would learn to master his passion—or at least better conceal it. Such was his hope.

Yes, his plan was a solid one. With this thought, he bent his head once again over his records.

A few minutes later, his butler entered and placed the day's post on one end of Darcy's desk. Glancing briefly at the pile, Darcy noticed a small packet wrapped in brown paper. He picked it up and sliced it open with his letter opener. The package had been sent by Clive Darcy, the uncle he and Georgiana had visited in Philadelphia.

Inside, he found Clive's letter explaining how the packet contained all of the letters for Georgiana and Darcy that had arrived after they had left Philadelphia. His uncle apologized many times for having neglected to send the letters sooner. Darcy was unsurprised; Clive was one of the most absent-minded people Darcy had ever met.

Inside the packet were some dozen letters, mostly addressed to Darcy on business matters, although there were a few to Georgiana from Elizabeth. He regarded Georgiana's letters somberly, knowing they would contain a chronicle of his cousin's illness and final days. Darcy set them aside; Georgiana could decide if she wished to read them.

He found three letters Elizabeth had written to him about Richard's illness. How he wished he could have been there to help her during such a difficult time!

Darcy arrived at the last letter in the packet. His heart raced wildly when he recognized the handwriting. He had forgotten until now that Elizabeth had posted a letter that Richard had written on his deathbed. Darcy held it in shaking hands.

It was almost like receiving a message from beyond the grave. It was an unexpected gift, but at the same time, Darcy experienced trepidation about the letter's contents. Then he snorted. What was he thinking? Richard had no deep, dark secrets. He was unlikely to reveal the location of some lost family treasure or the existence of an illegitimate child.

Smiling at his flights of fancy, Darcy opened the letter carefully. His cousin's handwriting was usually a sloppy scrawl, but the shakiness of the lettering was a sobering reminder that Richard had written when he was very ill.

My Dear William,

If you are reading this letter, it means I have died. No doubt you will have learned the circumstances from Elizabeth's letters to Georgiana. I do not wish you to mourn me. I had a good life. I could have wished for a glorious death in battle, but then there is something to be said for a death softened by laudanum and whisky and soft pillows.

I have left my affairs in good order. Thomas will, of course, inherit the estate, but I have settled an amount on Elizabeth and bequeathed her the house in Town, which is not part of the estate.

But that is not why I am writing this missive. I have a specific subject, one I thought to never raise with you but which now seems urgent.

I know that you love Elizabeth. In fact, you are in love with Elizabeth.

I am not angry. I can only applaud your taste and discernment. In hindsight, I realize that our engagement must have caused you some heartache, and I apologize most sincerely. I do not know how I would survive losing Elizabeth, and I am impressed at your discretion and endurance. However, at Rosings, I believed you disliked Elizabeth and thought her family beneath you. Only when I observed you in London following our betrothal did I begin to suspect the truth of your feelings. Your abrupt departure for America was confirmation of my suspicions.

Knowing your excessive sense of honor and guilt, you have undoubtedly, needlessly tortured yourself about your affection for Elizabeth. I never intended to breathe a word of this knowledge to you or anyone else. I had no desire to compound your guilt. Now on my deathbed, I understand how fortunate I am that the woman I love is loved by a man of honor whom I can trust.

I ask you to please help Elizabeth and take care of her. She is strong, but not always as strong as everyone assumes. My passing will be difficult for her. My parents will not be happy about my bequest and will make life difficult for her. You are the only one in a position to temper their disdain or help her with the legal issues. I thank God someone in my family will treat her with decency.

Elizabeth is a capable woman of good understanding, but her family situation is difficult. Many depend on her, but few take care of her. In many respects, she will be quite alone when I am gone.

Her father's health is precarious, and her family's finances even more so. The money I could free from the estate will help her support them, especially if she sells the townhouse. I believe Bingley has suffered some financial setbacks; his support for the Bennets cannot be relied on.

But the bigger problem is Wickham. Bingley sent regular support to the Wickhams for their extravagances. After Lydia's death, Wickham continued to importune Jane for money. I offered to take over the management of the problem from Charles since Jane was entering her confinement.

I need not tell you that Wickham's character has not improved over the past years. He is in his cups constantly and has run up considerable debts. I would be content to allow him to stew, but he has visited Longbourn and created all sorts of chaos for Elizabeth's family. He flirts with Kitty, fights with Mr. Bennet, and tells Elizabeth's mother tales of how you have mistreated him. He importunes the Bennets and the Bingleys for money and threatens to spread false rumors in Meryton about Lydia.

I granted him a small monthly income if he would keep a promise not to visit Meryton or say anything about the Bennet family to anyone. Yes, I know he is a worthless fellow and does not deserve any sum of money, but 'tis a small cost for Elizabeth's happiness.

Elizabeth never knew of my arrangement with Wickham. She would have suffered guilt and heartache for a situation she had no hand in creating. I have asked Thomas to continue the payments to Wickham after my death, but I have little hope that he will do so. He dislikes Elizabeth as much as my parents. I know not what Wickham's next course of action will be, but he may badger Elizabeth or attempt some other means of trickery— particularly if he learns of my bequest to her. I know I can trust you to watch over Elizabeth and beware of Wickham.

There is another matter, a delicate matter, but it needs saying. I also know I can trust you to love her as she deserves to be loved. Do not let me or my death stand between you. If you wish to declare your love for her, do so with my blessing. The thought that you and Elizabeth might make each other happy lightens my heart considerably as I contemplate leaving this earth. You are a good man who would make her an excellent husband. Do not let some misguided sense of honor to my memory stand in the way of your happiness.

I caution you, however, that I know nothing of Elizabeth's feelings toward you. While I did disabuse her of the notion that you dislike her, I know she has no suspicion of your true feelings. She once thought you proud, but I am unsure what sentiments she now harbors toward you. Perhaps I should have questioned her on the topic. However, I am only human and was never eager to discuss my love's possible feelings for another man.

I can tell you this: I believe she could love you. In many ways, you and she are quite similar. But you must show her the best of yourself and not the face that you present to the rest of the world.

Beloved cousin. My oldest and dearest friend. I am only sorry I cannot say goodbye to you in person. You have been far more than a cousin to me—far more a brother than those of my flesh. Knowing you has made my life happier in many ways.

With all my love,
Richard

Darcy was unaware how long he sat at his desk, staring at the letter in his hand. His heart was beating an erratic rhythm, and his eyes were moist. The fingers clutching the letter trembled slightly. A cold sweat had broken out all over his body.

He had been wrong. The letter's contents were far more shocking than hidden treasure or a bastard child. While reading it, Darcy had received shock after shock. Even now he struggled to absorb all the information it had contained.

Richard had guessed his love for Elizabeth. *Oh, Good Lord.*

Darcy dropped the letter and buried his face in his hands.

He should feel appalled at this revelation, and part of him was. But unexpectedly, he also experienced … relief. His darkest secret had been known and understood by the one person who had the most cause to resent it.

Darcy rubbed his face with his fingers, staring at the letter on the desk—yet more proof his cousin had been a far better man than Darcy could ever aspire to.

Even more surprising was Richard's tacit permission to court Elizabeth. It was the last thing Darcy expected to find when he opened the letter. He could hardly believe it still, despite rereading that passage twice.

But then Darcy envisioned himself in Richard's position. If Elizabeth were Darcy's betrothed when he was dying … Yes, he would be relieved to know she had someone like Richard who would love and care for her. Perhaps the letter was not so hard to understand after all. Richard had loved her dearly and wanted to ensure her happiness.

Of course, who knows if I could make her happy?

He laid the letter flat on the desk and smoothed it with his hand, perusing again the pertinent passage.

A great weight had been lifted from Darcy's chest, one he had not realized existed but which must have settled in during that awful day at Hunsford. For the first time since then, Darcy was free to admit his love for Elizabeth.

Free to love Elizabeth.

He smiled. Then his smile turned into actual laughter. "I love Elizabeth Bennet," he said to the empty study. "I love Elizabeth Bennet!" His voice grew louder.

It was such a relief to say it aloud, a relief to admit it, even if no one else heard.

He stood abruptly and shouted, "I love Elizabeth Bennet!"

He heard running feet, and the door was opened by a footman. "Mr. Darcy? I heard some shouting. What did you say?" *Thank God he did not understand my words.* Darcy actually laughed, and the servant regarded him oddly.

"Thank you, Prescott." Darcy sank into his chair, unable to suppress the foolish smile on his lips. "I do not need assistance at this time." Prescott bowed and withdrew, closing the door behind him. *No doubt he believes I have been consuming excessive quantities of brandy.*

Thank goodness I need not explain my behavior to the servants.

He ran both hands through his dark hair, staring down once again at the letter and sobering. *Richard did not know how Elizabeth feels about me*, he reminded himself. Darcy himself knew even less.

He was fairly certain she no longer disliked him and no longer feared he disliked her. But there was a large gap between the cessation of animosity and falling in love. She might never feel more than the mild affection of friendship for him. Might never love him as she had loved Richard.

Richard had always possessed easy manners in company, the ability to charm, and a friendliness that attracted everyone around him. No wonder the men in his command had been loyal to a fault and ready to follow him into battle.

Compared with his cousin, Darcy was an inarticulate hermit. No, Darcy was only superior in wealth, and that was a mere accident of birth. It also, Darcy was certain, meant absolutely nothing to Elizabeth. Darcy could never be a substitute for his cousin, and it would be the height of arrogance to attempt it.

A portion of Darcy's elation trickled away.

His cousin's letter might have removed most of his guilt, but being free to love Elizabeth raised a whole new host of anxieties. Ironically, when he had been on the verge of proposing to Elizabeth back at Hunsford, he had been utterly certain of being accepted and had given little thought to her feelings for him. Now that he understood her better, he was far less sanguine about being accepted and far more concerned about his chances of winning her affections. How he had suffered for his earlier arrogant presumption!

Darcy rested his chin in his palm and rubbed his jaw. Could he discern her feelings from her recent behavior? Unlike other women, she never flirted with him or tried to draw his attention. However, she listened seriously when he spoke and did not seem to shun his company. She had given him the book, but then she had given one to Georgiana as well. On the balcony, he had allowed himself to believe she hoped for his kiss, but he could not trust his judgment since his own desire had clouded his understanding.

Darcy hoped he could convince Elizabeth to at least accept his assistance, especially given the other unsettling revelation from the letter: Wickham. Darcy had assumed that Lydia's death had thrust Wickham out of the Bennets' lives for good. Now he recognized the naïveté of that assumption. Darcy could not blame Richard for paying Wickham to keep his distance. Darcy might have done the same.

But now that Darcy was aware of the danger, he worried about the possibilities. What if Wickham had already contacted the Bennets—or God forbid—Elizabeth? Wickham was clever; Darcy could think of many stratagems he might use to bleed money from Elizabeth or insinuate his way into her life. He shuddered when he thought of all the ways Wickham could harm Elizabeth. Her pride and desire for privacy might have prevented her from telling Darcy if she had word from Wickham.

The thought made Darcy want to call for his horse and ride directly for London. But there was no reason to think Wickham represented an immediate danger, and Darcy had only just arrived at Pemberley. He could hardly go haring off to London right away.

There was also the matter of the almost kiss. Although Richard's letter had mostly assuaged Darcy's guilt, he still did not know if she was disgusted or appalled by his actions.

The question of her feelings had suddenly become vitally important.

She still mourns Richard, he cautioned himself. She might not be prepared to be courted again. He could wait, but only if he had hope she would let him press his suit eventually.

For her, he could be patient.

But he would never learn these answers by hiding at Pemberley.

Yes, he must return to London. Not tomorrow, but perhaps the day following. London held all the answers.

Chapter 12

As Elizabeth's feet trod the path along the Serpentine, she sorely missed her solitary rambles in Hertfordshire. She visited Hyde Park almost every day, but these walks did not compare to the openness of the environs surrounding Longbourn.

Mr. Darcy had been away for five days, and Elizabeth's thoughts turned to him rather more often than she expected. Probably because he was so impossible to understand. He often avoided her company, yet seemed to enjoy her conversation. He sought her out for a dance and then pushed her away. He was happy with his sister's come out, but he disappeared immediately after. The man was a conundrum.

Although she still resolved on offering her friendship to Mr. Darcy, he was not making it easy. Particularly when he was not in the same town.

She had not been lonely during Mr. Darcy's absence. Richard's friends had visited frequently, particularly Lord Kirkwood. Elizabeth had visited the Gardiners and Darcy House almost daily. She had accompanied Georgiana to another ball, as well as luncheons and afternoon visits. Although her aunt also attended these events, Georgiana felt more comfortable in Elizabeth's presence and managed to procure invitations for her friend—no one would turn down a request from Miss Darcy.

But increasingly, Elizabeth wondered why she remained in London. When she had accompanied Richard, she had felt more at home in these ballrooms and drawing rooms as he introduced her to his acquaintances. However, she no longer felt part of that world, and it held little appeal. Only her loyalty to Georgiana prompted her to attend the events. Sometimes, she caught sharp looks or women muttering behind their fans when she entered. Many women of the *ton* probably believed she accompanied Georgiana because she was in search of a husband.

Elizabeth could be a "student of human folly," as her father would say, or enjoy the occasional witty conversation, but she wearied of the city. She was a perpetual outsider. At least in Hertfordshire, she was at home.

She missed Jane and worried about her father's health. Jane's baby girl, Anna, had been born during the summer, and

Elizabeth had enjoyed taking care of her. She longed to see her little niece again. Jane, Charles, and the baby made such a delightful family that Elizabeth had to restrain feelings of envy. She would not begrudge her sister one ounce of happiness; however, she could not help but muse how life would have been different if Richard had lived.

Yes, she resolved, she would give London another week, and then she would return home.

Her thoughts and her steps were interrupted by the sound of someone calling her name—her Christian name. Surprised, she turned and beheld Wickham striding up the path toward her.

He was wearing a fine suit and carried a walking stick, looking every inch the gentlemen he could never be—either by manner or station. His face held an amiable smile. Elizabeth was forced to admire his ability to smile, dissemble, and pretend, no matter what his offenses. In this way, he was the opposite of Darcy, who often scowled even when he was pleased.

"Sister! We are well met!" She believed neither his smile nor the coincidence of their meeting.

Elizabeth did not trouble herself to produce a smile for her erstwhile brother. In fact, she would have preferred dinner with Mr. Collins and Miss Bingley over a short conversation with Wickham.

"Mr. Wickham." Her voice held little warmth.

"Come, we are brother and sister! You may, of course, call me George." His smile was very ingratiating and inviting.

"You may call me Miss Bennet," she replied.

Wickham's face fell for a moment, but then he pretended not to hear here. "Well, this is a coincidence! I have scarcely been in London one day, and already I encounter you!"

"Indeed, quite a coincidence," Elizabeth murmured, certain she could guess the purpose behind this "accidental" meeting.

There was a pause as Elizabeth watched the sun glittering over the Serpentine. Wickham seemed to expect her to carry on the conversation, but she felt no obligation. While Lydia was alive, Elizabeth had felt a duty to maintain civil relations with her new brother, but with her sister's death, the obligation had ceased. His last visit to Longbourn had caused difficulties for every member of the Bennet family. She saw no reason to make the conversation easy for him.

"I heard that Georgiana's coming out ball was a great success," Wickham said finally.

"Yes, *Miss Darcy* did very well," Elizabeth replied.

A slight narrowing of his eyes indicated that Wickham noticed her tacit rebuke.

"I am very happy for her." He smiled like a large predatory animal. "I wish I could see her again. We were such good friends as children." His eyes found hers as if an idea had just occurred to him. "Sister! You see Georgiana frequently; could you arrange a time and place for me to meet her?"

Elizabeth's jaw fell open at the sheer audacity of the request. Of course, he had no reason to believe she knew the story of Ramsgate, but—

"Absolutely not!" Elizabeth cried once she had recovered her voice.

She turned, not knowing where she would go as long as her path took her away from Wickham. But before she had taken a step, she felt his hand on her shoulder, holding her in place. She reached up and forcibly removed it from her shoulder. Before she could leave, Wickham spoke: "If you wish me to avoid Georgiana, you will listen to what I have to say."

Elizabeth's shoulders slumped. Keeping Wickham away from Georgiana was of the utmost importance. She turned and regarded him with a stony face.

Wickham raised an eyebrow, but his smile had no mirth in it. "Your late fiancé and I had an arrangement ..."

"I know," Elizabeth said softly.

"You do?" Wickham's eyes widened in surprise.

Richard's solicitor had informed her of the payments to Wickham shortly after her betrothed's death. She had thought Wickham might give up the arrangement after Richard's death, but it had been a foolish hope.

Wickham recovered smoothly. "Well, yes. You know, I was discharged from the army. But the colonel was good enough to help me pay debts stemming from your sister's illness and funeral."

"I did not realize you paid for her funeral with card games," Elizabeth said.

Wickham blinked and forged ahead. "I-your sister, God rest her soul, was ill a long time, her entire pregnancy, and I only wanted the best care for her." Elizabeth wondered if Wickham had even once called the doctor to treat his wife.

"My sister has been dead for more than a year. Any expenses you incurred would surely have been offset by now, given how much money Richard has already sent you." Elizabeth struggled to keep her tone even.

"No, that is not so—" Wickham's voice was losing some of its smoothness in the face of Elizabeth's opposition, but he still managed to smile.

Elizabeth had never experienced an urge to strike another person, but she fantasized about giving Wickham a slap that would knock the smile from his face. Surely no one else had ever acquired so much in such an underserving a manner!

"The colonel paid you because he feared your presence in my life would cause me undue anxiety. I have no such qualms. You have already received far more from my family than you deserve. I will give you nothing more."

Rage granted her energy as she turned on her heel, preparing to leave Wickham far behind. But he grabbed her wrist. "I would advise you to reconsider, Sister. You do not know what I am capable of when provoked!" His voice was no longer charming but rough and low.

A small part of Elizabeth's mind warned her to beware of a man who was bigger and stronger, but she was too furious that he dared to threaten her. Wrenching her wrist from his grasp, she brought her other hand up and delivered a resounding smack across Wickham's face.

While he was still holding his cheek in shock, she turned and ran up the path, not stopping until she was out of the park and on her own street.

***

The devastation was complete.

Elizabeth stared at the destruction, while next to her, Gibbs, the gardener, mournfully shook his head. The townhouse did not have the largest garden in London, certainly, but it was a good size for such a house. Like many, it was surrounded by walls on all sides.

Elizabeth had poured love and energy into the garden. Anticipating that she would one day be mistress of the house, Richard had given her free rein to design plantings and make alterations to the previously neglected plot of land. She had worked with Gibbs to shape the space into a refuge—a place where she could retreat to escape the frantic pace of city living.

And now it was destroyed.

During the previous night, someone had climbed the fence and proceeded to butcher the garden. Flower pots were overturned and broken. A trellis was torn down, the vines trampled underfoot. A whole row of rose bushes had been hacked off at the roots, while a small tree had lost most of its branches. Everywhere she looked, vines had been torn out by the roots, leaves had been cut from plants, and bushes had been stripped of branches. Not a single plant had been left unmolested.

Who would do such a thing?

Elizabeth blinked back tears. The garden had not been close to finished, nor had it been at its best in January, but it had always reminded her of Richard. He had listened attentively to her plans for the garden, although he could not have been very interested. They had spent some enchanting evenings on the bench in the center of the garden. Now she felt as if she had lost another link to his memory.

"I am so sorry, ma'am," Gibbs said softly.

"I am sorry for you, Gibbs. All of your hard work destroyed through one malicious act. It is criminal!"

"I am sorry I didn't hear nothing during the night. You know, my window on the third floor overlooks the garden—"

"You were asleep. No one posts someone to watch over a garden." She stooped to pick up a crushed and broken leaf, which had somehow survived the autumn. "Such wanton destruction makes no sense."

"No," Gibbs murmured, running a gnarled hand over his chin. "I canna think of who would do such a thing."

"Nor I." Elizabeth's eyes traveled over the grounds, determining if anything could be salvaged. "The destruction is so thorough. This is not some random act...It is almost … personal. Designed to cause distress and pain."

As she said these words, Elizabeth recognized the truth in them. This was a message. But directed against whom? She could not imagine that Gibbs or any of her other staff had created such a vicious enemy. And they did not *own* the garden; she did. But how could she have engendered such animosity?

It made no sense.

Elizabeth sighed. "Well, see what plants you can rescue, and clear up what you cannot." She regarded Gibbs's wrinkled face and contemplated the work necessary to recreate the garden. "You should hire additional help, maybe that boy who helps out in the kitchen sometimes. Have Grayson make a list of the plants we need to replace. We must find a vendor. I suppose most planting must wait until spring."

Gibbs scratched behind his ear. "Some we can grow from cuttings. Many of the best plantings started so."

She patted his shoulder reassuringly. Those plants had been like his children. "I do not mind buying new if it is easier."

"Thank you, ma'am."

"And, Gibbs, do not work too hard. You are not as young as you once were."

He smiled, showing several missing teeth. "Yeah. But that's true for all of us, ain't it?"

Trust Gibbs to try to lighten her burden even under these circumstances. Elizabeth was still smiling at his rejoinder when she entered the house a moment later.

***

Darcy had only been home for ten minutes when his aunt sailed into the drawing room ahead of the footman who had intended to announce her—heedlessly interrupting the new piece Georgiana was playing for him.

Seeing Georgiana behind the pianoforte, she started speaking before the doors were even closed. "Georgiana, I have just heard the most awful story! Oh, hello, William. I was unaware you had returned from Pemberley."

"I only now arrived." He gestured the countess to a seat. "What is your news?" Darcy had little interest in *ton* gossip but knew she would not have brought it to Georgiana unless it concerned his sister in some way. However, now his aunt hesitated as if unwilling to share her tidbit with Darcy.

Darcy grabbed the arms of his chair to control his agitation. Of all the bad luck! If only Aunt Rachel had visited *after* he left the house. Since he had not seen Elizabeth for nearly a week, his need for her had reached a desperate pitch. Instead of visiting her townhouse, he would be compelled to hear his aunt's report on the latest rumors or—if he was fortunate— just her schemes for the design of Georgiana's next dress.

Finally, Aunt Rachel drew herself straight in her chair. "There are stories of an alarming nature about Georgiana's friend, Miss Bennet."

All of Darcy's senses immediately went into a state of heightened alert. "What stories?" Darcy asked.

Lady Matlock lowered her voice, confident she now had their rapt attention. "She has been seen in the company of that man who married her sister—whose father was the steward at Pemberley."

"Wickham?" All the breath seemed to leave his lungs. Was he too late? What had the blackguard done to her?

Sitting beside him, Georgiana flinched at the mention of Wickham's name, but their aunt was smoothing her skirt and did not notice. Her face creased with disgust. "Yes, that one."

"If she met with him, I doubt it was by choice," Darcy said.

The countess's voice lowered further to her most scandalous whisper. "But the rumor is that they are conducting an *affaire du coeur*. And she is his sister by marriage!"

"Never!" Darcy was suddenly standing and had to restrain himself from stalking toward his aunt. "She blames Wickham for ruining her sister. Eliz—Miss Bennet would never trust him!"

The countess shrugged. "They were seen together at Hyde Park."

Darcy could not help rolling his eyes. "One encounters all manner of people at Hyde Park."

"Yes, but there are rumors of other meetings, clandestine meetings, even at his lodgings." His aunt straightened her shoulders and folded her hands in her lap, apparently uninterested in considering the veracity of her gossip.

Darcy met Georgiana's horrified eyes; she was too stricken to speak in defense of her friend. But Darcy was not. "Vague rumors about secret *rendezvous*? I cannot believe you credit such talk!" Next to him, he could feel Georgiana relax against the back of the settee. At least he seemed to allay the worst of *her* fears. "Miss Bennet loathes the man—she would not give him her opinion on the weather, let alone entrust him with her virtue!"

His aunt was eyeing him shrewdly. "Why do you care so much about her reputation?"

Darcy seated himself once more, making an effort to appear relaxed. "I would not wish to see anyone unfairly maligned. And she was my cousin's betrothed. I care about her for his sake." God willing, his aunt would not examine the truth of that assertion!

"Hmmph." Lady Fitzwilliam sat back in her chair with an air of dissatisfaction. "I think it wise for Georgiana to discontinue her association with Miss Bennet, at least until these rumors die down. Georgiana cannot be linked to any scandal during her debut year."

Georgiana's eyes pleaded with Darcy, and he gave her a short nod to acknowledge the silent request.

"I do not believe these rumors have any merit, and I have no intention of separating our household from Miss Bennet's. To do so would suggest we believe such vitriol." He gave his aunt no more opportunities to object. "Now if you will excuse me, I have urgent business matters to attend to. However, Georgiana has a new piece which she might be prevailed upon to play for you."

Darcy stood abruptly and strode out of the room before his aunt could draw breath for another objection.

***

Elizabeth sipped her tea as she perused the list of plants which must be replaced. The magnitude of the damage still saddened her, but it was comforting that eventually they could restore the garden to its former glory. She was, however, no closer to ascertaining who might have caused the damage. Despite her initial fears, Elizabeth was now inclined to believe it was the work of a deranged individual, perhaps a vagrant.

The housekeeper, Mrs. Lawrence, marched in with a plate of lemon biscuits, which she placed on the table next to the tea pot. "Thank you." Elizabeth smiled up at the motherly woman. "You always seem to know when a craving for sweets has struck."

The other woman folded her hands over her plump waist and smiled briefly, but her eyes narrowed with worry. "Is there something else?" Elizabeth asked her.

"Ma'am ..." Lawrence's hands worried the edges of her apron. "I have not known you for long, but I want to say ... well, you are a good woman...The colonel knew what he was about when he chose you."

Elizabeth smiled faintly, a bit mystified where the conversation was tending. "Thank you."

The rest of the housekeeper's words emerged in a rush. "I want you to know I don't believe a word of them rumors—and neither does any of the staff here."

Elizabeth blinked rapidly, assimilating this information. "Thank you. I appreciate your faith in me. But which rumors do you mean?"

Lawrence's hand flew to her mouth so quickly it was almost comical. "I thought you knew, ma'am, or I would never have presumed—"

"It is all right. Sometimes the servants' gossip is the most efficient in London." Elizabeth was far more concerned about the content of the rumors than her staff's reactions to them. "Quite possibly, I ought to know about them."

Lawrence started wringing her hands as she realized she must now reveal the rumors to her mistress. "Well, I had it from the housekeeper over at the Browns, and Jenny heard the same thing from one of the footmen at Lady Pierson's house." Elizabeth nodded encouragement for the other woman to continue. "They're saying ...." Lawrence's hands moved even faster. "Forgive me...They're saying you've taken up with your sister's husband. The one who's a widower."

"Mr. Wickham!" Elizabeth cried.

"That's the one." Lawrence nodded. "We know such gossip is false, ma'am. We've never seen that scoundrel here or even heard mention of him."

For the first time in her life, Elizabeth was tempted to utter an oath. She swallowed the impulse and assumed a soothing tone, which did not match her mood. "Thank you for telling me." Lawrence gave her a worried smile. "And tell the staff I appreciate their faith in me."

Lawrence nodded, bobbed a curtsey, and disappeared quickly into the hallway, no doubt grateful to have such an awkward conversation at an end.

Once she was alone in the room, Elizabeth buried her face in her hands. She should have known Wickham would retaliate for her refusal to pay him. Slandering her good name was exactly the kind of stratagem that would appeal to him. Her social standing was already tenuous. No doubt this new calumny had spread quickly.

Women who had been betrothed were often considered "used goods" by the *ton* and somewhat less than virtuous, whether or not they had actually anticipated their vows in any way. This made it easier to spread rumors that she was giving her favors freely.

Knowing it must be Wickham's doing did little to solve the problem. She brushed a stray tear from her cheek, angry she had permitted that man to distress her.

Such rumors were frustratingly hard to refute—like grabbing a handful of water. The gossip was vague and difficult to trace to its source. She could refute the accusations but could conceive of no way to disprove them. While Richard was alive, such slander would never have been repeated, but no one of any social standing would defend her now. Richard's parents were more likely to repeat the rumors than refute them.

Elizabeth was unaware how long she sat in the drawing room, dwelling on her situation without coming closer to finding a solution. Minutes ticked away as she reviewed all the options over and over, only to discard them once more. She gave a deep sigh. Perhaps she should accept that nothing could be done. The inhabitants of the *ton* would talk behind their hands and titter behind their fans whenever she walked into a room—and she could do nothing but ignore it.

She had just resolved to collect herself and attend to her afternoon tasks when Grayson opened the door and intoned, "Mr. Wickham, ma'am." She could detect a note of steely disapproval even in those few syllables.

Elizabeth did not trouble herself to smile at her erstwhile brother but focused on a fruitless attempt not to scowl. She waited until Grayson had closed the door and Wickham had seated himself before she spoke. "Mr. Wickham, I gave you my answer the other day in the park. It has not changed, I assure you."

Wickham laid his walking stick across his knee in the studied pose of a gentleman. "But I believe we do have matters to discuss, Elizabeth." The grating sound of his voice uttering her Christian name made her skin crawl.

"So you are the source of the rumors."

Wickham never asked which rumors she meant. "I would never stoop to such stratagems." His knowing smirk implied otherwise. He paused for dramatic effect. "However … I did hear about the gossip, and I have no doubt I could identify the source and dissuade them from spreading such heinous lies … for the right incentive." He toyed idly with the head of his walking stick, regarding her with a raised eyebrow.

Blackmail? Elizabeth was aghast. She had not believed Wickham capable of such despicable behavior.

"I only require a small loan," Wickham continued. "Perhaps three thousand? And your reputation will remain intact."

Rage boiled through Elizabeth's veins. This scoundrel would stain her dear sister's memory by blackmailing her family! It could not be endured! She found herself suddenly on her feet, staring down at the still-seated Wickham. He seemed a little uncomfortable to be looking up at her in such close proximity. Good.

Elizabeth took a deep breath. "Richard may have paid you out of concern for my sensibilities, but I can be the judge of my own sentiments. My sensibilities would be far more offended by continuing to fund your villainy than by any trumped up rumors that people of sense would ignore!"

Wickham's face turned scarlet, and he appeared on the verge of exploding. He surged to his feet, nearly knocking Elizabeth over, and used his height to loom over her. She took an involuntary step backward.

"Do not make the mistake of supposing that the only threat is to your reputation," he snarled. "Such a shame about your garden ..." Elizabeth gasped; there was only one way he could have learned about that destruction. "It would be terrible if a similar fate were to befall your *horses*."

Elizabeth stared at the man. Every time she marveled at how low he had sunk, he found new depths. The mews on the other side of the garden, held Richard's curricle and horses, including his prize stallion. A groom slept in the mews above the stable, but he could hardly guard against determined ruffians who sought to hurt the animals.

Nausea swept through her. Would Wickham act on that threat? Everything in Elizabeth rebelled against giving this villain so much as a shilling, but the vision of Richard's beloved horses maimed or dead in their stalls was equally dreadful.

"Even you would never go that far!" She hated the weak, high-pitched sound of her voice.

"Oh?" His voice was silky and threatening. Wickham pressed forward, forcing Elizabeth back another step.

"Stand back!" she cried.

"Why? Do I make you uncomfortable?" Wickham took another deliberate step forward, once again pressing against her. But when she backed away, she encountered a bookcase. There was nowhere else to go.

She took a deep breath, hoping for a commanding, forceful tone in her voice. "Mr. Wickham! You must leave at once!" If she spoke loudly enough, Grayson would hear and investigate.

"Or else ... what?" Wickham smirked. "You are hardly in a position to give me orders, *Sister*."

Suddenly, the drawing room door flew open, and someone entered. However, Wickham's body blocked her view. Perhaps Grayson had heard her cries. There was a flurry of movement. Elizabeth barely had time to make sense of what she saw before Mr. Darcy was standing over the prone form of Wickham, who appeared somewhat stunned to find himself on the floor.

"Mr. Darcy!" Elizabeth exclaimed. How had he come to be there?

His eyes held a wildness she had never seen before. At that moment, she believed him capable of anything. He was breathing hard as he loomed over Wickham, undisguised contempt on his face.

He glanced up briefly. "Miss Bennet, please forgive the intrusion." His calm, polite words were at such odds with the situation that Elizabeth fought the temptation to laugh. "I heard raised voices and I feared—"

"Your arrival was quite timely, thank you," she assured him.

In one swift movement, Mr. Darcy swooped down and pulled Wickham up by his cravat so that the man's feet barely touched the floor. "What villainy are you perpetrating now?" His voice was low and threatening.

Wickham's face began to turn red, and Elizabeth feared for his safety. She had never seen Mr. Darcy quite so enraged. "He cannot answer with you strangling him," she observed.

Mr. Darcy grunted an acknowledgement and settled Wickham on his feet but maintained a firm grip on the cravat. "This does not concern you, Darcy." Wickham's voice was weak and raspy.

In the past, Mr. Darcy had expressed a sense of responsibility for Wickham because of his failure to reveal the man's true character. He also seemed to feel that the Darcy family had somehow been responsible for unleashing Wickham on the world.

So she was unprepared for Mr. Darcy's response.

"Anything which concerns Miss Bennet concerns me," Mr. Darcy growled, shaking Wickham a little by his cravat.

Elizabeth's eyes widened. Certainly that was taking his role as adopted cousin a little far!

"Indeed?" Wickham sneered. Elizabeth very much feared he would twist Mr. Darcy's statement into something that could be used to hurt him.

Abruptly, Mr. Darcy released his grip on the cravat, allowing Wickham to stumble backward. "Whatever scheme you have concocted to extort money from Miss Bennet will cease now. Leave her alone, or you will face my wrath!"

"I am not afraid of you!" Wickham's cough at the end of his assertion somewhat undercut his bravado.

"Do not threaten her again, or I will have you arrested!" Mr. Darcy grabbed the front of Wickham's coat in both hands and dragged him toward the drawing room door.

"For what?" Wickham managed a smile even as he was pulled, stumbling, across the polished wood floor. "I was simply having a conversation with my sister, my dear departed wife's sibling. That is not against the law."

"Stay away, Wickham, if you value your health," Mr. Darcy snarled. He opened the door and practically threw the other man into the entrance hall at the feet of a very surprised Grayson. Mr. Darcy looked up at the butler. "Ah, Grayson, could you make sure that Mr. Wickham finds his way back to the street?" Grayson nodded, helping Wickham to his feet and guiding him to the front door with a hand under one elbow.

When Mr. Darcy turned back into the room, he spied Wickham's walking stick sitting by the chair he had occupied. Without a pause, Mr. Darcy strode across the room, grabbed it, returned to the doorway, tossed the stick into the hallway, and closed the door.

When Mr. Darcy turned back to Elizabeth, his eyes searched her face with ferocious intensity. "Did that villain hurt you?" He crossed the room quickly, taking both of her hands in his.

"No, I assure you, I am quite well." Her statement would have been more believable had her voice been less shaky.

Mr. Darcy guided her gently to a chaise longue. "Come, sit. Is there nothing I can get for your present relief? A glass of wine?"

"I am well, thanks to your timely intervention. You have my gratitude."

Mr. Darcy scowled. "I should have been here earlier."

Elizabeth arched her eyebrow. "By all means, please castigate yourself for a failure to be omniscient. I intend to."

For a moment, Mr. Darcy seemed at a loss, staring at her. Then he burst into laughter. "Ah, Elizabeth, you always find the means of telling me when I take myself too seriously!"

Elizabeth was taken off guard. *Does he even realize he used my Christian name?* But he displayed no awareness.

Apparently reassured she would not collapse in a faint, Mr. Darcy finally seated himself. "I should have anticipated he would importune you once he knew of your bequest from Richard."

Elizabeth's heart ached for him, wishing she could ease some of his burden of guilt. "You could not have anticipated this. You take too much upon yourself, sir."

Mr. Darcy rested his forearms on his knees and ran his hands through his hair. "Would that I could find some means of removing that man from your life permanently."

"He is an annoyance, nothing more," Elizabeth said firmly.

"You do not realize how destructive he can be!" Mr. Darcy's voice had an almost desperate edge. "He is responsible for these appalling rumors—"

So he has heard them as well. Elizabeth grimaced. "I suspected he was the source."

"I only heard about them today, or I would have been here earlier." Mr. Darcy looked up at her earnestly. As if she would have reason to expect him to offer assistance with her troubles!

Mr. Darcy's hands flexed open and closed on his knees, and he smiled in a rather predatory manner. "For such lies alone, I could happily strangle Wickham—"

Elizabeth found this fey mood slightly alarming. "Please do not trouble yourself with murder. The opinions of the *ton* mean little to me."

"Do you not care about your reputation?" His voice betrayed surprise.

"Those who know me will recognize how patently false these stories are. I would never ally myself with Mr. Wickham in any respect." She focused her eyes on her hands as she smoothed her dress.

"It is not only the rumors that concern me. If he does not obtain what he desires, he may resort to more extreme measures."

Elizabeth sighed. She might as well reveal all. The servants' gossip would inform him eventually. "He has made threats against the horses."

Mr. Darcy's head jerked up. "The horses?"

There was nothing for it; she divulged everything: the meeting in Hyde Park, the damage in the garden, and Wickham's threats. By the time she was finished, Mr. Darcy was fairly quivering with barely contained rage.

"The blackguard! To threaten innocent beasts. And Richard's thoroughbred stallion!" He was now pacing the length of the room.

"I fear he might hurt one of the servants should they interfere," Elizabeth said.

Mr. Darcy nodded grimly. "I will send you another groom to help guard the horses." It was not a request but rather a statement. Elizabeth inclined her head. Accepting his help was prudent, and she did not have the strength to argue with him.

"I fear that Wickham views you as an easy victim. A young, unmarried woman living alone— one who has recently inherited. He expects you to be unprotected."

Elizabeth felt a chill at Mr. Darcy's assessment of her vulnerability, but she also felt the stirrings of anger. The independence Richard's bequest had granted her should not come with a price! "Perhaps I should return to Longbourn," she conceded. At least Richard's horses, and the staff, would be safe if she were not in residence.

"No, you cannot!" Mr. Darcy exclaimed hastily. Elizabeth regarded him, brows drawn together in perplexity. He took a deep breath and continued at a more deliberate pace. "You risk drawing Wickham's attention to your family. He might importune your father—or even threaten him."

"I had not considered that possibility." No, she should remain in London and keep Wickham's eyes focused on her.

Mr. Darcy placed his hat on his head and retrieved his walking stick. "I will visit Wickham and have a candid conversation." Elizabeth was happy Mr. Darcy's impressive glower was not intended for her.

"I hope that you will not pay him. His relationship with my family has already benefited him far more than he deserves.

Should he receive additional funds, it will only encourage further behavior such as this."

Mr. Darcy nodded briskly. "I agree. There are other ways to work on such a man. However, I should visit him now before he changes lodgings once more." He strode to the door, but turned abruptly before his hand touched the knob. "Oh, I had quite forgotten my purpose in visiting. Would you do us the pleasure of dining with us tomorrow night?" He regarded her with a peculiar intensity, awaiting her response.

Surely a dinner invitation could not be so important to him. "Yes, I have no other engagements."

Did his shoulders relax? No, it must have been her imagination.

"Excellent. I shall inform Georgiana. Good day, Miss Bennet."

Elizabeth bade him a good day and watched him leave the room. Only then did she permit herself to collapse back into the soft embrace of the chair's upholstery. By all rights, she should be considering the problems presented by Wickham, but instead, she was preoccupied with the puzzle of Mr. Darcy.

Why had he visited her—and without his sister? A simple dinner invitation could have been accomplished by post or by a note sent with a servant.

Just as bewildering was the warmth of affection she now experienced for him. Naturally, she was grateful for his assistance with Wickham, but these feelings went beyond mere gratitude. She knew he was concerned about her as Georgiana's friend and Richard's former fiancée, but did he care for her for her own sake? And why did she wish it so devoutly? Of course, they were friends, but perhaps some part of her longed for more?

No, she was being ridiculous! Richard had caused a minor scandal by choosing a country girl of no family as his betrothed, but Mr. Darcy, who possessed one of the greatest fortunes in England, would never choose someone like her.

He felt guilt over Wickham's actions. It was that simple. With that thought, she resolved to put the matter out of her mind.

***

By dinner time, Elizabeth was relaxed enough to enjoy her cook's excellent stew. After the meal, she retired to the drawing room. Sitting near the window, where she could occasionally glance out to see the lovely full moon, Elizabeth stitched embroidery on a dress for Jane's daughter. Absentmindedly, she enjoyed the murmur of voices and the sounds of horses and carriages on the cobblestones outside her door. Although she preferred the country, Elizabeth also took pleasure in the hustle and bustle of the city.

The peace of the evening was abruptly shattered by the sound of breaking glass. Elizabeth was showered with shards as a large rock crashed through the window!

Chapter 13

Throwing up her hands to shield her face, Elizabeth cried out and nearly fell out of her chair. A moment later, she heard racing footsteps as Grayson and Lawrence both burst into the room.

"Oh, Good Lord!" Grayson cried.

Lawrence simply gave a wordless exclamation and hurried to Elizabeth's side. "Are you hurt, ma'am?"

Elizabeth stood shakily, and shards of glass cascaded to the floor from her dress. She examined her arms and felt her neck, the areas with the most exposed skin. The few cuts were minor. "I believe I am unharmed."

"Oh, here is a cut!" Lawrence pulled out a clean handkerchief and applied it to a longer gash on Elizabeth's neck. "But 'tis a small one. Nothing to fuss about."

One of the footmen hurried into the room. "Another rock was thrown through the dining room window!"

"Another?" Grayson cried, looking greatly disturbed.

The footman continued, "Weston ran after the culprit, but he escaped."

"Was anyone in the dining room at the time?" Elizabeth asked. A shudder wracked her body as she realized how easily she, or someone on her staff, could have been seriously hurt.

"No, thank the Lord," the footman responded.

"But who would do something like this?" Lawrence asked, still applying pressure to her mistress's neck.

Elizabeth had her suspicions but did not wish to speculate. It was a horrible thought that anyone might hate her with such passion. "I must contact the authorities in the morning. Grayson, might someone install boards in the window frames in place of the broken panes?"

"Yes, ma'am." Grayson nodded. "I believe we have some boards that can be cut to fit." The butler took the footman with him in search of boards.

Elizabeth took the handkerchief from Lawrence and examined the splotches of blood. "Not a deep cut, I think."

"No, ma'am. It should stop bleeding on its own," Lawrence agreed.

Elizabeth pressed the cloth up to her neck again and slumped back into her chair, suddenly exhausted. A maid swept up the broken glass, while Grayson brought in someone with boards and a saw.

Abruptly, Elizabeth wished to quit the room and its negative associations. A wave of anger surged through her. This had once been her favorite room in the house, but now it was sullied by disturbing memories.

"Lawrence, I think I shall retire for the night."

"Yes, ma'am," the housekeeper replied. "You do that. You have had a shock, you have. You will be needing your rest."

But before Elizabeth stood, Grayson strode back into the room holding a small object wrapped in fabric. "Ma'am, the household has three pistols. I would like your permission to distribute them to the groom and footmen—just in case those scoundrels return."

"Yes, of course," Elizabeth replied, hating the necessity. "Good thinking."

"And there is this." Grayson handed her the small parcel. "The master would want you to have it about you for protection."

Elizabeth unwrapped it to reveal a small "lady's" pistol Richard had purchased for her. Although many in the *ton* viewed shooting as an unladylike pursuit, Richard had seen it as a useful skill for any woman, including his fiancée. So he had gifted her with the pistol and provided her with lessons in how to use it. She had never enjoyed shooting but had grown reasonably competent. Truthfully, Elizabeth had forgotten about the pistol. It had always remained at the townhouse, and she had never used it, save for practice with Richard.

She regarded it distastefully. "Grayson, I do not believe I should—"

"Ma'am, if you forgive my saying so, the colonel would want you to carry it with you under these circumstances. Perhaps in your reticule. He would be very concerned." Elizabeth hesitated. "For the colonel's sake, ma'am," Grayson repeated.

Elizabeth sighed and picked up the gun, its weight foreign in her hand. "Very well." Grayson smiled in satisfaction and handed her the reticule, watching as she inserted the pistol into it.

Elizabeth stood and made her way out the door and into the entrance hall. Lawrence gestured for a maid to follow Elizabeth up the stairs to her bedchamber, as if afraid her mistress was not competent to do so alone. After one stumble, Elizabeth was forced to admit Lawrence might not have been entirely wrong.

***

There was no room for doubt: Elizabeth was not pleased to see him.

Darcy, however, felt he had demonstrated remarkable restraint.

Having learned of the savage attack on Elizabeth's house the previous night, he had fought valiantly against an overwhelming desire to immediately appear on her doorstep. Fortunately, Georgiana had persuaded him that Elizabeth would not appreciate such gross impropriety and had reassured him that her staff was now alert to the danger.

Darcy had conceded to his sister's logic with poor grace and had mollified his concern by clandestinely instructing his butler to send four footmen to Elizabeth's house. This had permitted Darcy to sleep for a few restless hours, only to wake before dawn. He had deferred his visit to Elizabeth's townhouse until nine, which he felt showed considerable self-control under the circumstances.

At least Elizabeth had been awake and dressed when he arrived. However, she was unhappy to discover he knew of the previous night's events.

"How did you learn about the incident so quickly?" she asked over a cup of coffee in her breakfast room.

Darcy cleared his throat and examined the fascinating pattern of the tablecloth. "Er, my man in the stable sent word around soon after it happened."

Elizabeth scowled. "I did not realize you had placed a spy in my household."

Darcy colored. "That was not my intention." Elizabeth set her mouth in a straight line and said nothing further. Darcy wished to explain, but what should he say? At Darcy House, his duty had been clear, but confronted with an angry Elizabeth, he worried he might have overstepped his bounds.

"I visited Wickham," Darcy said.

She lowered her coffee cup. "You did?"

Darcy could not remain seated any longer. He shoved his chair back from the table and restlessly paced the breakfast room. "Early this morning. There can be little doubt of his involvement, but naturally, he denies any knowledge. And we have no proof. He seems to have fallen in with a crowd of ruffians, if my informants are correct. That makes the situation more complex. Even if I can find a way to stop Wickham himself, he may find others to carry out his mischief."

Elizabeth stood as well, regarding him steadily. "I appreciate your concern, but this incident does not warrant so much anxiety. I am unharmed."

"Oh?" Darcy strode to Elizabeth and reached out a finger to trace the cut on her neck. "This cut says otherwise." She flushed and pulled away from his touch. *Good Lord! How could he have taken such a liberty?* Abruptly snatching his hand back, he strode to the window, as far from Elizabeth—and temptation— as the room would allow. "Forgive me," he murmured, certain his face was a bright red.

There was a long pause. Would Elizabeth castigate him for his inappropriate behavior? She cleared her throat. "It is a shallow scratch, nothing to cause undue anxiety." Darcy said a silent prayer of thanks. Apparently, this was another incident they would pretend had never happened.

But he shuddered at the thought of how badly he had failed to protect her. "You are not safe until this situation is resolved. I will send you additional footmen, and you must come to Darcy House for the duration." He hoped she would not notice the additional footmen were already posted outside her house.

"There is no need," Elizabeth replied. "I have Grayson and two other footmen, plus a gardener and groom. Mr. Wickham would not be foolish enough to act directly against me in my own home."

Darcy sighed and ran a hand through his hair. Such stubbornness was not unanticipated. "I must insist. I will not rest easy until I know you are securely protected."

Elizabeth stood behind her chair, grasping its back with white-knuckled hands. "And I am perfectly in earnest. I am *not* a member of your staff, and I will not hasten to obey your every instruction." Her tone was light and teasing, but he detected a hint of irritation.

Damnation! He had offended her! Was nothing ever simple with this woman? His heart sank at the thought. Half of their conversations seemed composed of misunderstandings and conflict. Even now her frustration with him showed in every line of her body. Perhaps she could never get past her distaste for him. He had tried to become a better person for her, but he could not completely change everything about himself. Maybe she was not capable of loving the man who was Fitzwilliam Darcy.

Darcy pulled his thoughts out of this spiral of despair and struggled to formulate a response. "I do not think of you in those terms, Miss Bennet, I assure you."

Elizabeth lowered her eyes to the table. "I will accept the offer of additional staff. Thank you. But I do not believe it is necessary for me to abandon my home."

"Very well," Darcy said. Her concession would do for the moment, but they would return to the subject again. He would not compromise Elizabeth's safety, even if she hated him for it. At least she would be alive and unharmed to hate him.

***

Darcy glared at the newspaper before him. Despite important news about the war and the actions of parliament, the society pages drew the most attention from the *ton*. Today, Darcy would have cheerfully burned the paper's offices to the ground. Oblivious to the sounds of his club around him, he reread the offending article.

"We have learned that a certain Miss B., who stood up with the debutante Miss D., the niece of the Earl of ----- has been seen in the company of some unsavory characters. Recently, Mr. W., a cashiered army officer known for his debts and seduction of many misses, was seen leaving her townhouse at odd hours—despite their consanguineous relationship."

Goddamn! That last sentence was an inspired piece of rumormongering. Technically, the church would consider Wickham and Elizabeth to be brother and sister because of his marriage to Lydia. By referring to that, the gossip column made their supposed "affair" seem even more sordid and ensured that the insinuations would be repeated throughout every drawing room in London.

Pain in his right hand caused him to glance down; it was crumpling the edge of the newspaper in a death grip. Gingerly, he relaxed his hold. Perhaps Wickham had paid someone on the paper's staff to print the item, or maybe he had spread the gossip so thickly that the columns could not ignore it.

Rubbing his hand over his eyes, Darcy considered that the item's provenance was of little matter. The damage was the same. Elizabeth had no family name or fortune to protect her reputation or refute such accusations. Her association with the Darcys had provided no protection but rather earned her prominence to make her worthy of inclusion in the scandal rag. And her former fiancé's parents would do nothing to staunch the flow of such vitriol—in fact, they might encourage it. The paper would not dare make such insinuations about Georgiana or Aunt Rachel, but Elizabeth was defenseless.

He knew what the future held. Elizabeth's invitations to teas and balls would evaporate. When she did attend an event, the women of the *ton* would whisper about her behind their fans. Elizabeth did not care about the *ton's* opinion, but she would be distressed to have her reputation unfairly destroyed.

Darcy gritted his teeth against the impulse to utter a stream of profanity. Elizabeth was worth a hundred of those women, and he knew with absolute certainty she had done nothing wrong. Yet such accusations would destroy what little acceptance she had gained through her betrothal and association with the Darcys.

After the rock-throwing incident a week ago, Darcy had been seeking Wickham, who had abandoned his previous lodgings. After days of fruitless searching, Darcy had hired some Bow Street Runners. As they inquired about Wickham, the runners were warning decent merchants and landlords about Wickham's reputation, reducing the number of people the man might deceive in his schemes. However, Darcy had not thought to warn anyone on the staff of the newspaper.

Bitterly, Darcy reflected that he should have encouraged Elizabeth to return to Hertfordshire, where she would be insulated from some of the poison in the *ton*. However, when she had suggested the idea, Darcy had only focused on his own selfish desire to keep her in London.

Darcy stared at the stark white paper and the black words that persisted in spelling out Elizabeth's ruination. He could conceive of no way to prevent it. Darcy could fix many things, but gossip was frustratingly difficult to combat.

"Hello, Darcy!" Glancing up at the cheerful greeting, Darcy suppressed a groan. Lord Kirkwood was among the last people he wished to see.

Without awaiting an invitation, the handsome viscount's heir drew up a chair. Darcy hastened to fold up the newspaper, but Kirkwood eyed it meaningfully. "So you have noticed the latest gossip as well."

"It is all slander!" Darcy spat.

"Of course." Kirkwood sat back in his chair, watching Darcy as if taking his measure. "Fitzwilliam would be spitting mad. Appalling way to treat a virtuous young woman."

Darcy's opinion of Kirkwood rose several notches. "Appalling," Darcy agreed, lifting his brandy glass to his lips, only to realize it was empty. When had that happened? He signaled the attendant for another.

The other man steepled his fingers in front of him. "The difficulty is, many consider such a woman's reputation tarnished, if not outright ruined, when she has been betrothed but not married. It is not fair, but such is the way of the world. And then Miss Bennet insists on living alone when she is still unmarried."

Darcy scowled at Kirkwood. "Nothing about this situation is of Miss Bennet's making!"

"Of course not." Kirkwood dismissed this objection with a wave of his hand. "The problem is, she has no family name, no one to take her part, no standing." Darcy opened his mouth to contradict this statement, but the other man continued. "Oh, I know your sister is a good friend, but people will say Miss Bennet took advantage and all that rot."

Darcy did not respond. Kirkwood seemed to have a point, and Darcy wanted to hear it.

Kirkwood took a sip from his own glass of brandy, then he stared at the amber liquid contemplatively. "I have been ruminating on this situation. Fitzwilliam was a great man—a great soldier. Did service to our country in battle that no one appreciates, saved lives … and now he cannot be here to protect the woman he loved."

Guilt settled around Darcy like a blanket. Richard *had* been great man, who had provided immeasurable assistance to his cousin when needed.

"And the woman herself…." Kirkwood continued, unaware of Darcy's inner self-castigation, "I understand why Richard loved her. She is beautiful. Have you noticed, Darcy? Those eyes— Goddamn!"

As his teeth ground together, Darcy refrained from comment; the only words which readily came to mind were oaths.

However, Kirkwood's monologue needed no encouragement. "And clever. I could listen to her talk all day. She would be a wonder at running a household."

Darcy's eyes narrowed. Why would Kirkwood consider Elizabeth's abilities to run a household unless …

"So I have decided to offer her the protection of my name!" Kirkwood's smile invited Darcy to congratulate him. "I will visit her house tomorrow afternoon and propose."

Silence. Darcy realized Kirkwood was awaiting a response.

"W-What? Sorry, what did you say?" Darcy was having difficulty processing this pronouncement.

"I am getting married. Leg shackled. Tied down. The whole bit." The other man grinned, taking another swig of brandy and setting the glass down on the table. He regarded Darcy with such a broad smile one would think he had invented the entire institution of marriage. "I will marry Miss Bennet!"

Chapter 14

Everything inside Darcy was screaming denial, shaking in horror at the thought of another man proposing to her.

"Ah ... you ... she ... that is ... have you thought this through? The marriage, I mean?" Given the circumstances, Darcy was proud he managed a sentence that was even marginally coherent.

Kirkwood laughed with irritatingly good cheer. Darcy wanted to force the self-satisfied smile from the lord's face with his fist. "Thought of nothing but this for the last two days. She will make the perfect wife. Oh, I know you might not agree—"

You would be surprised, Darcy thought darkly.

"—But wealth and connections are not everything. I have little concern for the opinions of the *ton* and fortune enough." *So much for the rumors of Kirkwood's father's gambling debts.*

Despite his black mood, Darcy had to admire the man's declaration. If Darcy had arrived at similar realizations before Richard's proposal, they might now be married.

"As my wife, no one would dare slander Miss Bennet again." Kirkwood pounded his fist on top of the newspaper.

Darcy's thoughts were a miasma of disbelief, anger, and despair. But amidst the chaos, he seized on one irrefutable fact: he must prevent Kirkwood from proposing. It would be a disaster.

But as he gazed with hatred at Kirkwood's beaming face, Darcy could think of no means of thwarting the man's plans. Kirkwood was in every way an eminently suitable match for Elizabeth. Not only was his family old and established, but they apparently were financially stable. Kirkwood himself did not have a reputation for keeping mistresses, gambling, or drinking. But perhaps additional investigation would yield more information ...

Darcy immediately dismissed the thought as unworthy. Kirkwood had been a stalwart friend of Richard's and had supported Elizabeth during a difficult time. That should be recommendation enough of his character. Indeed, Darcy would have no concern about the man—if he did not wish to marry the object of Darcy's affections.

Darcy fought to keep panic from his face as he realized there was no obvious reason Elizabeth would wish to refuse

Kirkwood's proposal. The lord was every bit as eligible as Richard, even more so.

However, he reminded himself, Elizabeth cared nothing for fortune, particularly since she had her own source of income. *There* was a glimmer of hope.

Without mercenary considerations, Elizabeth would marry for love—or at least affection.

But … what if she *did* feel affection for Kirkwood? Certainly they were friends. Perhaps her feelings ran deeper. Darcy would not pretend to understand her heart, and he could not reasonably assume she would decline such a proposal.

Darcy felt pieces of his life slipping and sliding out of his control. He had not expected to face a rival for Elizabeth's affections so soon.

Belatedly, he realized Kirkwood was speaking. "I suppose Miss Darcy is concerned about Miss Bennet."

"We both are," Darcy said firmly.

Kirkwood seemed momentarily nonplussed by the other man's tone. "Yes, well, your sister's mind might be eased if she knows my intentions." Darcy said nothing, and Kirkwood cast about for a means of filling the silence. "Your support for Miss Bennet is quite admirable. I know it is what Richard would have wanted."

Darcy caught and held Kirkwood's eyes. "We consider Miss Bennet to be a friend in her own right."

Kirkwood blinked. "Of course, of course! She is blessed to have friends like you." Darcy did not reply, instead focusing on not strangling Kirkwood with his own cravat. "So, I thought you would be pleased, relieved, to know I will be lending my assistance."

Darcy simmered with rage. Kirkwood thought to bestow a favor on Elizabeth. He had not the slightest conception how fortunate he would be to secure her acceptance. *I thought similarly at Rosings*, he reminded himself.

"Miss Bennet may believe it too soon after Richard's death to consider another betrothal," Darcy warned.

Kirkwood's eyes widened, as though he had not considered the possibility. "But she cannot wait too long, or she will be on the shelf!"

Darcy sighed and rubbed his jaw. His opinion of Kirkwood was falling rapidly. "She may not wish to marry at all. She loved Richard."

"Huh." Kirkwood considered this notion for a moment. "Well, tomorrow will tell, eh?" He clapped Darcy heartily on the shoulder, while Darcy gritted his teeth. "I would do the deed today, but I have an important card game with Broad and Smallwood. Need to get some of my own back." Darcy made no response, certain he could not refrain from the foulest language. How could he view marrying Elizabeth as less important than a card game?

"Very well. I should be on my way." Kirkwood stood.

Darcy stood as well, forcing himself to shake the man's hand. "Thank you for sharing your plans."

"I thought you should know," Kirkwood repeated.

Darcy considered what he could say without committing outright falsehoods. "I am happy to know she has such friends."

"Of course, you must not breathe a word of this until I have the opportunity to visit her tomorrow afternoon!" Kirkwood placed his hat on his head.

"Please do send word of how you fare," Darcy requested. Kirkwood gave a nod as he departed.

Darcy sank into his chair, gulping his brandy. Damnation! What was he to do? He hunched forward in his chair, resting both elbows on the table. He recalled his feelings after her betrothal to Richard. Could he endure witnessing Elizabeth's betrothal to yet another man? Could he survive it without going insane?

America would not be far enough away. Perhaps India. Or China. Or the Arctic.

He felt as if he were witnessing a carriage accident he was powerless to prevent. His mind raced, considering and discarding ways he could prevent the disaster. The truth was inescapable: he could not stop Kirkwood from proposing. Nor could he prevent Elizabeth from accepting. Nothing could stop it.

Unless …

Darcy's eyes opened wide.

Unless he proposed first!

When he had been ignorant of Richard's intentions toward Elizabeth, Darcy had been at a disadvantage. Many times, Darcy had wondered how he would have acted if he had known of Richard's plans in advance. Would he have proposed first? Would he have bowed out in favor of the better man?

Today, however, he had been given a warning. He could not prevent Kirkwood from proposing, but he could preempt him.

Darcy pulled out his pocket watch. Ten o'clock; too late for a visit to Elizabeth that evening. But he could call on her the following morning. Kirkwood might not feel comfortable making a morning call, but Darcy had no such scruples. They had nearly become family; he could claim enough familiarity. Or perhaps he was simply desperate enough to defy convention.

After all, he had Richard's permission to woo Elizabeth. Kirkwood did not.

Yes, he would go in the morning and propose before Kirkwood was even awake. Eight was probably too early, but nine …. Would he seem too desperate? Should he wait until ten? It would be agony.

Then a sobering thought struck Darcy; he nearly bent under its weight. What if she still disliked him? He understood little about Elizabeth's feelings for him. He had returned from Pemberley with the goal of ascertaining the state of her affections, but he had expected to have weeks to learn her feelings and improve her opinion of him.

Their last meeting had not been auspicious and had left Darcy with the distinct impression that Elizabeth disliked his high-handed ways. Now Kirkwood was rushing in and forcing Darcy's hand before he knew the state of Elizabeth's heart. What if she felt nothing more for him than the distant affection one would bestow on an acquaintance? What if she actually disliked him?

Yet Kirkwood was correct. Elizabeth needed protection; she was too vulnerable as a single woman with a modest fortune living alone. All manner of perils could beset her. Servants might steal from her, unscrupulous men might seek to take advantage of her, or ruffians might invade her home.

She also required protection from the *ton*. They were ready to believe any gossip about a woman of no name and little fortune. But they would never dare whisper about *Mrs. Darcy*. Even the most vicious wagging tongue would know that Darcy would never marry a woman who had dallied with Wickham. No, their engagement itself would handily refute the rumors.

Elizabeth was a sensible woman. He would help her recognize the advantages in their union.

Yes, that was how to present it.

***

Elizabeth set down her coffee cup and stared at the day's newspaper lying before her on the table. She had opened it with some trepidation, but to her relief, it had contained no repetition of the previous day's scurrilous rumors. Likely it was only a short respite. The item in the previous day's paper was salacious enough that no doubt everyone in London was talking of it by now. She was little enough known in the first circles, but her association with the Darcys and the Earl of Matlock heightened her gossip value.

Already, one invitation to afternoon tea had been "postponed," and an expected invitation to a ball had not been forthcoming. For her own sake, she could certainly bear the deprivation, but she was anxious about the effect on people she cared about.

Mr. Darcy and his sister had been most kind, and she would not want their reputations to be tarnished by association. And then there was her family to consider. The news from London might not have reached Meryton yet, but it would, and she had no doubt the entire town would be talking of it. If only she could spare her parents such humiliation, so similar to what they had endured with Lydia!

Her eyes stung, and she blinked rapidly. She would not weep; Wickham was not worth shedding tears over.

Throughout the night, as she had tossed and turned in her bed, Elizabeth had considered whether she should have paid Wickham, but even now the thought made her ill. And in any event, the damage was done. Perhaps she should leave London altogether. If she were in Hertfordshire, the London newspapers would have little interest in her. Wickham might follow her there, but if she stayed at Netherfield, at least he would be unlikely to pester her parents.

Elizabeth added a little more sugar to her coffee. Yes, she would travel to Hertfordshire. It would solve many problems, and it would be good to be back with family.

There was a knock at the front door, and she heard Grayson's footsteps as he hastened to answer it. Who could possibly be calling at this hour?

The door to the breakfast room opened. "Mr. Collins, ma'am," Grayson intoned, his voice somehow managing to convey contempt in a mere three words. *I must ask him how he manages that.*

She wished to tell Grayson she was not receiving visitors, but Mr. Collins himself was hovering behind her butler.

"Thank you, Grayson." The butler ushered Mr. Collins into the room and closed the door.

"Cousin Elizabeth! It is fortuitous indeed that I happened to be in London today of all days!" Her cousin's smile somehow made her feel greasy.

Elizabeth had no idea what he meant by this but was certain she was about to be enlightened. "Indeed." She gestured him to a seat at the table and poured him a cup of coffee. "Is Mrs. Collins with you?"

"No," Collins simpered. "She remains in Hunsford. I accompanied Lady Catherine on an impromptu shopping trip. We arrived just yesterday and leave tomorrow."

Elizabeth nodded, wondering how much spiritual advice Lady Catherine could need when purchasing lace.

"But the timing of the trip was fortuitous indeed!" Collins clapped his hands together with delight. "When I saw yesterday's newspaper, I knew that it was incumbent upon me to render such counsel as was within my power to give. In which opinion I am joined by none other than Lady Catherine de Bourgh herself."

Elizabeth seethed inwardly at the picture of Collins and Lady Catherine discussing her supposed affair with Wickham and congratulating themselves on their moral superiority—without ever questioning the accuracy of the story. She assumed her most innocent expression. "Surely you recognize that the story in the newspaper was a slanderous falsehood?"

The man waved that concern away as if it were irrelevant. "You must take immediate steps to curtail this flood of rumor."

"I fail to see how I could possibly—"

Mr. Collins appeared not to notice she had spoken. "Lady Catherine and I agree that you must marry the man."

"Which man?"

"Mr. Wickham."

Elizabeth suddenly had difficulty breathing. "W-Wickham? Surely you are joking!"

Collins smiled complacently. "You must recognize it is the only certain method to stem the tide of gossip."

"But he is the *source* of the rumors!" Elizabeth spluttered.

Collins shrugged. "Come, Cousin, you cannot possibly have proof of that. And there must be some basis for his—"

"He is spreading the rumors because I refused to pay off his gambling debts!"

For the first time, she appeared to have shaken Collins's certainty that he understood the situation better than she did.

Grayson had silently entered the room behind Collins and began to set breakfast dishes on the sideboard. His face was mostly stoic, but his pursed lips told Elizabeth he disapproved of Collins's suggestions, and indeed his very presence.

Unfortunately, her cousin's acquaintance with uncertainty was brief. He cleared his throat. "Be that as it may—"

Elizabeth no longer had enough patience to permit Collins to finish a sentence. "And we cannot marry! The church considers us brother and sister."

Collins nodded in a manner he no doubt thought made him appear like a wise man of the cloth. "Lady Catherine and I discussed this impediment, but you could marry legally in Scotland. A trip to Gretna Green would not—"

Elizabeth's entire body shuddered with horror at the thought. "Let me make myself clear. I will not marry Mr. Wickham under any circumstances. I would sooner marry Grayson!"

A clatter rang throughout the room as Grayson dropped a large spoon on the floor. He stared wide-eyed at his mistress. Collins choked on the coffee he had just swallowed.

A fey spirit seized Elizabeth. "Grayson, you appear shocked," Elizabeth said. "Do not tell me you are already married?"

"No, ma'am." The butler seemed scandalized to discuss even this much of his personal life with his employer.

Elizabeth smiled broadly at Collins, enjoying herself for the first time that morning. "The problem is solved! If the scandal continues, I will marry Grayson—which will give the papers something else to write about. It is a far superior solution, since Grayson is not related to anyone in my family—as far as I know."

"C-cousin, I do not believe … I –" Mr. Collins had removed a handkerchief from his pocket and was vigorously mopping his brow.

"You can return to Lady de Bourgh and explain how you helped me devise this admirable solution to my dilemma. I am certain she will be vastly pleased with your interference."

Behind Collins, Grayson retrieved the spoon, a small smile replacing his look of utter shock.

"D-do you n-not feel it is a rather extreme solution?" Mr. Collins stammered.

Elizabeth tipped her head to one side, as if in consideration. "Well, I suppose I could wait; the scandal may abate on its own. Perhaps it would not be necessary for me to marry anyone immediately."

Mr. Collins removed a handkerchief from his pocket and mopped his brow. "That might be for the best."

"Very well." Elizabeth shrugged as if it meant little to her. She then stood, prompting Collins to stand automatically. "I will leave it to you to explain that to Lady de Bourgh."

She led Mr. Collins to the door before the man was aware he planned to depart. "I thank you for your concern for my wellbeing, and please extend my gratitude to Lady Catherine as well."

Grayson hastened to open the front door to the townhouse. Idly, Elizabeth wondered what he had done with the spoon—one of those eternal mysteries about the operations of servants.

Collins bowed his way out with expressions of delight and promises to convey her regards to Charlotte. Finally, Grayson could close the door behind the man. He regarded his employer with a raised eyebrow. She returned an ironic smile. "Do not be concerned, Grayson. You are safe from my matrimonial ambitions."

"So I concluded, ma'am."

"My cousin is a fool."

"It would not be my place to draw that conclusion," Grayson said drily.

Elizabeth laughed. "Richard knew what he was about when he took you into his employ."

The butler's eyes sparkled. "Thank you, ma'am."

She pivoted and strode back to the breakfast room. "Perhaps now I may eat my breakfast in peace."

"Cook was able to obtain some of the ham you particularly fancy, ma'am."

"Excellent."

However, Elizabeth had only eaten a few bites of ham when she heard another knock on the door. Heavens! Another early morning visitor. Who could it be this time? God forbid Mr. Collins had returned!

She heard Grayson open the door and then Mr. Darcy's unmistakable deep voice. Why would he visit so early? Her first fear was that it was an emergency involving Georgiana, but no, he would have sent a messenger.

Then a panicked thought gripped her. Was he angry about the item in the newspaper? Georgiana had been linked with Elizabeth's name in the article, perhaps damaging her reputation by association. Maybe Mr. Darcy intended to discontinue the acquaintance between their households, at least for the present. She would hardly blame him and had even considered offering to do so.

However, the thought of being separated from Georgiana and Mr. Darcy cut through her with a sharpness she did not expect. She realized she would miss their acquaintance dreadfully without frequent visits. But when had this occurred? When had she come to depend on friendship with the inhabitants of Darcy House?

Grayson ushered Mr. Darcy into the room. "Miss Bennet, forgive the early hour of my arrival." Mr. Darcy's words were rushed, and his agitation caused her to reconsider the fear that some ill had befallen Georgiana.

"There is nothing to forgive," she assured him. "I enjoy company with my breakfast." She gestured to the sideboard. "Please, help yourself."

Mr. Darcy eyed the food as if the very thought made him ill. "Thank you; I have already breakfasted."

"Would you care for some coffee? Tea?"

"I thank you, no." He put his hand on a chair as if preparing to sit, but abruptly turned and began making a circuit around the room. It was not a large room, and he soon had completed a full tour without voicing the reason for his unexpected visit. Perhaps he had more to say about the attack on her house and ensuring her safety? But why was he having such difficulty raising the subject? Every line of his body suggested anxiety and tension.

"Are you quite all right? Is there anything I can do for you?" she asked.

He viewed her distractedly. "No, thank you. There is nothing. That is—I—You—"

Elizabeth watched him with a growing sense of alarm. She could not understand the source of his present state of agitation. Was Wickham responsible for another egregious action?

"Is Georgiana well?" she asked.

Mr. Darcy completed his third circuit of the room. "Very well, thank you."

"Are you angry about the item in the newspaper? I cannot express how I regret that my troubles should harm Miss Darcy's reputation."

Mr. Darcy stopped pacing abruptly and stared at her, leaning over the dining table. Elizabeth flinched backward. He must be very angry indeed! "I *am* angry, Miss Bennet. I am livid, furious. But not at you. This is not of your doing. And I have no concern about Georgiana's reputation. People of sense will know she is blameless."

She is blameless, but not me, Elizabeth thought.

Nevertheless, she experienced some small measure of relief that his anger was not directed at her. But she was still at a loss about the purpose of his visit or the reason for his extreme agitation.

Finally, Mr. Darcy sighed explosively, pushed both hands through his hair, and positioned himself behind one of the breakfast room's chairs.

"I am concerned about *you*. You are so vulnerable as a single woman living alone. You have already been subjected to malicious gossip and have become the target of even more dangerous behavior. I am endeavoring to stop Wickham, but he has moved lodgings, and the men I hired have not yet located him." Mr. Darcy's mouth was set in a firm line. "I fear these attacks will escalate unless you give him what he wants. And even then—he has friends who know about you and may view you as easy prey." As if he could not stand to look at her, he lowered his gaze to the table.

Elizabeth sighed. Apparently, Mr. Darcy was building an argument for her to relocate to Darcy House or to the Gardiners' house. Although she herself had contemplated traveling to Hertfordshire, she chafed when others sought to plan her life for her.

Mr. Darcy lifted his head, and his dark eyes caught hers; she almost gasped. He was obviously laboring under the influence of some strong emotion. "I feel in some ways responsible. I brought Wickham into your life, and your continued association with my family has made you an object of his greed."

Elizabeth pursed her lips against the exclamations of frustration that threatened to burst forth. "You take too much upon yourself, sir. I do not hold you or your family responsible."

Mr. Darcy's hands grasped the wood of the chair back so tightly his knuckles were white. "But you also would not be in this tenuous position if it were not for your engagement to Richard and his subsequent death." Mr. Darcy bit off every word as if he hated to say them. "He would despair to see you alone and unprotected."

"I am neither—"

Mr. Darcy raised a hand to forestall her protest. "I am aware you do not see yourself this way, but others do because of your situation. I cannot rest for worrying what slander or malicious behavior you will be subject to next. You have already been subjected to violence in your home!" He ran one hand across his face as if to calm himself, while the other gripped the chair as if his life depended on it.

Elizabeth regarded him with open-mouthed shock. He could not rest for worrying about her? What could he possibly mean?

Abruptly, he abandoned his post, striding down the length of the table and sitting in the chair beside her. His proximity was rather alarming. This close, she was keenly aware of his intense gaze, his masculine smell, the lock of inky hair falling over his forehead. And the extreme agitation of his emotions. Elizabeth swallowed hard, confused about Mr. Darcy's behavior and her reaction to it.

"I cannot leave you defenseless, Elizabeth. Do not ask it of me." His voice was low and rough. "I must protect you—for your own sake as well as in memory of my dear friend and cousin. The best protection I can offer you is my name and my hand, if you would take me. Would you accept my hand in marriage?"

Elizabeth's mind was absolutely blank.

She realized her mouth was open, but no sound was forthcoming. She closed it with a snap.

Although Mr. Darcy had led up to the proposal quite logically, Elizabeth had been taken quite by surprise.

No, surprise was not a strong enough word. Astonishment? Stupefaction?

She was also surprised by her own reaction. The thought of marrying Mr. Darcy should make her laugh at the ridiculousness of it; she had only recently accustomed herself to not expecting his disdain. However, part of Elizabeth felt an unexpected warmth at the thought.

Unfortunately for Mr. Darcy, the other part of her was angry.

How could he propose in this cold and practical manner? Every conclusion was laid out quite logically, but clearly his feelings were not engaged. Oh, he must experience *some* concern for her, anxiety even. However, that was hardly an emotion on which to build a life. No doubt he felt a certain fondness—for Richard's sake at least—and perhaps she should be grateful he seemed to tolerate her company. But she could never enter into a marriage which offered no more than tepid affection. How could he believe she would?

"Miss Bennet?" Mr. Darcy's voice intruded on her thoughts. She recognized that she had been silent a long time and struggled to find the right words for a reply.

Her mouth felt suddenly dry and her tongue impossibly thick. "I thank you for the honor of your proposal, but it is impossible for me to accept." She attempted to maintain an even, moderate tone that did not betray the disturbance of her emotions.

Mr. Darcy's expression altered little, confirming her sense that his emotions were not engaged. "I beg you to consider—"

Elizabeth ignored the interruption, her indignation gathering force. "I do not consider security of any kind to be a suitable reason to wed. If so, I would have accepted Mr. Collins's proposal two years ago."

"Mr. Collins made you an offer?" Horror was plain on Mr. Darcy's face.

Under other circumstances, Elizabeth might have found his disgust amusing, but she was too caught up in her own agitation. "I appreciate your concern for my safety, but I must believe there are other, less extreme steps which would address the potential danger."

A red stain had appeared in his cheeks. "I beg you to reconsider. You would be doing me a great service as well. As you know, Pemberley needs a mistress, and I need an heir. I am sure you would suit the role admirably."

Elizabeth supposed she should be flattered by these compliments, but it felt as though she was being hired for a position on his staff.

"And of course, I would do my very best to appreciate and cherish you." He reached out and took her hand in both of his.

With a shock, Elizabeth realized that he had removed his gloves. The feeling of skin on skin was unexpectedly … new. Naturally, she had often clasped hands with Richard, and she treasured the memories of the warmth and companionship they had shared in those moments. But Mr. Darcy's touch was … shocking, exciting, electric. Somehow that single touch sent thrills coursing throughout her body and made her painfully aware of his proximity.

Some deep part of Elizabeth responded to him and *wanted* him to cherish her.

No, she chastised herself. He obviously did not desire her in *that* way.

He wanted a mistress for Pemberley, a mother for his heirs, and an opportunity to be of service to his dead cousin. He had said it quite plainly. She could not allow inexplicable and unexpectedly warm feelings to overcome her discernment or judgment.

But ... his thumb caressed the back of her hand, creating the most delightful sensations. How did he do that? He regarded their clasped hands as if amazed. However, his words were at odds with the feelings. "It would settle much of the scurrilous gossip about you, and the Darcy name would help insulate you from future rumormongering. Your family at Longbourn would be protected as well."

The longer she contemplated the rational and unfeeling nature of his words, the angrier she became. She must quit the room before losing the reins on her temper!

"Again, I thank you for your concern—"

Mr. Darcy continued, his voice soft, "A single woman living alone faces many dangers—"

"Mr. Darcy!" Elizabeth raised her voice to get his attention. "I do not wish you to make such a sacrifice!" His head jerked up as his eyes fixed on her face. "With a marriage contracted under such circumstances, I cannot believe we could make each other happy." Immediately, she mourned the loss of warmth as his hands retreated to rest in his lap.

Mr. Darcy's eyes shifted away from hers, and his head turned as he focused on the door, but for a moment, did she detect a glimmer of despair? No, she must be in error. He felt nothing beyond friendship; her refusal could mean little. She spoke again: "I do not desire to occasion you pain. Your friendship is meaningful to me, and I hope we can continue it." She paused, but he made no reply. "I thank you for the honor of your addresses."

A muscle in Mr. Darcy's jaw twitched, and his eyes blinked rapidly. Otherwise, his face, in profile to her, might have been carved from stone.

She stood on legs shaking so violently they could barely support her. "I beg you to excuse me. I have an urgent appointment this morning."

"Of course." A polite, indifferent expression settled over his face. *Obviously, his feelings were not touched.*

His chair jolted back from the table with more force than necessary. "I apologize for detaining you. Good day." Mr. Darcy gave a very proper bow and hastened from the room.

Rather than climb the stairs to ready herself for her invented appointment, Elizabeth sank back into her chair. Her heart pounded, and every nerve in her body seemed alive with agitation. Her entire body thrummed with excitement, confusion, anguish—and anger. But she did not completely understand why.

After all, Mr. Darcy's reasoning could not be faulted—and he *had* done her a great honor. His family would object to an alliance with her, but he would overlook them for the sake of her comfort and security.

Yet nothing in his address suggested that he wanted *her*, Elizabeth Bennet. He needed a wife. She needed protection. He sought to solve two problems with one marriage.

Such a cold, disinterested analysis actually provoked a shiver down her spine. Somehow, the unfeeling nature of the proposal was … distressing to her.

Of course, most marriages within the *ton* were arrangements for mutual benefits rather than love matches. Why then should it disgust her when Mr. Darcy thought of her so dispassionately? Perhaps because he was already her friend, she longed for a more emotional connection?

Despite her efforts, Elizabeth could not understand her own feelings. Every emotional thread she examined became hopelessly entangled in other considerations—and led her once more to the same confused snarl. Finally, Elizabeth's agitated thoughts brought about a headache, and she decided to retire to her bed chamber for the remainder of the morning. Perhaps sleep would bring some clarity.

***

Darcy had been drifting aimlessly some time before he thought to wonder about his location. By then, he was already at the river, staring at Westminster Bridge. The sun was high in the sky, making the white stone of the bridge gleam and emphasizing the dingy color of the bridge's footings near the water. The shouts of river men and merchants who populated the streets near the bridge carried over the gentle lapping of the water on the banks.

Elizabeth had refused him.

The awful memory occupied his mind, leaving no space for any other thoughts. He had been prepared for a declaration she did not love him; he had expected it. Nevertheless, he had believed the proposal would appeal to her reason...her desire to provide security for her family. In truth, he had not prepared for rejection.

Nor had he been prepared for anger.

When he had recognized how fury fueled the paleness in her face and the trembling in her hands, he had felt ill—sick with despair. How had he offended her? The words of his proposal had been so carefully selected with the design of explaining his reasoning and demonstrating the desirability of their alliance. How had his plans gone awry so completely?

Black despair seized his chest and rendered breathing difficult. He leaned against a tree, taking deep breaths that he hoped would calm his wildly beating heart. It was a beautiful day; the sun made the waters of the Thames glisten and shine. Usually, Darcy found the moving current of the river and the gentle sway of the plants on the bank to be soothing, calming. But today, nothing would help.

Since reading Richard's letter, Darcy had allowed a small seedling of hope to grow in his chest, but in the space of only a few moments, it had withered and died—and, he was certain, would never be resurrected.

He could never permit himself to nurture such hopes anew.

Dear God, can I ever show my face in her house again?

What a fool he was to think he could take Richard's place in even a limited role.

A carriage bearing a nobleman's crest clattered over the bridge, provoking thoughts of Kirkwood.

Blast and damnation! *Kirkwood.*

Now nothing would prevent the lord from proposing.

Nothing would prevent Elizabeth from accepting.

How could Darcy survive it? Watching her engaged once more to another man? Watching her marry another man?

It could not be borne.

Perhaps she would not accept his offer. She might not desire Kirkwood's protection any more than she desired Darcy's.

But that would mean nothing if Elizabeth felt true affection or, God forbid, love for Kirkwood.

The conclusion was inescapable. Kirkwood might employ the same arguments as Darcy and receive a very different reception for the simple reason that Elizabeth was already predisposed toward him.

Darcy closed his eyes and pressed the heels of his hands against his eyelids as if he could shut out this vision. He could strive not to fix his mind on such possibilities, but his heart still plummeted painfully at the thought.

Opening his eyes, Darcy massaged his forehead, trying to ward off an impending headache. He knew he must find a way to accomplish the impossible and accept the reality, no matter how unacceptable. One thing was certain: whether Elizabeth accepted Kirkwood's proposal or not, she was forever lost to Darcy.

Chapter 15

By midday, Elizabeth had concluded that staying abed with a headache only worsened her tendency to obsess over the problem of Mr. Darcy. So she resolved on a long walk after luncheon. Perhaps fresh air would provide the clear head she required to better understand Mr. Darcy's behavior. Vexing man!

Refusing him had been the proper decision, of course. Why then could she not stop thinking about him? Again and again, she pictured the expression on his face as he had proposed. Such tenderness. Such genuine concern for her wellbeing. And more …

Had passion flared in his eyes? The night of their waltz at Georgiana's ball, he had seemed on the verge of kissing her. Was it possible he felt more than friendship? No, surely he would have declared any such sentiments when paying his addresses.

Her mind wandered, recalling his broad shoulders, his strong hands, and the blue-black strands of hair falling carelessly across his forehead. Her body hummed with excitement at any thoughts of his desire for her, but he might just as easily desire any reasonably attractive lady.

What if her rejection caused him to retire to Pemberley, and they never met again? Why was the idea so deeply distressing?

She sighed as the headache pounded anew. Her thoughts were in such a tangle, they were impossible to unwind. She needed a walk. A long walk.

However, she had not even tied her bonnet ribbons when Grayson announced Lord Kirkwood at the door. Sighing, Elizabeth removed her bonnet and repaired to the drawing room with the hope the viscount's heir would not stay long. The man bounded into the room like a big puppy, wide-eyed and eager to please. Lord Kirkwood was of an age with Richard, but he always seemed younger.

"Miss Bennet!" he exclaimed, executing a small bow. "You are a looking exceedingly well. I trust you have been in good health?"

"Yes, I have enjoyed the best of health, thank you." Elizabeth wondered that Lord Kirkwood had visited alone; in the past, he had been accompanied by other friends of Richard's. Perhaps no one else had been available to visit the poor, grieving almost-widow.

"I am very pleased to hear it!" He sat in one of the brocade-covered chairs but perched at the very edge of the seat as if excessive energy prevented him from more restful sitting.

Their eyes met, and he gave her a wide smile. *He really is quite an attractive man,* she thought. *And about as different from Mr. Darcy as possible.*

Am I now comparing every man to Mr. Darcy? She thought with disgust.

Lord Kirkwood was oblivious to her internal debate. "I have a particular design in today's visit," he confessed.

"Oh?"

His expression turned abruptly solemn, and his eyes locked on hers. "I know this may seem abrupt to you, but I have admired you for a long time…."

Merciful heavens, no! Elizabeth only just prevented herself from crying out.

This was not possible! It was a cruel joke. Two marriage proposals in one day? She schooled her features into a semblance of calm; perhaps he intended something else entirely.

But this hope was destined to be dashed as her visitor continued. "It has come to my attention that you have recently been the victim of scurrilous accusations and threatening behavior. I cannot be happy knowing you are at risk—not when I can be of assistance to the beloved of my dear friend."

"That is not necessary. I am certain all will soon be forgotten." she demurred hastily. Perhaps she could prevent the entire uncomfortable scene.

But the lord was not to be deterred from his full share of awkwardness. "I do not believe so. Please allow me to say my piece."

Elizabeth wished she could somehow prevent the coming disaster, for his sake as well as for hers. However, she could conceive of no polite way to prevent a man from offering marriage.

No longer able to contain his energy, Lord Kirkwood sprung from his chair and almost bounced among the room's various pieces of furniture.

"I feel a great deal of fondness for you, and I flatter myself that you return some measure of my affection. I would like to offer you my hand in marriage, to protect and cherish you for the rest of my life." His pacing brought him in front of Elizabeth, where he smiled endearingly at her. As she contemplated the necessity of declining his offer, she felt as if she was planning to kick a small, eager animal.

For a moment, Elizabeth was actually tempted to swear. Why did everyone assume she needed protection? Taking a deep breath, she tried to relax the tightness in her shoulders. Lord Kirkwood wished to help; he did not deserve to suffer her frustration.

Best to dispense with the unpleasantness as quickly as possible. Elizabeth steeled herself. "I am very honored by your offer, Lord Kirkwood, but I cannot accept."

His face fell so dramatically that Elizabeth struggled not to laugh. He resembled nothing so much as a small child who had been deprived of his favorite toy. Indeed, the whole situation was somewhat ridiculous given that it was not the first proposal of the day.

"I do not believe I am in need of such protection as you are offering," she said softly.

He appeared quite crestfallen. "I beg you to reconsider!" Were those not the same words Mr. Darcy had used?

Elizabeth recalled the tangle of emotions she had experienced earlier in the day; at least Lord Kirkwood did not inspire such a confusion of feelings. "It is too soon after Richard's death. I cannot offer my heart to another man."

Lord Kirkwood's shoulders slumped as he fixed his eyes on the floor. "Darcy said as much, but I did not wish to believe him," he muttered.

"You discussed your proposal with Mr. Darcy?" She cried. *What could that possibly mean?*

The lord blinked. "Well, yes, I saw him at White's yesterday and mentioned my plan. I thought he would be relieved—in case his sister has been anxious for you." Elizabeth smoothed her skirts with palms that were suddenly damp with sweat.

Lord Kirkwood continued, "He tried to dissuade me, but I decided to try my luck." Apparently, the lord viewed her as akin to a particularly elusive deer he was stalking.

Why would Mr. Darcy propose to her on the morning of a day when he knew another man planned to make her an offer? She almost addressed the question to Lord Kirkwood, but he obviously knew nothing of Mr. Darcy's attempt to preempt him, and the poor man already looked so defeated that she did not wish to compound it.

Perhaps Mr. Darcy somehow disapproved of Lord Kirkwood and sought to rescue her from him? Did he know of gambling debts, a drinking problem, or some other deficiency rendering him an unsuitable husband?

No. Why would he not simply warn Elizabeth against the man?

Mr. Darcy's avowed goal was protecting her from scandal, but as far as Elizabeth knew, the Kirkwood family name was untarnished, thus serving the purpose admirably. Why not simply allow Lord Kirkwood to propose?

Oh, that vexing man! Every time she believed she understood Mr. Darcy, he showed how she was in error.

Lord Kirkwood's anxious stare brought her to the realization she was scowling. "I hope you are not angered with Mr. Darcy. He cannot be faulted for failing to sway me from my course," he said.

"No, no, of course." Elizabeth carefully applied a smile to her lips. "I do not blame him for that." *However, I do hold him accountable for other actions.*

Suddenly the absurdity of the situation struck her. Two proposals in one day. It would make an excellent plot for a comic opera! She stifled an irrational impulse to laugh and covered her mouth with her hand.

Lord Kirkwood's expression was bemused, and Elizabeth struggled to appear appropriately solemn lest he believe she was laughing at him. He glanced to the door. "I believe it is past time for me to depart."

Elizabeth rose to escort him toward the entrance hall. "Lord Kirkwood, I am very touched at the care you demonstrated for me. Someday, you will fall in love with a woman and will be very happy I refused you today."

He grimaced. "I pray you are right." He stopped and gazed deeply into her eyes. "But I am pleased we may part friends."

Elizabeth smiled at him. "As am I."

After bidding her a good day, Kirkwood slipped through the door and was gone. She almost missed his presence, for now she would have to address the troublesome problem of Mr. Darcy.

***

Darcy truly did not wish to know about Kirkwood's proposal, but he also could not stomach remaining in ignorance any longer. By midafternoon, he had worked himself up into such a fine state of agitation that he was not fit for human company. So naturally, he chose to visit his club.

Perhaps Kirkwood would be at the club, drowning his sorrows—or God forbid, celebrating. Darcy both desired to the see the man and desperately wished to avoid it.

Upon his arrival, he wandered through the rooms at White's. He happened upon Lord Kirkwood, ensconced in a chair, behind that evening's paper, and with a glass of port at his elbow. Not caring if he was intruding on the man's privacy, Darcy seated himself opposite.

"Kirkwood, well met."

The lord lowered his paper and gazed curiously at Darcy. He did not appear to be flushed with the joy of the newly affianced, but Darcy did not know the man well. Perhaps he was not particularly demonstrative. He did not seem especially distraught either. How could proposing to Elizabeth fail to provoke strong emotions? What was wrong with the man?

"Hello, Darcy," Kirkwood said mildly.

"Kirkwood." He paused, but the other man did not appear inclined to say any more. "Momentous day, eh?"

"Hmm?" Kirkwood blinked. "Oh. I suppose." He reached for his glass. "Miss Bennet refused me."

"I am sorry to hear that." Darcy had not realized how tense his entire body had been until all of his insides relaxed simultaneously. His body was suddenly so loose he felt he was in danger of sliding off the chair and onto the floor. He sent a little prayer of thanks to the heavens. "Did she say why?" The worst of his fears was past, but had Elizabeth mentioned Darcy's morning visit to Kirkwood? No, then the other man's expression would be quite different.

Kirkwood took a sip. "She does not feel the danger to her reputation, and she also cannot consider an offer of marriage so soon following Richard's death."

"Oh?" Darcy's heart sank. She had not given that as a reason for rejecting him, but perhaps it was because of his close friendship with his cousin. What a fool he was to think she would contemplate replacing his cousin— even for the sake of security!

Darcy shifted in the chair, trying to find a comfortable position. He wanted nothing more than to escape the conversation, but he was eager for every shred of information he could obtain. "Was Miss Bennet angry about the proposal?" Darcy asked.

"Angry?" Kirkwood echoed in bemusement. "Why would she be angry? No, she was very gracious, said she was honored, and so on." Kirkwood watched the port swirl in his glass. "In point of fact, she seemed rather … amused."

"Amused?" Darcy echoed incredulously. His proposal to Elizabeth had provoked many emotions, but amusement was not among them.

Kirkwood shrugged. "She is apt to discover the humor in every situation. She said someday my wife would thank her for refusing me." The slight smile on the lord's lips transformed into a grimace.

It was hard to reconcile the reaction Kirkwood described with the tight-lipped anger Darcy had faced earlier. If he and Kirkwood had made substantially the same argument in favor of marriage, why should his proposal be received with anger and Kirkwood's with *amusement*? Yes, Elizabeth would enjoy the irony of receiving two proposals in one day, but she *should* only grow angrier each time someone espoused the idea that she needed protection.

"Did you tell her you had spoken with me yesterday?" Darcy asked.

Kirkwood blinked. "Y-yes. I said I had discussed the proposal with you."

Darcy barely caught himself before swearing aloud. Elizabeth would suspect he had proposed marriage only to steal the march from his rival. Just when he believed her opinion of him could not sink any lower.

"Actually," Kirkwood mused, "she did seem a bit put out then. You would think she would be flattered." He shrugged. "Eh, women!" He tossed back the rest of the port.

So she was angry when his name was mentioned. Darcy dropped his head into his hands. She must truly hate him. What a fool he was. Any relief he had experienced now dissolved into a new sense of anxiety. Would she even speak with him again?

"Darcy? I say, are you feeling ill?" Darcy looked up into Kirkwood's concerned face.

"A touch of queasiness." *All too true.* "Perhaps it is best if I go." Darcy managed to push himself into a standing position and stumble out of the room with a modicum of dignity.

Once more in the privacy of his carriage, he dropped his head against the back of the seat and marveled at the mess he had made of his life.

***

Elizabeth stared at the door to Darcy House and breathed deeply, trying to calm the agitation in her stomach. She had, upon occasion, ignored some of the lesser rules of propriety but never one as large as this. An unmarried lady should never visit an unmarried gentleman alone. If Georgiana were home, Elizabeth's visit would have a veneer of acceptability, but she could not say what she must in Georgiana's presence.

After Lord Kirkwood's departure, Elizabeth taken a long, vigorous walk, trying to untangle and decipher everything that had transpired that day. While she could easily believe Lord Kirkwood had been straightforward with her, she was still mystified about Mr. Darcy. Had he intended to preempt Lord Kirkwood, and if so, why?

Again and again, she had ordered herself to ignore the problem. Did it matter if he had additional motivations that he had not revealed? She had refused Mr. Darcy and was confident in her decision. Of course, it had been the best choice. Even if she regarded him in a different light, she could not possibly consider a different answer to his question.

Of course not.

However, as she mused about the day's events, the questions surrounding Mr. Darcy only multiplied and grew more difficult to ignore. She considered that Mr. Darcy's bizarre behavior might indicate some deeper emotional attachment, although it was difficult to credit. But for a moment, she allowed herself the indulgence of imagining he did have romantic feelings for her. How would she feel about him?

Her relationship with Richard had been simple and effortless. It had always been easy to discern his thoughts and sentiments. They thought alike in so many matters and had established an easy camaraderie. And Richard had been a soldier: straightforward, holding nothing back. She had appreciated these qualities in him.

In many ways, his cousin was Richard's opposite. Silent and brooding, he rarely revealed his thoughts and never his feelings. He seemed to dislike assemblies of people, particularly large groups. But now that she thought on it, he always seemed to seek her out, even as he seemed uncomfortable in her presence. Perhaps he did value her company; he simply demonstrated it in a very different way than Richard had.

The walk had resulted in two hours of thinking in circles, which reached no conclusions. Finally, Elizabeth decided she could only enjoy peace of mind if she spoke with Mr. Darcy in person.

As she stared at the smooth cherry wood of the Darcy House's front door, however, her resolve wavered. How could she even initiate a conversation on such a delicate subject? Would he judge her too forward for visiting him?

No. Elizabeth straightened her shoulders. Mr. Darcy had set these events in motion, and she *must* understand what had transpired—and why. Some of her earlier anger flared. Instinctually, she knew he had concealed something from her, something which concerned her. And she was tired of being vexed and perplexed by this man!

Resolutely, she grabbed the knocker and banged it. The butler opened the door and nodded. "Miss Bennet, I will tell Miss Darcy you are visiting."

"No, I—"

Before Elizabeth could say another word, the butler disappeared down the hallway, while a footman helped remove her cloak. Elizabeth fussed with her gloves and her reticule, silently berating herself for not immediately speaking up.

"Elizabeth! You arrived in time for tea." With a welcoming smile, Georgiana glided down the hallway and ushered her friend into the drawing room. Elizabeth followed Georgiana and seated herself in one of the beautifully embroidered chairs.

As she poured out the tea, Georgiana chatted about the latest piece she was learning on the pianoforte and about her aunt's insistence on a white dress for the next ball she was to attend. After a few minutes, Miss Darcy noticed her friend's uncharacteristic silence. "Are you quite well?"

"Yes, I thank you. I am very well." Feeling unequal to the needs of subtlety, Elizabeth asked, "Will your brother be joining us for tea?"

Georgiana's eyebrows rose, but she was too polite to comment. She turned to the maid who had brought in a tray of biscuits. "Mary, has Mr. Darcy been alerted to Miss Bennet's visit?" The maid indicated that she did not know but would inform him.

Elizabeth immediately had misgivings. Now she had ensured she would encounter Mr. Darcy! Her anger surged through her again. No, it was for the best. She must have some answers from him.

Georgiana regarded Elizabeth curiously as they spoke of the frequent rain. But feeling unequal to meeting her friend's gaze, Elizabeth fixed her eyes on her teacup. She would be mortified if Georgiana made assumptions about her feelings toward Mr. Darcy.

They soon heard a quick step outside the door, and Mr. Darcy entered. His cravat was askew and his coat rumpled as if donned in haste. He looked as discomposed as Elizabeth felt. His eyes found her face immediately with a questioning look, but she could not allow her expression to betray anything in Georgiana's presence.

Meeting a blank look, he glanced away as he bowed. "Miss Bennet." The words were directed more toward the floor than toward her. Mr. Darcy seated himself and received the cup of tea Georgiana proffered.

The conversation ranged from the weather to the health of the inhabitants of Hertfordshire to the wellbeing of the Darcys' various relations. Once these topics had run their course, the three seemed to have exhausted every available subject. Elizabeth's mind was too full of questions that she dared not ask Mr. Darcy to fix her thoughts on more trivial matters.

Georgiana found herself in the unusual position of making most of the conversation. She bravely essayed several subjects; however, trapped in their separate discomforts, the others were unable to sustain her efforts. Mr. Darcy barely made an attempt, as he alternately glowered at the floor and directed puzzled glances at Elizabeth.

This is ridiculous, thought Elizabeth finally. *Someone must end this impasse—despite Georgiana's presence.* "Lord Kirkwood came to visit today," she mentioned during the next lull in the conversation.

Mr. Darcy's head shot up, and he regarded her with a piercing glare. "Indeed?"

She regarded him steadily. "Imagine my surprise at learning you knew he intended to visit me."

Several expressions passed over Mr. Darcy's features: discomfort, guilt, and perhaps a bit of embarrassment. However, he did not seem angry she had raised the subject. His eyes slid to Georgiana. Elizabeth could not help gazing at her as well.

"Why?" Georgiana looked bewildered. "Was his visit of particular significance?" Suddenly, she seemed to intuit if not the subject of Elizabeth's visit, then its sensitivity. Her hand flew up to cover her mouth. "Oh!" Her eyes darted from Darcy to Elizabeth, immobile, with tension emanating from their bodies.

"Dear heart, I believe Miss Bennet and I have something we must discuss privately," Darcy said gently.

Georgiana's dilemma was written plainly on her face. Unmarried men and women were never left alone, except for one purpose. Could it be that? But her brother would visit Elizabeth to make an offer of marriage, not the other way around. And Elizabeth did not appear eager to accept a proposal.

Georgiana clearly could not penetrate the oddness of the situation; however, she was too obedient to question her brother. She nodded and swiftly exited the room, closing the door softly behind her.

The moment Georgiana was gone, Elizabeth turned the full force of her gaze on Mr. Darcy. "You knew Lord Kirkwood was preparing to make me an offer, but you deliberately arrived beforehand to preempt him."

Mr. Darcy inclined his head stiffly. "I did."

Elizabeth swallowed, pleased he admitted it. "Why? If you were only concerned with my safety, surely marriage to Lord Kirkwood would do just as well. Unless you have some objection to the man?"

Darcy looked at his hands. "No, I have no objection to him. His character and family situation are impeccable."

"Then why?" She demanded.

Darcy launched himself from his chair and strolled to the windows, gazing at the street outside without any particular interest. "As I said, Pemberley needs a mistress. I need an heir."

"And I would do as well as another women?" She could hear the indignation in her own voice.

He rested his arm on the window frame and ran his free hand through his hair. "I - I believe – you are well suited to the role. I admire you. We are friends. You would be an excellent mistress of Pemberley."

"So you did not want to let this opportunity go? You did not want to let Lord Kirkwood have me?" Her hands shook, and she hastily set down her teacup.

Mr. Darcy colored, but his expression did not change. "I suppose you could say so." The muscles clenched in his jaw, and his lips pressed tightly together. Perhaps he wished to contain his disgust at her forward behavior.

What did it matter? He had answered. She understood his feelings—or lack thereof. She was a convenience, an opportunity he did not wish to lose to another man. Slowly, her anger drained away. What did it gain her to be angry with this man? But in its place, she experienced an unfamiliar emptiness. Perhaps she had been hoping, just a little, that he had deeper feelings for her.

Now there was no need to linger—at Darcy House or even in London. Yes, it was past time to return to Hertfordshire.

Her eyes burned, and she blinked back tears of humiliation, refusing to cry in his presence. She cleared her throat, staring at the door and longing for escape. "Thank you for your explanation, Mr. Darcy." She stood, calculating how many steps would free her of the room and this frustrating man.

"I must be going. Please give Miss Darcy my regrets." Her voice was hoarse and thin.

In the back of her mind, she wondered how she could maintain her friendship with Georgiana while avoiding her brother for the rest of her life. But that was a question for another day.

After crossing the room without incident, Elizabeth had reached out to the door knob when Darcy's voice stopped her hand. "Why were you so angered?"

She did not touch the knob, but she could not turn around to look at him. "I beg your pardon?" Her head lowered, she stared at the bottom edge of the door and the room's fine woolen carpeting.

"When *I* proposed you were furious, but Lord Kirkwood reported to me that you refused him graciously and with humor." Darcy's voice was rough and low.

Elizabeth blinked; she had not noticed the difference in her reception of nearly identical proposals. Her hand rested on the brass door knob; one quick twist and she would be free of this man and his intrusive questions. Free of his vexing contradictions. If she pretended she had never heard his question, she knew instinctively that he would let her leave without a protest.

But she could not do it. If she had any hope of retaining her friendship with this man, she must address his difficult questions. Reluctantly, she removed her hand from the knob and turned to face Mr. Darcy.

His face held a desperation she had never seen before, and an almost wild fierceness lit his eyes—completely at odds with his refined clothing and the elegant furnishings.

"Why, Elizabeth?" *This is the second time he has used my Christian name. What does it mean?* "Is it simply that you prefer him to me?" Now his voice held a hint of pain.

The hurt in his voice made her heart throb with empathy. But had she merely wounded his pride, or had she somehow spurned his tender feelings?

"No!" The protest sprang from her lips without thought. She struggled to articulate her meaning. "If anything, it is the opposite. That is—I do not know Lord Kirkwood well. I was honored by his proposal, but my feelings were not touched." Too late, Elizabeth realized the implications of her words and wished she could recall them.

Mr. Darcy's attention was completely focused on her face. "And *my* proposal touched your feelings?" Leaving his post at the window, he swiftly closed the distance between them. Suddenly, the room seemed too small.

"N-naturally," she stammered. "You are my friend. Richard's cousin. I f-feel affection for you and Georgiana."

"Affection." Mr. Darcy bit off the word disdainfully. His eyes would not waver from hers. "That does nothing to explain why my offer angered you!"

As Mr. Darcy loomed over her, Elizabeth instinctively backed away. His face paled when he noticed her reaction, and he abruptly turned away, blindly walking back toward the window.

Elizabeth used this time to examine her own emotions. Why had she been so angry with Mr. Darcy and not with Lord Kirkwood? What was different about them? Why was the lord so easily dismissed from her thoughts, while she felt compelled to confront Mr. Darcy?

Dismissing Lord Kirkwood's proposal had been simple; it held no appeal, despite the good intentions behind his offer, and she had felt nothing more than regret for disappointing his hopes. However, she had found it far more difficult to credit *Mr. Darcy's* good intentions, and the proposal itself was … more disconcerting.

Despite these disquieting emotions, she forced herself to examine the question. Mr. Darcy was far different from Lord Kirkwood. Despite the mode of his offer, betrothal to Mr. Darcy held … appeal. Certainly he was attractive—and kind. If she were truthful with herself, Elizabeth reluctantly admitted that under different circumstances, she might have been tempted to *accept* Mr. Darcy's offer.

The thought rushed in with the suddenness of a tidal wave, washing away all other notions and knocking aside all of her earlier assumptions. The truth and clarity of her realization left her staggered. *She desired Mr. Darcy.*

How had her feelings about him changed? *When* had her feelings changed?

Could I be in love with him?

For a moment, the thought struck her with dizzying ecstasy—joy and wonder filled her heart to overflowing.

And then memory left her dashed back on the rocks of reality.

Richard.

How could she have forgotten about Richard for one moment?

Her hand flew to her mouth in horror. How could she consider replacing him in her heart so soon? Only a week ago, she thought she would never consider marriage again. Even *contemplating* such feelings about Mr. Darcy seemed like such a betrayal.

No. Impossible. Those feelings had died in her when she had buried Richard. She had been so certain.

"Elizabeth? Are you well?" Mr. Darcy was staring at her again, his eyes wide with concern.

Awareness returned. She had walked several steps into the room and was clutching a chair with one hand, while the other covered her mouth in a gesture of despair. "I must go. I beg you to forgive me," she mumbled as she lurched toward the door, pausing only for a moment by her chair to collect her reticule. "Give my regrets to Georgiana." Dimly, she was aware that Mr. Darcy was stepping closer to her.

"You are not well. You should not venture out—" Mr. Darcy's hand on her elbow arrested her progress. "I pray you, sit, and I will have some water brought."

The room had grown stiflingly hot, and her stays compressed her lungs until she could barely breathe. *I must leave now!* Passing one more minute in Darcy House would be intolerable.

Elizabeth pulled her arm from his grasp without looking at his face. "Thank you, no. I must leave at once!"

Darcy released her arm abruptly, and she almost lost her balance. Keeping her eyes fixed on the doorway, she stumbled forward until she could grasp the door knob. As she opened the door, she glanced back at Darcy over her shoulder. His expression was so perplexed that she was almost tempted to return and comfort him.

But then I might never leave.

If only she could say something to reassure him and demonstrate that she wished to maintain their friendship, but she could think of no words that were not fraught. "I-I—" she stammered. "I beg you to give my regrets to Georgiana." *Had she said that before?*

His mouth set in an unhappy line, Mr. Darcy merely inclined his head. "I will."

The need to escape threatened to suffocate her. She darted through the doorway into the hall, closing the door firmly behind her. She was halfway to the main entrance when she remembered her cloak. But the day was mild, and the walk was short; she made the hasty decision to sacrifice it. The cloak could be collected by a maid later. Swiftly, she hurried out the door of Darcy House into the sunshine.

Chapter 16

Darcy stared at the plate of breakfast in front of him, willing his appetite to return. The eggs and ham should have provoked rumblings from his stomach, given that he had not been able to choke down a single bite of dinner, but the food's aroma only rendered him slightly nauseous. He had slept fitfully, as his thoughts constantly returned again and again to the scene with Elizabeth the previous day. The disgusted look on her face as she realized Darcy intended to press her for an answer about her feelings toward him. What had possessed him to such foolishness … such offensiveness? He could well recall the echoing sounds of her boot heels racing through the entrance hall.

Yes, I am the man who prompts women to flee his presence. Any discussion of marrying me is so disturbing it causes one to race into the cold without a cloak.

Although to be fair, it is not all *women who flee—only the one I* wish *to marry ....*

Yes, no doubt there were any number of women who would not run from him. For instance, Miss Bingley …. Darcy shuddered.

He had realized too late—must he always be too late?— that Elizabeth had given him a perfect opportunity to reveal his feelings when she had demanded he account for the manner of his proposal. But he was so accustomed to concealing his love for her, it had not occurred to him to reveal it. And to be honest, her refusal had piqued his vanity, and his temper had flared.

Of all the times to lose my hold on my temper!

He had never before made an offer of marriage, but he was certain that anger was not supposed to be part of it.

He had been rough, demanding, angry—when he should have been gentle and understanding and loving. She was, after all, grappling with her grief for Richard.

No wonder she had fled. She had probably run all the way back to her townhouse.

He had compounded his offense by growling at Georgiana when she inquired about Elizabeth's visit. Sometimes, he wondered how she could bear to live with him. He could hardly bear it himself.

On days like today, he was disgusted with himself.

Darcy had already informed his butler and valet he would be returning to Pemberley today, no longer caring what they thought of his abrupt comings and goings. *I never should have left Derbyshire.*

Once there, he might never leave again.

Conceding breakfast as a lost cause, Darcy pushed back from the table at the same moment his butler entered, followed by Bannon, the groom he had sent to Elizabeth's house to watch over her horses. Gloomily, Darcy mused she had most likely ordered Bannon to quit his post, unwilling to have any reminders of Darcy about her house.

Then he noticed unease twisting Bannon's features. "What is it, man?" Darcy asked, standing immediately. Had something happened to Elizabeth?

"Mr. Darcy, sir." Bannon tugged off his hat and held it before him. "I came as soon as I could. Miss Bennet ...well, she—"

Anxiety knotted Darcy's gut. "Has something happened to her? Is she injured?"

"She is gone!" Bannon blurted out. "She left at first light this morning. Took some of the colonel's horses and hired a carriage."

Darcy grabbed the edge of the table for balance. She was running away, escaping him. Oh, Good Lord, what had he done to her?

Bannon was babbling. "I came as soon as I can, but there was all these doings—"

Darcy interrupted. "Where did she go? Hertfordshire?"

Bannon solemnly shook his head. Darcy was at a loss. Where else would Elizabeth go? She knew few people outside London or Hertfordshire. "Carter, the footman she took with her, said she was bound for Matlock."

"Matlock?" Darcy echoed. Why would she go there? Richard's parents were not in residence and would not welcome a visit from her if they were.

Bannon just shrugged. "Carter said she been there before. For the colonel's funeral."

Oh, Good Lord! Darcy sank slowly into his chair as understanding dawned. Of course. Richard's grave was on the grounds of the Matlock family chapel. Disgusted by Darcy's proposal, she was seeking refuge in memories of Richard's love.

Darcy felt like a prize idiot. How could he have ever hoped to measure up to Richard? Replace Richard?

Suddenly, Darcy felt exhausted. "Thank you, Bannon. I would like you to stay on at Miss Bennet's for now."

"Will you go after her?" Darcy frowned up at Bannon. He did not appreciate intrusive servants.

"No, she is entitled to her privacy."

"But the thing is, Mr. Darcy," Bannon's hands anxiously worked the edge of his hat, "Mr. Grayson found out after the lady left that one of the kitchen boys told Mr. Wickham where she was going to. He'd been paid off, the scoundrel!" Bannon's eyes were open wide in earnest concern. "What if Wickham goes after her?"

Darcy shot to his feet. "Good God, Bannon, why did you not say so at first?" He yelled for his butler, who immediately opened the door.

"Saddle my horse at once. I ride for Matlock!"

***

There had been no snow on the way to Derbyshire, but the roads were pitted and bumpy—and the hired carriage was not the best sprung, communicating every bump and hole to the occupant. The entire journey, Elizabeth's body had been jostled and bumped around, fittingly mirroring the tumultuous nature of her inner thoughts. For propriety's sake, Elizabeth supposed she should have brought a maid, but privacy had given her time to think.

The night after her visit to Darcy House, she had stared at the ceiling of her bed chamber, attempting to sort through her feelings for Mr. Darcy. She sighed. It had been so much simpler when she had just been angry with the man for proposing so insultingly. If she had never visited Darcy House to demand an explanation, he would never led her to consider that he genuinely cared about her.

Even more disturbing was the way her heart leapt at the thought that he might have romantic feelings for her. Yes, life had been easier when she had been blissfully unaware of those sentiments.

Did she truly feel love for him, or was she confusing friendship with something else? How could she feel that way about another man so soon after Richard's death?

She could not. That was the answer. It was some sort of temporary madness—perhaps brought on by grief itself. A visit to Richard's grave would clear her head, remind her whom she loved. It would restore her equilibrium and help her forget all this nonsense.

Lost in her reverie, she was startled when the carriage jerked to a stop. When Carter, the footman, opened the carriage door, she gave him a puzzled glance. "Hello Carter, why have we stopped? Is there a problem on the road?"

He grinned. "No, ma'am. We're at the Matlock chapel." He positioned the steps and held out his hand so she could descend.

Elizabeth gratefully straightened up after the confined quarters of the carriage and glanced around. It was indeed the grounds of the Matlock churchyard—less green, but otherwise just as she remembered them on the sweltering June day when they had laid Richard to rest. "I cannot believe we are here already! You made very good time, Weston," she said to the groom who was hitching the horses to a nearby fence.

"Thank you, ma'am." Weston smiled, then turned away shyly.

In June, the graveyard had been shaded with weeping willows and birch trees and carpeted with thick grasses. But this time of year, the trees were bare of leaves, and most of the grass was a dull brown. Nonetheless, she heard a cheerful birdsong in the distance, and the sun shone brightly. The graveyard held the kind of peaceful quality often found in such places.

It was a lovely spot for Richard's final resting place. Blinking back incipient tears, she murmured to Carter, "I would like to visit the colonel's grave alone."

Carter frowned, scanning the deserted churchyard. "Very well, ma'am. Weston and me will take the horses to that stream to water 'em. But we'll be back in a trice. You won't want to stay out long in this cold."

Elizabeth nodded. The sun had warmed the air, and the temperature was mild for January but still chilly. She drew her cloak about her as she climbed the hill toward the Fitzwilliam family gravestones. The small hill on the east side of the churchyard was home to a mausoleum and several grand effigies of prominent members of the Fitzwilliam family, but Richard's grave marker was a plain gray marble with his name and the years of his birth and death. He had expressed a desire to avoid anything too ostentatious. However, the grave's simplicity set it apart from the far more ornate markers surrounding it.

Grass had grown around the grave, but Elizabeth could still see the outline where the earth had been disturbed. There was a rather flat gray rock next to the grave, and Elizabeth sat on it, not caring about the state of her skirts. Gathering her cloak about her, she set her reticule down and leaned forward to better view Richard's gravestone.

The letters carved in the marble grew blurry and wavy, frustrating her desire for a clear view. Tears fell freely down her cheeks.

Sometimes, she had difficulty not being angry at this vexing situation. Loving Richard had been simple; he had been her best friend. Why did he have to be taken from her and leave her with these complicated questions about Mr. Darcy?

She tried to guess what Richard would say about this situation, but her imagination failed her. It was impossible to envision confessing feelings for someone else. But what if she spoke to him not as a fiancé, but as a friend? As she would speak to Jane?

She sent up a silent plea to the heavens. *Richard, I might be falling in love with your cousin. I am so sorry. I did not mean for it to happen. What should I do?*

A divine message would be welcome at this moment. Perhaps a bolt of lightning or an angel would appear to give her a sign. She would have settled for a dove. Or a sparrow. But nothing happened.

She imagined a Richard who had never loved her romantically, who had only ever seen her as a friend. How would *he* have felt if she loved his cousin?

Well, of course, he would be overjoyed. If he believed Elizabeth would be a good match for Mr. Darcy. Richard had loved his cousin.

Would Richard have seen me as a good match for Mr. Darcy?

In an instant everything became clear to Elizabeth. Richard had wanted the best for her—he would want her to be happy. *She* might believe she was betraying Richard, but *he* would never have felt that way. In fact, he had expressed concern over his cousin's isolation and wished he would find a woman to love. What if Elizabeth could be that woman?

She blinked the tears from her eyes, and the engraved letters and numbers grew clearer. Then just for a moment, the entire gravestone seemed to glow with a soft white light. Elizabeth gasped. Richard had given her the guidance she sought—without an angel or a burning bush. She blinked again, and the gravestone looked utterly ordinary in the bright wintry light. *Did I see anything at all?*

Elizabeth stood and stepped toward the gravestone, needing to feel it under her fingers. Removing her glove, she laid her naked hand on the top of the smooth marble. It should have been cold, but it felt warm to her touch.

"Thank you, Richard, dearest one. Even now you continue to give me gifts." A tear rolled down her cheek, but she was no longer overwhelmed by grief. Instead, she felt a tiny seed of hope beginning to grow. She straightened and smiled.

Now she was ready to return to London and face William again. As she tugged on her glove, she dabbed her face with her handkerchief, hoping her red-rimmed eyes would not alarm Weston and Carter. Elizabeth turned away from the grave, wondering if they had finished watering the horses.

There was a tall figure blocking her way, silhouetted by the sun. For a moment, her heart leapt in the hopes Mr. Darcy had met her. But when her eyes adjusted to the sunlight, Elizabeth gasped. It was Wickham!

Chapter 17

"Hello, Sister," Wickham sneered. "I thought this might be a good day for a family reunion."

Elizabeth could not imagine Wickham's presence was an accident. Somehow, he must have learned she would be here—alone.

Swallowing hard, Elizabeth nodded a curt greeting. "Mr. Wickham, what a coincidence." She tried to brush past him. "If you will excuse me, I must—"

"I am afraid I will not excuse you, Lizzy." Wickham's hand shot out and grabbed her upper arm like a vise.

She attempted to pull away, but he only tightened his already bruising hold on her arm. Taking advantage of his superior strength, Wickham yanked her toward him and whispered in her ear. "*Someone* has been telling stories about me to Darcy. He's got Bow Street Runners looking for me and stirring up trouble with the London merchants. Suddenly, my word is no good, and no one wants to give me credit. And everyone believes me one step from the gallows!"

Elizabeth's brow creased with worry. She was unaware, but not surprised, that Mr. Darcy had undertaken these measures. Elizabeth set her jaw. She refused to show fear to Wickham. "I said nothing to Mr. Darcy that was not true."

Wickham continued on as if she had never spoken. "Now I cannot return to London, and I may need to flee England altogether." He whirled her around to face him, grabbing her other arm in a painfully strong hold. "And. It. Is. Your. Fault." He punctuated each word with a bone jarring shake of Elizabeth's body.

Her instincts cried at her to fight the man and run for her life, but she fought back this panicked reaction, knowing it would be useless. *Focus, keep your head, Elizabeth.* "Mr. Darcy will not be happy to learn you have treated me thus. He is not a man to cross. Perhaps you had best leave."

Wickham laughed harshly. "By the time Darcy learns of this, I will be long gone."

Elizabeth lifted her chin as she looked at him. "What do you want from me?"

He sighed. "If only you had given me the money when I first asked so politely, things would not have come to this pass."

Despite the perilous situation, Elizabeth's temper flared. How dare he blame her? "You destroyed my garden and threw rocks through my windows! How is any of this my fault?"

"Do not blame me!" Wickham roared. "You drove me to it!" He released one of her arms only so he could deal her a violent slap across the face that sent her careening backward and falling onto the dead grass of the churchyard.

He is a madman! Elizabeth thought, clutching her hand to her cheek. Momentarily freed from his grip, she scrambled backward awkwardly, heedless of the dirt and mud. Wickham advanced slowly, towering over her menacingly. *He is enjoying this*, she realized. *Relishing his sense of power over me!* Elizabeth looked desperately over her left shoulder. There it was! Her reticule, abandoned on the flat rock where she had been sitting.

In no hurry, Wickham simply smiled like a cat anticipating fun with a mouse. "You will pay for the way you have treated me!"

She did not want to take her eyes off him, but it was necessary. Lunging toward the reticule, she grabbed it as she scrambled further back, her boots gaining little purchase in the dry grass.

Wickham laughed at the sight. "Yes, by all means, get your handkerchief! I will give you something to cry about."

Elizabeth pulled out the pistol and pointed it at him. His smile died. "Leave me alone!" She shouted.

Wickham swallowed and seemed to regain his equilibrium. "What? A present from your dear departed betrothed? But I doubt you know how to use it."

"Do not make assumptions, Mr. Wickham." Without daring to glance away from him, she tried to stand. But as she was getting her feet under her, her boot heel caught on the hem of her dress, upsetting her balance. Wickham took advantage of her momentary distraction to lunge forward.

Elizabeth reacted instantly. She could not allow Wickham to hurt her again! She squeezed the trigger.

The blast from the pistol was deafening as the smell of gunpowder filled the air. The pistol's recoil pushed Elizabeth back onto the grass, but she stood hastily, ready to fend off Wickham. But it was not necessary. The man was lying on the ground a few feet away from her.

For an awful moment, Elizabeth thought she had killed him. Then Wickham screamed—an awful, blood curdling sound. "Damn you to hell, woman! You shot me!"

Relief washed through Elizabeth. The man could not be too badly hurt if he could curse. Clutching the pistol, which was useless as a gun but could make an effective projectile if necessary, she carefully approached Wickham's prone figure.

He was clutching his right leg, below the knee, where blood seeped through his fingers. "Damn you! You shot me!" He repeated.

For a moment, Elizabeth was struck with an absurd impulse to laugh. What had he expected? "I warned you."

"But I never thought you would do it! You're a *woman*!" This was followed by some more unsavory language. "Damnation, it hurts!"

Elizabeth rolled her eyes. Underneath all the bluster, the man was such a coward.

Peering down the hill, she could see the carriage had not returned. Why were they taking so long? She supposed they would have to take Wickham to a doctor. Undoubtedly, he would try to persuade the authorities she had attacked him without provocation. She sighed.

Well, there was nothing for it. Turning back to the still-cursing man, she knelt next to him and examined the wound. She shoved down his stocking and pushed up his trouser leg, but every time she touched his leg, Wickham would moan and curse.

The wound needed binding, and she must sacrifice a petticoat to tear into strips. Making quick work of the project, she started binding up the wound to the best of her ability; it seemed to staunch the bleeding, at least for the moment.

As she worked, the sound of approaching hoofs rose from the road, but they were coming from the wrong direction; it could not be Weston and Carter. The rider was pushing his horse to run. Did Wickham have a henchman? The thought made her sick with worry. She looked up, but the angle was wrong, and she could see nothing.

Elizabeth finished tying the last knot in her makeshift bandage, but before she could stand to get a better view of the road, Wickham grabbed her arm. Using it as leverage, he flipped his body over hers and pinned her to the ground.

Elizabeth tried to strike out at him with her fists, but he held down her hands with his—and straddled her hips with his legs. The indecency of the position made Elizabeth blush. "I was trying to help you!" She hissed at him.

Wickham's face was white and drawn with pain. "After shooting me!" He snarled. Pulling a length of rope from his pocket, he held Elizabeth's wrists together over her head with one hand. No, she could not let him tie her hands! She fought to buck him off while looking around frantically for the gun. There it was, only three feet away, but it might as well have been on the moon.

Closing her eyes in concentration, she focused on bringing up her right leg as leverage against his wounded leg—in the hopes she could push him off her. Then she heard a loud *thump*. All of Wickham's weight unexpectedly landed on her. Opening her eyes, she was peering directly into his unconscious face. Good Lord! She rolled his limp body off hers and into the dirt. What had happened to Wickham? She squinted up into the sun.

There stood Mr. Darcy, dark against the bright blue sky, after having apparently punched Wickham. Mr. Darcy's clothing was disheveled, his cravat askew and his hair a mess. He looked quite wild. However, the expression on his face was an intense mixture of relief and anxiety as he gazed searchingly at her. "Elizabeth!"

"Mr. Darcy?" Her voice squeaked embarrassingly. What must she look like, sprawled in the dirt? Quickly, she scrambled to her feet. "Thank you for your assistance!"

Mr. Darcy closed the distance between them even as his eyes quickly scanned the hillside, taking in the scene. "I heard a gunshot and screaming. I feared the worst."

Elizabeth felt her face heating. What would he think of her? "I shot Mr. Wickham when he attacked me."

A corner of Mr. Darcy's mouth quirked upward. "*You* shot Wickham?"

What must he think of her? "I warned him to stay away, but he kept coming toward me."

Mr. Darcy chuckled softly. "You never cease to amaze me."

Relief flooded through Elizabeth; at least he did not seem appalled by her behavior.

"Did he hurt you?" His eyes searched her frantically. He frowned at her face, where Wickham's slap had undoubtedly left a mark. "No wonder you were screaming." Gently he reached out to touch her cheek.

Despite herself, Elizabeth was indignant. "That was not me—"

A groan alerted them that Wickham was recovering his senses. "Darcy?" Wickham cried. "She shot me! The damn woman shot me!" He rolled to his side in the dirt, looking imploringly up at Mr. Darcy.

"Good for her," Mr. Darcy replied.

"Christ, it hurts like the devil!" Wickham moaned.

"The screams were Wickham's?" William asked her, and she nodded. He laughed.

William looked about them and then took Elizabeth's hand in his. Drawing her away from where Wickham writhed and groaned, he led her behind a tree for some privacy. Elizabeth was mystified by his actions but gave no objection.

"Oh, thank God, you are unharmed!" He cried. Before she could blink, William had pulled her into a bone crushing embrace, one hand pressed against her back, while the other stroked her hair. "Elizabeth! My Elizabeth."

She stiffened for a moment in shock—although she hardly knew whether to be more surprised at his touch or his words.

The warmth of his body following the tension of the past days was indescribable. She knew it was highly inappropriate, but she melted completely into his body—where she fit quite comfortably. *I have been longing for his touch*, she realized with a shock.

When he loosened his hold on her waist, she wanted to protest the loss of warmth—despite the impropriety. But he did not release her. Instead, a gentle hand under her chin tilted her face up, and his lips descended onto hers.

She had a second to realize he was about to kiss her before their lips met—and she was caught up in a maelstrom.

Her first thought was that William kissed nothing like Richard.

Richard's kisses had been gentle, loving… and careful.

William kissed her with absolute desperation. As if he had waited his whole life for this precise moment—and he had *only this moment* in which to express all his cares, desires, passions.

His lips were fierce on hers. Demanding reassurance that she still lived. Insisting that she respond to him. Expecting a return of his passion.

When his tongue brushed the seam of her lips, she parted them without thought and was amazed at the new onslaught of sensation as his tongue explored her mouth. No, Richard had never kissed like this.

Distantly, she heard someone moaning in passion and only belatedly realized it was her. The feelings his tongue provoked …. Who would have believed the sensations from one small place could reverberate so thoroughly throughout all of her body, racing up and down her spine and even into her fingers and toes? She had not known such exquisite pleasure existed!

When he finally released her, she was dizzy from loss of breath and reeling from the events of the past few moments. *I suppose now I know how he feels about me.* She stifled a slightly hysterical giggle that threatened to erupt.

Elizabeth was certain her expression was dazed, and her cheeks were bright red. William could not meet her eyes but stared at a point over her right shoulder. "Forgive me, I take unconscionable liberties," he murmured, dropping his gaze to the stunted grass under their feet. "In my defense, I can only claim temporary madness brought on by the tremendous relief of seeing you unharmed."

Elizabeth's lips twisted. Only this man could kiss her so passionately and then apologize so abjectly for it a moment later. "It is quite all right," she said softly. "I am capable of defending myself from unwanted embraces. My pistol is somewhere about here."

William's eyes shot anxiously to her face, but then he chuckled. "I am pleased my embraces were not *so* unwelcome."

Elizabeth was on the verge of confessing exactly how much she welcomed his advances when they were interrupted by a groan from Wickham. "What are you about over there?" Wickham called out peevishly. Fortunately, a well-placed shrub and a sturdy tree trunk obscured the man's view of their compromising activities. "When is someone fetching the doctor?"

William took her hand again as they stole around the tree to regard Wickham's prone figure on the ground.

William regarded her with a hint of a smile. "What do you think, Miss Bennet? Should we leave him here? Eventually, he might drag himself to the church."

Elizabeth enjoyed the way his eyes lit with amusement. "Well, he has caused me quite a bit of trouble ...."

"You cannot leave me!" Wickham cried. He might be unable to stand, but his lungs were perfectly healthy. "I shall bleed to death! Where is your Christian charity?"

"Hmmm...." Darcy said thoughtfully. "If he were to die, it would save both of us quite a bit of vexation."

Indignant noises were coming from Wickham's direction. Elizabeth met William's eyes with a similar conspiratorial glee.

"Indeed," she replied. Her attention was caught by activity at the bottom of the hill. "But it appears that my carriage has returned. Perhaps we had best take him to the doctor. If he did die, there would be tiresome questions."

Darcy sighed heavily. "Very well. If you wish." He gave her a broad smile and strode down the hill to collect her servants.

***

Darcy sat across from Elizabeth, attempting to discern her mood from her shuttered expression, but it was fruitless. Her eyes were downcast, and her face a mask. Was she angry with him? She had every right to be. Not only had he failed to protect her, once again, from danger, but he had behaved with a total lack of propriety.

On the hill in the graveyard, Darcy had—for perhaps the first time in his life—acted wholly on impulse, without any consideration for the consequences. His heart had overflowed with relief at finding Elizabeth unharmed, and he had not checked the compulsion to embrace, even kiss her. Now that a cooler head was prevailing, he was heartily ashamed of his precipitous behavior but not the sentiments behind it.

Elizabeth had seemed happy to see him and appeared to return his affection, but perhaps she was only grateful for his assistance, belated though it was. Although she had denied being offended at his completely inappropriate behavior, she had grown more solemn since reuniting with her servants and had said little since then. Perhaps she had second thoughts ...

He had said nothing about renewing his offer of marriage—it had seemed wrong to do so under those circumstances and in that place, but what if she believed he did not intend to? What if she believed he would compromise her reputation and cared nothing for her?

If possible, he ached for her even more than he had before. He had held her in his arms and knew how perfectly they fit together. He knew the softness of her skin and remembered the silkiness of her hair. His fingers, lips, every part of his body, wanted to touch her again.

Darcy rubbed his chin with his hand. After they had left Wickham in the company of the magistrate and under the care of a doctor, he had convinced Elizabeth to spend the night at Pemberley. Then he recognized the need for a proper chaperone, so he had dispatched Elizabeth's footman to the home of Mrs. Devries, an elderly neighbor who always enjoyed his hospitality.

Once they arrived at Pemberley, it would be more difficult to hold a frank dialogue, so he knew they must clear up any misunderstandings now. However, a moving carriage was hardly the location he would have selected for a conversation of some delicacy.

And it was a damnably awkward conversation to initiate. How was one to begin? *Perhaps, um, if you recall our kiss earlier ...? Miss Bennet... you may have noticed I kissed you .... Elizabeth, do you remember that marriage proposal you earlier found so disgusting ...?*

Perhaps not.

How could this this be so difficult? He had kissed the woman, and she had not pushed him away—or used her pistol on him. Yet somehow, he remained completely in the dark about her feelings.

Elizabeth shifted her head slightly and wet her lips with the tip of her tongue; he barely suppressed a groan, recalling the taste of those lips. Her smallest gesture was mesmerizing to him. His mind was immediately preoccupied by thoughts of how and when he could touch her again.

How had Richard even managed to hold an intelligent conversation with the woman—all the while knowing she would let him kiss her if he wanted?

Richard. Darcy closed his eyes, silently chastising himself.

In all the excitement, Darcy had overlooked the fact that Elizabeth had indeed visited Richard's grave. Did that mean she missed her betrothed and believed no one could replace him? Yet she had kissed him back …

He glanced over at her still downcast eyes. Did she regret the kisses? Or feel guilt? Was that why she would not meet his gaze?

She must have grown aware of his gaze on her; as he watched, her blue eyes rose to meet his. His heart thumped nervously in his chest, knowing that his fate would be decided in the next few minutes.

"I am grateful for your assistance, Mr. Darcy, but how did you happen upon me?" She asked.

Darcy swallowed. "Bannon, that is, the groom who was working at your townhouse, told me you had gone and that a boy in your kitchen had reported your departure to Wickham."

"He did?" Elizabeth asked faintly, looking a bit sick.

"I am afraid so. I left London immediately." He grimaced. "I hoped to overtake you on the road. You spent the night at a coaching inn?" Elizabeth nodded. "My second horse went lame and I had to walk it to the nearest town. Otherwise I would have arrived far earlier and prevented the unpleasantness with Wickham. I cannot express how sorry I am."

Elizabeth gave him one of the arch smiles he loved so dearly. "And if it rains tomorrow, will you also apologize for that?"

How does she manage to provoke me to laughter even now? Darcy abruptly sobered as he contemplated what could have happened if he had been delayed even further. "I was so fearful that—Well, I am grateful you are unharmed. You were correct in asserting that you could defend yourself." He gave her a small smile.

She appeared discomfited by the praise. "I would have been in dire straits indeed without your assistance—and Richard's pistol."

Darcy *was* grateful for the pistol, but the sound of his cousin's name made him flinch nonetheless. "I fear Wickham's unwanted arrival prevented you from finding the peace you sought at Richard's grave." His eyes searched her face for some indication of her feelings.

She turned her head to watch the scenery passing by the window. "I had concluded my—" She paused and swallowed. "I found the answers I sought."

Darcy desperately wanted to know which questions she had asked but instead cast about for an appropriate response that could not be construed as presumptuous. "Good," he said finally.

Elizabeth's hands fidgeted in her lap, but she seemed to have no intention to say anything further.

Darcy cleared his throat. "I owe you an apology." She turned her attention back to him, her eyes wide. "I took terrible advantage of you in the churchyard. You would have been within your rights to slap me or retreat to the chapel for protection."

Elizabeth laughed. "I must admit, sir, such thoughts did not occur to me."

Darcy felt himself relax slightly. "No?"

"No, indeed." Her expression was more playful now. "Your kisses are quite persuasive."

Darcy raised an eyebrow. "Oh? What did they persuade you to want?" *Oh, good heavens, am I flirting with her now?*

She gazed coyly up at him through her lashes. "More kisses." Her glance had a profound and immediate effect on Darcy; he now found himself growing uncomfortable for a completely different reason. He ached to touch her, run his hands through her hair, feel her curves, crush her against his body …

"That could be arranged," he said hoarsely.

She appeared slightly alarmed by the intensity of his response.

Darcy swallowed, hoping his voice would not shake. "Elizabeth, I hope you recognize by now that when I offered my hand, I did so not for the sake of protecting you—not solely for the sake of protecting you—but because I am violently in love with you."

Her lips parted slightly, and she blinked rapidly. "Y-you are?"

Darcy kept his gaze fixed on hers. "And I would be very honored if you would accept my hand in marriage."

The shine in her eyes and the flush of her skin suggested she was not unaffected by his words, but she looked down at her hands, obviously troubled. "Mr. Darcy, I must ask you—" Darcy hated the sound of his formal name on her tongue. How could he persuade her to address him by his Christian name? "Do you offer marriage out of some feeling of obligation?"

Darcy looked at her sharply. What could she possibly mean?

Her hands were twisting a ribbon from her dress into torturous shapes. "Many perceive that Richard's death left me in a precarious position—not quite a wife, but almost a widow, practically a ruined woman." She held up a hand to still his protest, raising her eyes to his. "Do you make an offer now to help alleviate the awkwardness of my position?"

Darcy wanted to reach out and hold her, caress her— anything to remove the pain from her eyes. He knew she would hate to wed anyone under those circumstances.

"No!" He said firmly.

She smiled wistfully. "I wish to believe you, but I admit I sometimes find your sudden interest difficult to credit."

He could not prevent the harsh laugh that escaped. *Sudden!*

"Mr. Darcy?" Elizabeth seemed alarmed at his reaction.

He experienced an epiphany at that moment. If they were to move forward as husband and wife, he must reveal *everything*— even the details he found painful or humiliating. Very well.

He gritted his teeth and leaned forward, spanning the gap between them by engulfing her hands in his. "There is nothing 'sudden' about my interest in you. I—" He swallowed hard and started again. "Do you remember the night that Richard proposed to you? When I arrived at Hunsford Parsonage?"

Elizabeth nodded, her eyes fixed on his face. "To inquire about my health, yes."

"No, I had not visited to inquire about your health." Elizabeth's brow knitted in confusion. "I went with the intention of asking you to marry me."

One hand flew to her mouth, and her eyes were wide with shock. Darcy fought an impulse to laugh at her horrified expression. "Oh! I am so sorry! I had no intention of causing you pain. I had no idea!"

"Of course not," Darcy reassured her. "Even Richard did not recognize my feelings, and he knew me far better than you. I believed I had made my feelings clear to you, but in hindsight, I realized I did not."

"But—" Elizabeth looked mortified.

"Please, rest easy, my love. It is for the best. If I had offered my hand that day, how would you have responded?"

A blush stained her cheeks as she glanced away uneasily.

"I know you did not hold a high opinion of me at that time, and I have endeavored to improve your opinion since then. Perhaps it was for the best that I did not have an opportunity to voice my sentiments that day." He smiled gently.

Elizabeth regarded him with wonder in her eyes. "I had no thought of ... all this time you ..." She shook her head, bewildered.

"I have loved you for years," he told her simply.

"I have been so blind!" She cried.

Darcy clasped her hands more tightly. "Shh, love, do not say so. I did not wish you to know. You were my cousin's betrothed. I concealed my feelings from everyone, even Georgiana." Darcy took a deep breath. He had decided to reveal all, but he was taking a great risk. "However, Richard guessed."

Elizabeth's eyebrows rose. "He did?"

"I did not discover this until recently, when the letter he had written on his deathbed finally arrived at Pemberley." He pulled the letter from his coat pocket. "I would like you to read it."

The letter was well-worn and creased from having been reread multiple times during the past weeks. He laid it gently on Elizabeth's palm, noting a slight tremor in her hand. She unfolded it so slowly he thought she might decide to forego reading it altogether, but finally, she bent her head to the task.

Elizabeth scrutinized the letter, while Darcy scrutinized her expression, noting every slight widening of her eye or movement of her lips as she read. Tears collected in the corners of her eyes, but she did not weep. Was that a good sign? He could barely breathe, awaiting her reaction. By giving the letter to Elizabeth, he was taking the chance Richard might come between them once more. *Richard* might have wanted Darcy to care for Elizabeth, but *she* might have different ideas. She might even resent the thought that she needed care.

Darcy resolutely shifted his gaze to the scene outside the window, reminding himself that all of these worries mattered little in the end. The only question of import was if Elizabeth loved him. If she did not, Darcy's feelings and Richard's opinions mattered not at all.

He returned his gaze to Elizabeth when she sighed softly and set the letter down in her lap. She bit her lip, looking down at the letter, and wiped away tears with her fingers. Giving her the letter was the right thing to do, but he regretted causing her even a moment's uneasiness.

Darcy leaned toward her again. "No matter what our future holds, Richard is in your heart and in mine. He has helped to bring us together—in a way that might not have happened without him. I believe we should cherish that as a gift."

Elizabeth stared soberly at the letter, absorbing his words. "Richard understood your feelings so much better than I did. I was so blind, so certain I understood you—and I was so wrong!"

"Richard had known me since childhood," Darcy reminded her gently.

Her face was in shadow, making it impossible to read her mood. He was in agony, needing to know how she felt about the letter—and him.

"I want your hand and your heart, but only if they are freely given," he said. "Richard knew nothing of *your* feelings for me and if you could ever love me. And I find I hardly know any better. But if you choose me, it should be for your own sake, not out of some sense of obligation to me or to Richard." He wished to reach out to take her hand again but feared his touch would be unwelcome.

Her lips parted, but she did not speak for a moment. Finally, she met his eyes. "It occurred to me that my reaction to you and to Richard has ever been quite different. Perhaps that is why I have been so slow to recognize ..."

Her voice trailed off, and she turned her gaze to the window. "My relationship with Richard was like an outing on a placid lake, smooth, entertaining, and untroubled. However, everything about my friendship with you has been a storm tossed on turbulent seas—thrilling and a little wild. Our reactions to each other have always been ... extreme." Darcy's heart clenched painfully. This did not sound like the speech of a woman accepting a suitor.

"When I misunderstood your character, I disliked you, and I was angry with you, and now I ..." Elizabeth's eyes turned on him, large and serious. "I believe that is why I did not recognize the true nature of my feelings for so long. I expected if I loved again, it would feel as it had before—it would resemble the feelings I had for Richard, but it does not." She swallowed and managed a small smile. "However, that does not mean the feelings are weaker because of it. Simply different."

Hope had started to sprout in Darcy's breast. "Are you saying you *do* feel—?"

Elizabeth gave him a blinding smile. "I am saying, yes, Mr. Darcy, I love you. Yes, I will marry you. Yes."

Darcy experienced such a flood of intermixed emotions — relief, joy, overwhelming love, even the impulse to laugh—that he hardly knew what to do or say. Competing impulses warred within him until he could no longer withstand the building emotions. *Propriety be damned!* He surged across the short space between their seats.

Elizabeth startled at his unexpected action, but her body melted into him as he settled next to her and took her in his arms. "You have made me a very happy man today," he murmured as he gently untied her bonnet ribbons and removed the offending garment, gaining access to her hair.

Darcy paused for a moment, watching her reaction. However, she did not seem at all alarmed by this egregious breach of propriety but gave him an arch look that further emboldened him. He quickly located the hair pins that kept her complicated coiffeur in place and removed a few in strategic places. The remaining pins rained down on the floor as her dark tresses tumbled down over her shoulders.

Darcy exhaled, soaking in the sight. He had never before seen her with her hair down, and it was a magnificent view. Dark curls framed her face, falling midway down her back. This forbidden sight accelerated his breathing and caused his heart to pound out a more rapid rhythm. Despite the chill in the carriage, sweat dampened his cravat. With one arm, he tucked her closer to his body, but it was not enough. It could never be close enough. Although if he could rid them of these offending layers of clothing

…

No, Darcy cut off that line of thought. Envisioning the two of them naked, even in a jostling carriage, simply made him too uncomfortable.

It must wait for the wedding night.

Darcy focused on admiring how the weak afternoon sun reflected in her hair, creating light and dark highlights. Very deliberately, Darcy peeled off his gloves and plunged his hands into the silken mass of hair, provoking a gasp from Elizabeth. Her slightly parted lips were too great a temptation. He leaned forward and pressed his mouth against hers.

It was not a polite kiss, but a demanding one. It demanded she respond to his passion—and revel in the sensations when she did. As they kissed, his hand skimmed down her body to her lower back, pressing her into him. The other hand held the back of her head. Elizabeth moaned against him, stoking his desire.

Fearing that Elizabeth was made uncomfortable by the awkward position of her body, Darcy started to pull away, but then Elizabeth shifted. Without breaking contact with his lips, she repositioned her body so she was now seated in his lap.

Oh, Good Lord! Darcy could hardly believe her boldness or his good fortune. His hands freely explored more of Elizabeth's body, stroking the curves of her back and the sides of her waist. How he wished he could feel her soft skin instead of clothing!

It was ecstasy, but it also strained his control. He wanted so much more from her than was wise before their wedding.

Given the heat of his blood, the chaperone might need to station herself at the entrance to Elizabeth's door that night. It would be difficult to restrain himself, knowing Elizabeth was only a few doors away and that she indeed desired him …

Reluctantly, Darcy pulled back away from the ecstasy of Elizabeth's mouth, although he could not bring himself to remove his hands from her waist. Elizabeth's lips were red and swollen, her face flushed with desire, and her hair tousled. The wantonness in her look almost made him groan.

Fortunately, she did not seem at all angry over the liberties he had taken; in fact, she seemed rather bemused that he had stopped. "Mr. Darcy, I—"

"Elizabeth," he interrupted. "You are sitting on my lap. I believe you may call me William."

A delicate blush spread over her features. "Of course." She made a move to slide off his lap, but Darcy's hands held her in place. "I apologize. I did not mean to behave in such a wanton manner," she said. "I do not know what came over me."

Darcy put a finger to her lips. "Never apologize for your passion with me. It is one of the things I love about you and hope you will never change."

She raised her eyebrows playfully, and one side of her mouth curved up in a wicked smile. "Very well, sir, if you *wish* me to be wanton, I will make the effort."

Desire surged through Darcy's blood as he imagined the possibilities. "Miss Bennet," he said in a hoarse whisper, "I think it would be best if we had a very short betrothal."

Epilogue

"A toast to the new couple!" Elizabeth's Uncle Gardiner had a voice that boomed even above the hubbub of the celebrants around the breakfast table. Everyone fell silent as he spoke about how worthy a husband William would be for his niece. Elizabeth knew some of his words were intended to reassure her father, who had initially resisted the idea of such a "difficult, unpleasant man" marrying his daughter, but a hearty endorsement from her uncle had allayed most of his fears.

She smiled when her father glanced her way, letting him see the joy shining in her face. Indeed, the day was all the more joyous because he had been well enough to make the journey to Pemberley for the wedding in the small Darcy family chapel. Her wedding day would not have been complete without his presence.

As she glanced around the table, Elizabeth noticed the Earl of Matlock and his wife only taking tiny, disapproving sips of their champagne. Believing Richard's death had banished the "upstart country miss" from their lives, they had been dismayed to find her foisted on them by their nephew. No doubt they were wondering how potent her "arts and allurements" must be to entrap *two* wealthy and discerning men.

She pushed any misgivings from her mind. Perhaps over time, they would come to believe she truly loved William. At least they had attended the wedding; Lady Catherine and her daughter had simply refused the invitation.

Elizabeth watched as Georgiana conversed with Jane, whose gentleness was helping to coax Darcy's sister out of her shyness. Aside from the principal participants, no one had been more excited about their union than Georgiana. The prospect of having Elizabeth as her sister had made her giddy with joy for the past three weeks, and she had been essential in helping Elizabeth prepare for the hastily scheduled wedding.

William had been conversing with her father, seated on his other side, but now he turned to her and clasped her hand in his, raising it to his lips. His eyes smoldered as they held her gaze. "Mrs. Darcy," he murmured. The delicate sensation of his lips brushing her hand sent shivers up her arm and down her spine—

and she could not help imagining that evening…when he would finally embrace her in the marital bed.

She had expected to be nervous, but instead, she felt delightful anticipation, even eagerness. She loved him, and she trusted him. He stoked a passion in her she had not known existed. And tonight, she would have an opportunity to express that passion.

Elizabeth smiled at William, willing her eyes to convey all her love. However, she could not withstand such an intense look from him without also desiring his touches—in places not appropriate for a wedding breakfast. To distract herself, she glanced about the room once more.

Charles was smiling serenely at Jane; he had been shocked, but thrilled, at the news that his best friend was to marry his wife's sister and had immediately commenced a search for houses near Pemberley. Apparently, Jane believed one could sometimes be "too close to family."

As Elizabeth watched, a nursemaid entered the dining room and brought baby Anna to Jane. Dressed in a long white dress and a lace cap, Anna was simply adorable. Jane looked over at Elizabeth, smiling. Jane knew her sister wanted to hold the baby. She and Charles stood and brought their bundle to Elizabeth's seat.

Elizabeth happily took her niece from Jane's arms. "I knew you would want to see her before it was time for her nap. You might leave before she wakes up," Jane said.

Elizabeth smiled down at the plump, happy baby and said directly to her, "I will miss you! You simply must move to Derbyshire!" Anna babbled and grabbed at one of Elizabeth's curls.

Charles and William laughed. "You already have Jane on your side; you need not enlist my daughter as well!" Charles said.

Anna turned her gaze to William and smiled sunnily at him.

"I know this is your child," Elizabeth observed to her sister and brother. "No one else could have such a gentle disposition. Even when she is tired, she smiles and coos."

"I am sure your children will be much the same," Jane said diplomatically.

Elizabeth glanced at her new husband over the bundle of baby and saw his eyes crinkle as he smiled. "No, I do not expect so." Jane looked puzzled. "I believe any child of ours would be...passionate."

"And full of opinions," William added.

Charles clapped his friend on the shoulder. "Well, Darcy, fatherhood is wonderful. I wish you well. But you best prepare now. We had a devil of a time choosing a name. You should start considering your choices now!"

William's face grew serious. "Perhaps we would have difficulty selecting a girl's name, but I think we know what we would name a boy."

Elizabeth looked at him in puzzlement. During their brief engagement, they had barely discussed raising children, let alone naming them. Then suddenly, she understood him quite clearly. She met his eyes, nodding her agreement.

Without speaking, they were in perfect accord. There was only one possible name for a boy—because the person who had brought them together was still with them in spirit.

Charles watched them curiously. "You would name him George after your father?" He asked.

"No." William shook his head, smiling at his wife. "His name will be Richard."

The End

About Victoria Kincaid

As a professional freelance writer, Victoria writes about IT, data storage, home improvement, green living, alternative energy, and healthcare. Some of her more…unusual writing subjects have included space toilets, taxi services, laser gynecology, bidets, orthopedic shoes, generating energy from onions, Ferrari rental car services, and vampire face lifts (she swears she is not making any of this up).

Victoria has a Ph.D. in English literature and has taught composition to unwilling college students. Today she teaches business writing to willing office professionals and tries to give voice to the demanding cast of characters in her head. She lives in Virginia with her husband, two children who love to read, and an overly affectionate cat. A lifelong Jane Austen fan, Victoria confesses to an extreme partiality for the Colin Firth miniseries version of *Pride and Prejudice.*

Thank you *for purchasing this book.*

Your support makes it possible for authors like me to continue writing.

Please consider leaving a review where you purchased the book or at Goodreads.com.

Learn more about me and my upcoming releases:

Website: www.victoriakincaid.com

Twitter: VictoriaKincaid@kincaidvic

Blog: https://kincaidvictoria.wordpress.com/

Facebook: https://www.facebook.com/kincaidvictoria

The Secrets of Darcy and Elizabeth

Victoria Kincaid

In this Pride and Prejudice variation, a despondent Darcy travels to Paris in the hopes of forgetting the disastrous proposal at Hunsford. Paris is teeming with English visitors during a brief moment of peace in the Napoleonic Wars, but Darcy's spirits don't lift until he attends a ball and unexpectedly encounters…Elizabeth Bennet! Darcy seizes the opportunity to correct misunderstandings and initiate a courtship.

Their moment of peace is interrupted by the news that England has again declared war on France, and hundreds of English travelers must flee Paris immediately. Circumstances force Darcy and Elizabeth to escape on their own, despite the risk to her reputation. Even as they face dangers from street gangs and French soldiers, romantic feelings blossom during their flight to the coast. But then Elizabeth falls ill, and the French are arresting all the English men they can find….

When Elizabeth and Darcy finally return to England, their relationship has changed, and they face new crises. However, they have secrets they must conceal—even from their own families.

Amazon Top 10 Bestseller in Regency Romance
Amazon Top 10 Hot New Release in Regency Romance

Average of 4 stars on Amazon (almost 120 reviews)

Made in the USA
Lexington, KY
22 October 2015